DEATH IS THE INHERITANCE

Paul Newland and his flash BMW have been missing from Rainbow Caravan Park in Cornwall for two days and the park's owner is convinced he has committed suicide. Desperate to avoid official police involvement, she asks John Reynolds to make enquiries, but then Mrs Newland turns up at the site confident Paul is well. When Em, a local employee who befriended Paul is found murdered, and with various cracks appearing in what first seemed an unsuspicious situation, Reynolds soon realises it is not just Paul Newland he should be worrying about—but those he's left behind ...

DEATH IS THE INHERITANCE

DEATH IS THE INHERITANCE

by

Mary Clayton

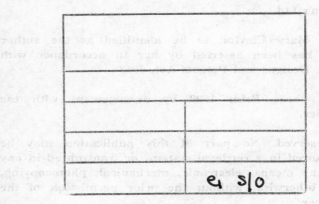

Magna Large Print Books
Long Preston, North Yorkshire,
England.

British Library Cataloguing in Publication Data.

Clayton, Mary
  Death is the inheritance.

  A catalogue record for this book is
  available from the British Library

  ISBN 0-7505-1499-X

First published in Great Britain by Headline Book Publishing,
1998

Copyright © 1998 by Mary Clayton

Cover illustration © Tim Gill by arrangement with Headline
Book Publishing Ltd.

The right of Mary Clayton to be identified as the author
of this work has been asserted by her in accordance with
the Copyright, Designs and Patents Act, 1988

Published in Large Print 1999 by arrangement with the
copyright holder.

Magna Large Print is an imprint of
Library Magna Books Ltd.
Printed and bound in Great Britain by
T.J. International Ltd., Cornwall, PL28 8RW.

To FRC. With grateful love.

I should also like to thank my family and friends for all their loving help. And to my American agent, Arnold Goodman, and my English editor, Andi Sisodia, my constant gratitude for their patience and advice.

Chapter 1

It was dusk when the car crept through the gates to the site, pausing for a moment before drawing up in front of one of the caravans. As the couple emerged, quietly, almost subdued—'No noise after nine, no radios or television'—Marge Clithero twitched her curtains back angrily.

'It's not him,' she snapped at her husband. 'I told you so.'

Her face, smeared in white cream, stiffened, and her tone made Derek sink even further into his corner, where he was hiding behind a paper, pretending to read. Short and stocky, with a head of wiry tan-and-white hair like a Yorkshire terrier, he knew that when Marge was in a mood it was better not to argue.

'I knew we shouldn't have rented to him on the off chance.' Marge was aggressive. 'From the start I said there was something odd about him. What did he want with a family caravan, a single man, with never a word to say for himself?'

Derek's muttered defence, 'He talked his way in easily enough,' was lost in Marge's next outburst. 'And now gone for two days without a trace, and all his belongings left behind. I tell you, it's peculiar.'

She was speaking of one of their 'guests'. Last Saturday he had turned up at the site and asked if he could rent a caravan. He wanted it for a couple of weeks at least, he'd said; he'd heard Rainbow Park was quiet, well run, just what he'd been looking for, on the north Cornish coast where he planned to hike along the cliffs ... His fulsome explanations, his ready smile, had overcome Marge's original objections. She'd preened.

All their caravans were usually booked months in advance, she explained, of course word gets round. Frowning at Derek in case he contradicted her, for those happy times were gone, she went on to say that Rainbow Static Caravan Park, owned and managed by herself and her husband, wasn't like other sites nearby, where the owners lived abroad and relied on someone local to keep an eye on things. She was from the north of England originally, she confided, and good northern common sense had told her that wasn't the way to go about it. People liked the hands-on approach, the personal touch. Twice now she'd been awarded a Gold Star for excellence, had once been voted the best site in the area—although she didn't specify how long ago that was. Instead, with scarcely a pause, she had suggested that as there was an unexpected vacancy, perhaps in this one instance she might make an exception.

The sight of the money the new arrival produced had overcome any last scruples. There were introductions and handshakes all round. His name was Paul Newland, he told her, from up-country, here on holiday. He had an air about him, a real gentleman with his city clothes. And, 'Double the usual,' Marge had boasted afterwards. Derek didn't argue. He seldom did, but his expression showed he didn't like it when she broke with routine. There was always trouble. And now trouble had come, big trouble, if Paul Newland really was missing.

'Said he wanted to hike the cliff path,' Marge was saying in the peeved voice that sent shivers down Derek's spine. 'Well, for starters, the Cornish cliffs are dangerous. And God knows where he took that car each day. Out early every morning, and never back till late.'

The car too had originally been an attraction. Large, shiny blue, worth a packet, Marge had gloated. Gave the upmarket touch they needed, probably good for a general increase in the weekly rental. She had scarcely stopped congratulating herself when Paul Newland had driven his new BMW off early Wednesday morning and failed to bring it and himself back that night—or this.

Another car came through the gate but she didn't bother to look. She recognised its sound: it was the decrepit Ford belonging to the young Alderans, who were only welcome because little Mrs Alderan's father had been one of her first 'guests'.

'It's no use just sitting there and saying nothing.' Marge returned to the attack. 'If you don't do something soon, we'll be in a right old pickle. Why don't you ask that friend of yours, that Reynolds fellow, to come over, quiet like, and advise us on our next move?'

And as Derek, finally goaded into a response, again muttered into his paper that he didn't want to impose, Marge retorted, 'Isn't being a policeman what Reynolds did for a living? And doesn't he owe you a favour? You're always on about your army days, boasting about saving each other's lives and such. Otherwise,' here her eyes narrowed and she gave a determined tug to her floral blouse, 'it'll be a case for the real police—and scandal.'

Scandal was the last thing a caravan site needed, especially one whose Gold Star was somewhat tarnished. Her voice sank at the very thought. And so it was, when after hours of nagging Derek finally plucked up the nerve to telephone Reynolds, that the mystery of the missing Paul Newland began to unfold. But what Marge didn't tell Derek, or Reynolds, didn't intend to tell anyone, was what had really prompted her show of anxiety—and what she hoped to get out of it.

Chapter 2

Marge was right that ex-Inspector Reynolds and her husband were friends, albeit unlikely ones. In almost everything else she was wrong. The two men had met in the Middle East, during one of those crises

15

in the sixties. Reynolds was fresh out from England as a young officer, and Derek, a regular private in the same battalion, had taken him under his wing. As to saving lives, whatever Derek had done or not done, Reynolds had certainly saved his life when a mission into enemy territory had gone horribly wrong.

Derek, though, had never mentioned any of these details, so his 'boasting' was all Marge's invention. It was true, however, that when he'd learned much later that Reynolds had retired early from the Devon and Cornwall Constabulary and come to live nearby, after long and silent deliberation he had driven over to St Breddaford and reintroduced himself. He even seemed proud of Reynolds' new occupation as a writer of detective stories, which had won him as much fame and certainly more fortune than his previous career.

Their relationship was perhaps unusual; famous authors and old soldiers don't often move in the same circles, but Reynolds never stood on ceremony. Besides, he had a kind heart and immediately sensed some deep unhappiness in a man he remembered as a typical soldier, full of good humour coupled with a determination that matched his terrier-like appearance. Whether it was being displaced so far from his native Yorkshire in what was after all a foreign environment, or whether civilian life in general, and domestic life in particular, had changed the older man, he recognised how much Derek came to look forward to their infrequent meetings, although the two had little in common except their shared memories of army days—and a love of gardening.

He himself never ventured into the world of Rainbow Park, where he sensed he might not be welcome, and had never met Marge. More from what Derek didn't say he'd come to suspect she might be a real tartar best avoided. He hadn't seen Derek now for several months—the summer season always kept the older man busy—but it wasn't only kindness that caused the ex-inspector to react so promptly to Derek's request. Added to the natural instinct to help a friend was a less admirable characteristic—Reynolds' own insatiable curiosity, about life and people in general and mysteries in particular, and what Derek told him made him very curious indeed.

He was well aware of the dangers of such

inquisitiveness. But there it was, impossible to resist. Promising Derek he'd be over first thing Friday morning, and hoping that Marge might prove more amenable than he'd given her credit for, he felt the familiar rush of expectation.

On reaching Rainbow Park, Reynolds wasn't impressed by what he saw: a seedy line of permanent caravans, some badly needing attention, spaced around the perimeter of a field that sloped gently towards the cliffs. Subdued sounds came from the occupied caravans, like a well-ordered beehive, as various couples, all apparently childless, prepared to go about their holiday pursuits.

The Clithero's own caravan stood broadside to the gate, effectively preventing anyone entering or leaving without running the gauntlet of Marge's scrutiny. She herself was a large-boned, grim mouthed woman, heavily made up even so early in the day. Her tinted hair and painted eyes added to the hardness, although she tried to dispel it by smiling often, and her manner was positively coquettish as she invited Reynolds in. The way she fluttered her eyelashes alone put the ex-inspector on his guard. A middle-aged woman who flirts under her husband's nose must want something badly. What that something was he didn't yet know, and wasn't sure he wanted to find out.

Uncomfortably perched on a hard chair in the living area of the caravan (painted a bilious green and smelling of cigarette smoke), he felt out of place, much too tall and much too broad to fit easily into the limited space. He stretched his long legs tentatively under a nest of tables loaded with china figurines, and, afraid of knocking something over, stuck his hands in his pockets while he listened patiently to Marge's chatter and Derek tried to make himself as inconspicuous as possible.

Her habit of referring to Newland as the 'missing person in question' began to grate, especially as she seemed to suggest that by the very act of disappearing, Newland had insulted her. Putting a stop to her complaints, Reynolds asked some sensible questions, the first one, whether she knew Newland's home address or telephone number, eliciting a long and complicated explanation of why she didn't.

'Usually it's the first thing we ask for,' Marge eventually confessed. 'I mean, you can't be too careful these days, can you,

John? Our guests are usually vetted, we don't take in just anyone.' Her fluttering eyelashes, suggesting that Rainbow Park wasn't like other places, she had good taste, failed to convince.

Taking all this with the proverbial pinch of salt, and flinching at her over-familiar use of his name, Reynolds cut short her list of the virtues of Rainbow Park by asking her if it were possible Newland had met with an accident. He might not have had any identification on him, or anything connecting him with the park, he suggested. Marge replied curtly that she'd already thought of that. She'd got Derek to ring the local hospitals before he'd phoned Reynolds.

'Then perhaps he's just skipped off home.' Reynolds tried to be positive. 'The weather's supposed to break. In any event, it's a bit premature to jump to conclusions.'

Marge bristled. Presumably in Reynolds' honour she was dressed to impress, in white linen trousers, brightly coloured blouse, and high-heeled sandals, more suitable for a Caribbean holiday than the unreliable Cornish August. His lack of admiring response was having an effect.

'Our guests are supposed to let us know where they're going, especially if they'll be back late,' she said reproachfully. 'The gate's always locked by ten. It's in the instruction book we give them on arrival. As for leaving, when he'd paid all that money for a two-week rental ...' Her shrug suggested disbelief. 'Besides, he's left all his clothes.'

That did make a difference. About to suggest she wait a while before she panicked, Reynolds glanced at Derek. He was sitting in a corner by the window but the way he knotted and unknotted his fingers hinted at the strain he was experiencing. 'She's been on about Newland being under stress,' Derek had finally admitted on the phone, his voice so low Reynolds could scarcely catch the words. Reynolds heard his feet shift in embarrassment but he didn't elucidate. Presumably he meant suicidal. But if the missing man had spent most of his time away from Rainbow Park, what had given Marge the idea he was emotionally disturbed? Curbing his growing impatience, he asked instead if he could look at the caravan for himself, and while Marge fussed with a large bunch of master keys, he flashed a sympathetic look at her husband.

The two men walked slowly behind her as she trotted across the manicured grass. In spite of the rundown appearance of the caravans, the actual site was immaculate. The caravans were numbered in order and the one Paul Newland had rented, number four, stood closest to the cliffs. As well as the number, a name was painted on it in faded green: 'Bide-a-Wee'. Perhaps that's exactly what Newland's done, Reynolds thought cynically as he climbed the shallow steps. Took the place on a whim, got bored quickly and shoved off somewhere new, intending to pick his gear up later. He noted the neat flowerbeds on either side of the door, even late in the season still a blaze of colour. 'Your work?' he was about to ask Derek admiringly when Marge forestalled him, as if she couldn't bear Derek to be complimented on anything.

'This isn't Derek's doing,' she snapped. 'I expect my guests to look after their own little gardens.' She gave a vicious twitch to an offending weed, adding meanly, 'Most people are very willing, they like the sense of belonging, makes them feel at home. But Newland didn't bother. Not interested, I suppose.'

This time her reproachful glance was levelled at her husband as he followed her and Reynolds inside. The caravan was dark and smelled of mildew. Even with the curtains drawn back and the door and windows thrown open, it gave Reynolds the sense of being shut up in a tin box. the sort of claustrophobia he experienced in planes and trains. There was nothing personal, not even papers or books, only a couple of ugly vases and an even uglier ashtray. He had the impression of dull brown furniture. carpets and walls, and when Marge threw open other internal doors to reveal a small bathroom ('All mod cons') and bedroom with double bed, he felt overwhelmed by the same depressing colour.

'Look here,' Marge was saying. She struggled with a built-in cupboard, its door swollen with damp. Inside, a grey suit, polyester, and several shirts hung on a sagging rack. A pair of shoes was stowed underneath along with several pairs of dark-grey socks. Certainly not the clothes to go hiking in.

'Nothing in the pockets, I went through them first thing,' Marge was saying smugly.

23

'Although he had a lot of cash on him when he arrived.'

If she's already rung the hospitals and examined the clothes, Reynolds thought irritably, what does she need me for? He took the trouble to go over the things himself, taking them out and holding them against himself to check the size. The suit apparently fitted a tall man, almost his own build and height, and the shirts were the same neck measurement. There were no distinguishing marks, no specks of dandruff, for example, no stray hairs, and the pockets were empty as Marge had said. Even the shoes were spotless and well brushed, never used for country walking. But as for being a wealthy man, a closer look showed that Newland's suit was the Co-Op's cheapest and the shirts came from Asda, the sort of garments which would make most men who could afford new BMWs turn up their noses. Had Marge and Derek noticed this strange discrepancy? Or had the clothes been deliberately purchased to put people off the scent? He looked at them again, and decided they were well used. If they had been recently bought, they must have been second-hand. He glanced from Marge to her husband.

'Please come,' Derek had finally pleaded. 'She's taken against him for some reason and won't listen to sense.' His voice had trailed off despondently. What's Marge done to him? Reynolds now wondered. What's happened to the reliable soldier I knew, the sort who used to be called the salt of the earth? But suppose her flirtatiousness is part of a pattern and she's been making amorous advances towards Newland—presumably without success if she's 'taken against him'? Derek might not be willing to accept her interest in another man with his usual long-suffering fortitude. Suppose he knows more than he's letting on ... But if either of them is involved in Newland's disappearance, why, for heaven's sake, draw attention to the fact when it would be to their advantage to keep quiet as long as they can?

Once more on the point of saying that if Newland had really vanished the matter should be handed over to the police, he thought better of it and turned to Marge, who seemed to be waiting for him to conjure up the missing man out of nothing, like some modern Sherlock Holmes.

'Could he have made contact with some old friend, say, someone who lives in the neighbourhood? And what about the other campers—was he on speaking terms with them?'

'He never spoke to anyone that I know of, certainly none of my *guests,*' Marge interrupted, raising plucked eyebrows at the word 'campers'. 'And the message isn't getting through to you, John. I don't want my guests involved if I can avoid it. That's why I asked for you.'

She straightened her blouse in what he was coming to recognise as a buckling-on-of-armour gesture. 'I can't help wondering,' she burst out, 'suppose he came here with the intention of doing away with himself? We'll be held responsible, see if we aren't.'

About to argue that if Newland had committed suicide she was more likely to be blamed for trying to hide the fact, Reynolds bit his lip. Her concern, if it really was concern, was so self-centred, so without regret or pity for the missing man, he might as well save his breath. But women like her sometimes said one thing and meant another. Again he fixed his gaze on her. The impression that she knew more than she was admitting was growing stronger by the moment. Stifling

26

his mounting irritation, he rephrased his question, asking specifically about the staff, did they have any helpers? He was surprised to hear Derek unexpectedly find his voice.

'There's no one else except us,' Derek said firmly. 'Marge and me, we do all the work.'

Marge immediately contradicted him with another vicious snap. 'You're forgetting Em Tregurion,' she said. Ignoring Derek's protests, she addressed Reynolds. 'Just a local who does the cleaning and so on.' The contempt in her voice showed clearly. 'Change-over days, things like that. And some of my guests like having what they call "maid service", one of the specialities I was telling you about earlier.'

I bet, Reynolds thought sarcastically. Whatever fastidious clientele Rainbow Park once attracted, they aren't much in evidence now. 'Em wasn't here much this week,' Derek broke in, forestalling the next question. 'And she was always gone long before Newland returned at night. Anyway, Newland wasn't about to let anyone clean up after him, not even with the sort of lolly he had. You said so yourself.'

'John isn't interested in all this chit-chat.' Marge became even more chill. She flashed one of her smiles, trying to dazzle Reynolds. 'Besides ...'

'I think we should talk with this Miss Tregurion, just to be on the safe side,' Reynolds interrupted. Suddenly he was beginning to be very interested in the start of what looked like a family row. 'Is she anywhere about now?'

While Derek went reluctantly to find her, and Marge moaned on about how Newland had let her down, and what was she to do with his caravan, she couldn't re-let it with his stuff inside, yet it was a shame to have it standing empty, Reynolds looked thoughtfully out of the window. All the other caravans were presumably like this one, past their prime, despite Marge's claims. If Rainbow Park was the sort of place that rested on its former reputation, frequented by loyal clients who returned year after year out of some sense of loyalty, it wasn't the best place for a man with a guilty secret. The mere fact of being new would make him stick out like a sore thumb. Moreover, Marge gave the impression of keeping such a close watch over all her guests, there wouldn't be much that escaped those beady eyes. Over the feathery tops of the tamarisk bushes on the hedge, he caught glimpses of the sea, today a blue-grey flecked with white. At least the view from 'Bide-a-Wee' earned full marks. But why would a man who claimed he wanted to walk the cliff path drive his car off every day when the path was waiting for him on the other side of that hedge?

When Derek arrived back with Em Tregurion in tow, part of the old soldier's protectiveness was explained. To begin with, Em was younger than Reynolds had imagined, and in a strange way vulnerable, the apron she wore over jersey and leggings giving her an almost childlike look. Although her garments did little to enhance her figure, she was so attractive, Reynolds was amazed that Marge had ever hired her—he had the impression that the older woman wouldn't take kindly to competition.

Em's skin had a glow to it, the sort that sun-worshippers strive for and seldom achieve. Her hair, again startling, was a vivid red; the ringlets escaping from the bun at the nape of her neck reminded him of an Italian Renaissance painting, although her eyes, sloe black, bold yet watchful, like a young robin, were completely Celtic. Not a typical cleaning woman, Reynolds thought, as he asked her if she knew who Newland was; and not your typical shy Cornish girl, as she replied, with a forceful toss of her head, that she had spoken with him 'a few times'.

'Did you see or speak with him on Tuesday evening, or early Wednesday morning, the last time he's been seen for a while?'

'We chatted on the Tuesday evening.'

Em's answer was accompanied by another toss of her head. Beside him, he heard Marge suck in her breath. Ignoring her and slipping more easily into his former-inspector role, Reynolds continued with his questions. At least they were getting somewhere at last. 'Did he give you any indication of his plans for the next day?' he asked, to have Em reply forthrightly that as far as she knew he'd decided to drive towards Land's End in the far west of Cornwall. Or at least that's what he'd said.

Marge's cry of 'Well I never,' followed by. 'He should have told me first. They all tell me their plans,' was lost in Reynolds' next round of queries, 'Did he say when he'd be back? Did he mention anything about himself, where he was from, anything like that?' foremost among them.

Before Em could answer, Marge broke in. 'I don't see the need to ask her all these questions,' she said pettishly. 'I can't imagine he told her anything significant. And if you make her feel important,' she added in a lower tone, 'she'll go blabbing to everyone. You know what these local girls are like, John, give an inch they take a mile. I don't pay her to stand round all day yakking.'

This was supposed to have been an aside, but Em Tregurion heard. A flush crossed her face and her black eyes burned. 'I don't spend my time yakking, as you call it,' she countered. 'You work me to the bone. And what I do in my off hours is my own business. The same for Mr Newland, come to that.'

Marge gave another little gasp as Reynolds, trying to soothe Em's feelings and bring the questioning back on line, asked again, 'Did he seem upset, for example, or …'

'Depressed, I suppose you mean.' Em was still angry. 'No, he didn't.' Her eyes flared a fresh challenge at Marge. 'In fact I have reason to know he was in a very good mood. He spent the night with me.'

With another toss of her head she glared at the three people in the caravan before addressing Reynolds. 'As for being local, I'll tell you something else. She may be from the north of England, but she's the biggest gossip I ever met. Ask anyone on the site, they'll tell you the same thing. If they aren't too afraid of her to speak out, that is.'

With that she ripped off her apron and threw it in a ball on the floor. 'You can take your bloody job and stuff it,' she shouted. 'I don't need it that badly, thanks for nothing.'

Before they could stop her, she was out of the door, slamming it behind her. They watched her stump across to the main gate, where she stooped to pick up a bicycle and then pedalled off, not without first loosening her hair so that it flared defiance behind her.

'Woo!' Reynolds drew in his breath, while Marge, recovering her voice, cried, 'The sly slut. I knew she was up to something, but ...' She clamped her lips shut. Behind her, Derek's chair creaked and a look of abject misery passed over his face. Though quickly hidden, it gave Reynolds a new insight. Once more the mystery surrounding the missing Paul Newland began to intrigue him on another, more personal, level.

'It seems to me,' he said slowly, 'if Miss Tregurion is correct—and so far she's the only witness we have—you should wait a while before raising the alarm. But if you have some reason to think something's gone wrong,' here he gave Marge a look, the sort that had often made hardened criminals tremble, 'then you should contact the police immediately. They're your best hope of finding him.'

An unbecoming flush covered Marge's cheeks. 'You don't understand,' she snapped again. 'I don't want to *find* him. I only want to know where he is.'

The difference was subtle, but Marge didn't bother to explain. Instead she went on even more angrily, 'I told you I wanted nothing to do with the police. That's why I asked for you. I thought you'd be discreet.' Her tone heaping more reproach, she continued, 'Derek said you'd be good at that. He insisted you were the right man.'

Realising perhaps too late that anger

wasn't the best way to elicit Reynolds' support, she summoned up her false smile and cooed, 'But of course, Derek and I have faith in you, John. Derek counts you as a friend.'

Her change of attitude, almost a complete about-face, was disorienting, and her belated attempt at flattery failed. It was her repeated mention of Derek that had the desired effect. Against his better judgement, Reynolds let himself be manoeuvred into making enquiries about Newland's possible whereabouts without consulting anyone official. He knew he was being conned into promises he didn't want to keep.

After Reynolds' departure, Marge rounded on her husband. 'He wasn't much cop,' she snarled. 'And you were just as bad. Why did you have to bring that bitch into it?'

When Derek failed to defend himself with the obvious answer that in fact she'd done the bringing in, he'd done his best to keep Em out, she went on, 'Well, if your precious John can't help us, we'll have to help ourselves. For a start, clear out this place. Store Newland's things somewhere. If he returns, we'll say we know nothing about them.' And ignoring

Derek's sensible objection that how could they do so when they'd just involved an outside witness, an ex-police inspector to boot, she stalked away, leaving him to deal with the problem—and wrestle with his own thoughts, among which Em's unfortunate revelation vied with even more unpleasant ones.

In spite of her air of assurance, Marge was not as confident as she seemed. If anything she was floundering. The Marge Clithero who had so often in the past struck terror into the souls of her hapless guests was out of her depth. Reynolds' observations had been sound. On several points.

To begin with, she had been attracted to Paul Newland, seeing him as a cut above her present run of clients, who, although loyal, lacked class. Newland's failure to follow up his promising start when he had been so open, so chatty, so—she searched for the word—so receptive, had been galling. Em Tregurion's statement about his liaison with her, if correct, only added insult to injury. It was demeaning, his attraction for a mere girl, a cleaning woman, when she herself, as she would have put it, was 'interested'. But it was

35

Em's attack on her personally that was hardest to accept.

Marge had always been so sure she knew everything there was to know about her guests, had even prided herself on their affection and trust. To be told by this slip of a thing that they actually disliked her was a bitter blow. If added to all this was another complication, no wonder Marge felt things spinning out of control.

It had been gnawing at her since yesterday. A phone call. Long distance. Informative and frightening. Sufficiently so to put the search for Paul Newland into top gear. If only Reynolds would co-operate, all might yet be well. She had the sinking feeling that whatever else she might wish for, the ex-inspector wasn't likely to play along with her.

Chapter 3

As he drove slowly inland, in the direction Em Tregurion had taken, Reynolds began to reassess his options. Although instinct told him trouble lay ahead, he felt a strange protectiveness towards his old friend, as well as the more familiar curiosity. And once that curiosity was roused, he found it hard to let go without answers to questions that began to appear more interesting than the main one of where Paul Newland had gone.

The same questions gave him a valid reason why he should talk to Em quietly, without Marge's unhelpful interference, and hear her side of the story clearly. And after he'd done that, he promised himself, the sooner he persuaded the Clitheros to contact the police and withdrew from the case himself, the better for all concerned.

The road he was following narrowed to a single track, continuing down a steep hill to a crossroads. Here five equally twisting lanes met. A signpost, half hidden in the summer grasses, pointed to several small villages, all within a mile radius, each distinct from the others and each, as Reynolds knew, fiercely independent. Typically Cornish, all had names that sounded similar. Cursing the narrowness of the lanes, lined with brambles and gorse that scratched the sides of his car, he negotiated his way to each village in turn, finally discovering the one where Em

Tregurion lived by the simple expedient of identifying her bicycle outside a cottage gate.

Hamlet was a better word for this cluster of cottages, most of them tucked away behind high hedges of flowering fuchsias. Em's stood at the far end, and when he opened the gate, a dog appeared in the doorway of the cottage porch, barking furiously as he advanced. A Dobermann. Black and tan. Big. By reputation a vicious breed, not friendly to strangers. He retreated behind the safety of the gate, and waited for its mistress to appear.

The path was edged with rose bushes, badly needing attention, and the scent of the different varieties was overwhelming as he leaned on the gate, while the dog kept up its infernal barking.

'Spying on me, are you?' Em's opening salvo was not exactly auspicious. Arms akimbo, she eyed him suspiciously from the porch, her hair tied back now into a plait which made her look even younger. She'd had time to change into jeans and open-necked shirt, which suited her better than her working clothes, but her attitude made it clear she didn't want anything to do with him and was still smarting from her exchange with her former employer. Reynolds sighed again. A hostile witness needs pandering to, but this young woman seemed all spikes.

'You took a bit of finding,' he admitted with a smile, 'but what a find.' He gestured to the roses and the garden beyond, which extended in a wild tangle to the side of the house. Yet someone had once lavished care on this place; he had the impression that buried in the undergrowth were all sorts of botanical treasures which in a normal way he'd give anything to get his hands on. 'Are you the gardener?'

Her dark glance didn't alter, but she did hush the dog. 'My father was,' she said, answering his question factually. 'I've had too much to do since he died.'

'I can imagine,' he said soothingly. 'I expect the Clitheros keep you busy. And,' he pointed to a surfboard, which he had spotted leaning against the cottage wall, half hidden under a cascading wisteria, 'that must keep you even busier in fine weather.'

To his relief she laughed. 'Not any more,' she told him. 'I've given up on surfing this year. But you're right about

39

work; the old cow is a slave-driver. Wants her pound of flesh, doesn't she just. Mind you, the pay was good or I wouldn't have stood it this long.'

'Mr Clithero's more sympathetic, I take it.' Reynolds' voice was bland, but she looked at him guardedly before replying that yes, Mr C was all right.

'And what about Paul Newland?' he began, only to have her retreat into the shadow of the porch. She was about to slam the door when he added, 'I'm just one of Derek's friends. Making enquiries on his behalf. He's worried about Newland, that's all there is to it. I thought you might shed some light.'

Her retort from the shadows, 'And what's it to you?' was justified. He hesitated for a moment, thinking out his reply. He'd already stretched the truth somewhat; better be honest. Besides, he had the impression that Em saw through sham.

'I'm just an old bloodhound on the trail,' he admitted with a wry grin that wasn't all pretence. 'Can't give up. Comes with the training, I imagine. Sorry about that.' Giving his name and former rank and profession, he waited for her to tell him again to clear off, but to his surprise she

40

said unexpectedly. 'I've heard of you. I'm no fan of detective novels, but my friends say yours are good.'

Funnily enough, her praise, slight as it was, pleased him. 'I'm off duty these days,' he told her. 'As I said, it's only to give Derek some peace of mind.' He almost added, 'Poor Derek,' but she said it for him, or rather she looked it, turning down her mouth as if to say, 'He's a loser.'

'For what it's worth,' her answer came softly, 'I'll tell you what I know. Not that it's much.'

She came out from the porch, the dog at her heels, and walked down towards the gate. 'I only said what I did to get my own back,' she admitted when she reached him, as if she had been thinking out what to say. 'The old cow made me that mad. And I'm sorry now. It wasn't nice. To Derek, I mean. I think he took what I said in the wrong way.'

When he made no answer—because, after all, what would have been the right way?—she began to pick at the rose bushes, snapping off the faded blossoms and the rounded seed pods with decisive jerks.

Her hands were brown, the fingers square-tipped and strong. 'My dad showed me how to do this,' she said. 'Called it dead-heading. Said it makes more flowers. But I haven't once, all summer.

'There wasn't anything to it,' she repeated finally. 'And Derek was just trying to be kind. Hen-pecked to beggary, mind you,' she added in an even lower voice, 'and only helping on the sly when the workload was extra heavy, and the old cow wasn't looking. Generous too,' she concluded thoughtfully. She tossed her plait. 'Even offered to lend me money if I wanted, but I wouldn't take advantage, knowing how fond he is of me and all. I'd told him what I've been working for,' she went on, elaborating, giving Reynolds one of her piercing looks, 'and why I put up with his wife this long. I've won a place at uni this autumn, to study Cornish history, and need all the cash I can get.

'And that was all Newland was interested in,' she went on. 'Honest. On the Tuesday evening, after work, when I was supposed to have gone home, the evening before the old cow now says he

42

went missing, we talked about Cornish legends, Cornish places, things like that. Where? Behind the hedge back of number four, along the cliff path. Well off site, so Ma Clithero wouldn't spot us. It was a fine evening, nothing else to it at all.'

'And what about his driving down west the next day—that would be the Wednesday, I take it?'

'He only asked about the roads,' she replied quickly, 'what was the fastest route, that sort of thing. I can't be sure. But I am certain he was in a good mood, almost excited. I don't know why.'

She looked past him through the roses. 'Perhaps it was just the chance to talk to someone who shared his enthusiasm for Cornwall,' she continued after a while. 'Although if you asked my opinion I'd have said he wasn't really that keen. In fact, I felt he was putting it on; it made me dislike him.'

This version of the meeting, if correct, didn't produce much fresh information, except to suggest the Clitheros' concern was grossly exaggerated—and that Reynolds had been right about Em's dislike of sham. Before he could come up with other questions to ask her, she went on more fiercely. 'I suppose you're like everyone else, think there's nothing worth looking at in Cornwall. Another Marge Clithero, believing Cornish is a dirty word. Well, you're wrong. There's plenty of interest in its history and language. I've even been making a collection of books on those subjects. Mind you, I suppose it isn't much of a library yet. I can't afford to buy in a regular shop like some, but it's surprising what you can pick up here and there for a song, if you search hard enough.'

She looked at him, her eyes intense. 'And when I'm through I'll use what I've learned,' she went on, even more fiercely. 'You can call us the lunatic Celtic fringe if you want, but if other Celts like the Welsh and Scots and Irish can fight for independence, and win it, so can we Cornish. We need to. We're the lowest paid, have the largest numbers of unemployed, all our old traditions are ignored by the rest of England, what have we got to lose? And when we're free I mean to run for parliament. Not Westminster, but the Stannary Parliament, the old Cornish tin miners' parliament, here in Cornwall where it belongs.'

To emphasise her point she ground her foot into the pile of rosehips she'd dropped on the path, reducing them to pulp. Reynolds had a vision of her leaning over her chariot, sword in hand, leading her men to the charge. He sighed. He'd heard about Cornish nationalism before but never really met a practising member. It was an abrasive experience.

Again she misinterpreted his silence. 'And we're tired of having all you outsiders coming down and telling us what to do,' she concluded. 'Why don't you go back home where you belong and mess that up instead?'

With this last salvo she disappeared round the side of the house into the overgrown garden, while the Dobermann, which had been lying patiently at her feet, scratching for fleas, leapt up and began to bark again.

After hearing Reynolds' car start, Em relaxed. Trembling with passion, she walked through the garden, where great swaths of flowering bushes concealed her from view and caught in her hair. The dog padded beside her, poking its wet nose into

45

her hand until she patted its head. Why had she been so foolish to blurt out all her dreams and aspirations to a stranger who meant nothing to her? And why had she become so angry with him, when he didn't deserve it? It wasn't his fault he wasn't Cornish. But after Ma Clithero's comments, she saw insults everywhere, even when none was intended. And she'd found from hard experience that if she didn't speak her mind, people wouldn't take her seriously, especially as she was a woman, and a local woman at that. She frowned.

She hadn't meant to deceive Mr Reynolds when he asked her about Derek; it'd just come out the way it had. True, Derek didn't understand her either, and was always asking why she wanted to go off to college, but at least the old dear was willing to sit and listen. What would Ma Clithero say if she knew her precious husband, her lap dog, had been making eyes at her cleaning woman, her 'maid', as she had the cheek to call it, printing it out in the brochures for everyone to read? Em had seen Marge herself making eyes at some of her guests, the last in line Paul Newland. And it was certainly true that some of the guests enjoyed a little giggle at Marge's expense, although most of them felt too sorry for Derek to show it.

Her expression took on a far-away look. As she strolled with her dog through the jungle of flowers and grass stretching to a stone wall that marked the end of her property, she began to calm down. This was where she felt most at home. Leaning on the wall, staring through a little copse of trees to the sunlit fields beyond, she could pretend her dad was still alive, and could hear his soft voice telling her, 'Slow and steady wins the race,' and, 'If you can't lick 'em, join 'em,' two of his favourite sayings. Well, that was what she meant to do. She was older than the average incoming student but she'd work hard to catch up. And when she had, when her diploma was in her pocket, then she'd take on the world.

The sound of the gate and footsteps roused her from her reveries. She turned. The dog was growling faintly, showing its teeth but not exactly snarling. 'Oh,' she said bleakly. 'It's you. What do you want now?'

47

Chapter 4

Feeling more deflated than ever, Reynolds returned to Old Forge Cottage where he lived in St Breddaford. What had started as an interesting enquiry had suddenly degenerated into a harangue about Cornish independence from a young woman less than half his age. Her matter-of-fact explanation had equally downplayed any theories he might have indulged in about the relationship between the Clitheros and the missing man, and reduced Paul Newland himself to the stature of a tourist. The only bright spot was Em Tregurion herself. Although part of the 'lunatic Celtic fringe', at least she had the virtue of being genuine about her patriotic sentiments; he wished her luck. Whether she had told him everything she knew, or had altered her story a second time round to make it more palatable, he no longer really cared. As he'd already told himself, his growing dislike of the whole affair, and Marge Clithero in particular, made him more certain than ever that he should bow out while he could. Next morning, as he braced himself to pass on this decision, two unexpected phone calls made him change his mind.

The first was from Marge herself. In hysterics. 'She's turned up.' Her voice had never sounded more northern. 'Newland's wife. With a couple of children. Says she's come to join him. She's taken over his caravan. What am I to do?'

This information alone would have convinced him he'd made the right choice, except that it was followed by an even more urgent call. From Sergeant Derrymore. Derrymore was the local policeman, and his friend. Together they had solved more cases than most official partnerships.

Derry too sounded agitated. When he explained that a body had been discovered, murdered, and could the ex-inspector assist, Reynolds could scarcely refuse. Not when he heard who the victim was. Because it wasn't Newland; it was Em Tregurion.

As he drove through the hamlet, past the craning neighbours, Reynolds felt his usual repugnance for his former profession. After all his years in the force he had never become reconciled to violent death, and the sight of those avid, staring eyes

49

made him feel guilty. He was only a cut above them, masking his curiosity under pretended detachment.

There had been rain in the night and the morning sun released the scent of the roses, stronger than ever. Em's still figure on the kitchen floor seemed especially poignant in contrast to his memory of her the previous day. She was dressed in the clothes he'd last seen her in, sprawled on her back, her neck twisted at an impossible angle, as if someone had picked her up, shaken her violently and then tossed her aside like a rag doll. Her hair was spread beneath her, its vivid colour all the more shocking against the waxen skin, all that luminous glow extinguished. He felt a stab of pity and anger.

The doctor had just finished his examination and was pulling off his gloves. Death had been caused by strangulation, he said unnecessarily, time of death sometime yesterday afternoon; he'd know better after further tests. In the meanwhile they ought to look for a right-handed person strong enough to leave those marks around her throat.

While he and Derrymore conferred, Reynolds moved to the porch, where Em had retreated and looked back down the path. A few hours ago she had been full of vibrant life, putting him in his place with gusto and yet at the same time revealing her own aspirations and dreams with all the vulnerability of the young. What or who had attacked her in this fashion, what enemies could she possibly have? Against his will, the look on Derek's face came back to haunt him. As did Marge's spite. And then there was what Derek had mentioned about Newland 'being under stress'. Could it be the missing man was so unstable he had returned stealthily to attack Em? Even in Em's second version of their meeting, she'd insisted he'd been in high good humour—could his mood swing be typical of psychological imbalance, depression turning to overexcitement ...? Hold on, he warned himself. This is sheer guesswork. Because Newland and she had some furtive little rendezvous behind a hedge doesn't mean he's a murderer. But something was still nagging at the back of his mind, another something that didn't feel right.

He was about to tell Derrymore about his own visit to the cottage, and why he'd come here, when a police officer drew the sergeant to one side, their sudden serious expressions suggesting the news was bad. Turning back to the doctor, Reynolds asked instead what was known about the victim.

'I only meet people after they're dead.' The doctor sounded sarcastic, his way, Reynolds supposed, of dealing with tragedy. He snapped his bag shut and lumbered to his feet, smoothing greying hair away from his narrow forehead. 'But as it happens, I've seen her. On a street corner. Handing out leaflets about the latest fad. Cornish independence, they call it, I mean, what a load of crap.'

'Any family?' Reynolds brought him back to the subject.

'No. Her father died some time back. Famous for his roses.' Here the doctor allowed himself a smile, showing yellow teeth. 'Garden gone to rack and ruin since. Look at her hair.'

He bent to move one of the strands. Caught among the red were some leaves; together with small white flowers. Olearia, Reynolds thought, kneeling down and, close up, identifying it by the typical musky scent of the leaves. Olearia Scilloniensis. Normally blossomed in late spring, so this was unusually late. But he hadn't seen any flowering olearia by the front path.

'If you ask my opinion,' the doctor was saying even more sarcastically, 'you'd do no worse than interview the local youths. Specifically the surfing gangs.'

He straightened up and stood for a moment looking at the body. But whether he felt pity or was too hardened to feel anything, he merely returned to his grievances about the surfers, his sallow skin reddening with vexation.

'Myself, I avoid them on principle,' he said, with a vicious snap. 'If they aren't drunk, they're into drugs, so stoned they don't know where they're at. Make our lives a misery. And if they can cause trouble, they do, over and over again.'

It was not until he'd finished that Reynolds remembered the doctor lived in what he called a 'villa' near one of the main surfing beaches. More than that, last summer the surfing community had tried to enlist the help of local doctors in their fight against sea pollution. Without success. But he was remembering too the surfboard against the wall. 'I've given up,' she'd said.

Derrymore had come back at the end of this exchange. He observed the doctor morosely before turning towards Reynolds. 'A word, sir, if I may,' he said, in a voice that brought Reynolds to full alert. When Derrymore became formal it meant trouble was brewing. And sure enough, after he and the sergeant had moved out of earshot, 'There's a neighbour,' Derrymore said. 'Claims she saw you and your car. Claims you were here yesterday sometime after twelve.'

Damn, Reynolds thought angrily, not another Marge Clithero, sticking her nose in where she isn't wanted. He glanced at Derrymore.

Physically, the sergeant hadn't changed much from the young constable he'd met on his arrival at St Breddaford, and the very way Derry's large figure blocked the doorway, his round face creased in a determined frown, his legs braced in a typical Cornish wrestler's stance, reminded Reynolds what had originally attracted him and led to their unusual but effective partnership.

Although by now they'd come to rely on each other and understand each other's way of doing business, being older and more cynical Reynolds knew one should never take anything for granted, not

54

even friendship. And for all the bond between them, there was still room for disagreements. With another pang he recognised the approach of one of those moments.

He would have preferred to discuss the case rationally, rather than spend his time explaining his involvement with the Clitheros and their strange concern about Paul Newland—surely irrelevant now. Eventually he settled for the lame excuse that he'd stopped to chat with Em about a missing man from the caravan park where she worked. He glossed over the possibility of a meeting between Newland and Em, partly because of Em's own changed story and partly because he still wasn't convinced the man was really missing.

The expression on Derrymore's face didn't alter. All he said in the same formal way was, 'Time to check out this missing person caper when I talk to the Clitheros and their guests about Em herself. At the moment my real concern is this. According to the neighbour, you may have been the last person to see Em alive.'

He stopped to let that sink in.

'She says she heard angry voices,' he

55

added. 'Arguing. And the dog began to bark again.'

Reynolds felt himself flush. Then Derrymore's last remark reminded him of the unnamed thing that had been nagging at him. 'The dog,' he said, starting for the door. 'Where's her damn Dobermann? I couldn't get near the cottage yesterday without it threatening to tear me limb from limb.' And as Derrymore confessed he hadn't given the dog a thought, 'It wouldn't let anyone close to do her harm,' Reynolds told him. 'It was quiet when we were just talking, but if she was in danger, look out.'

Without further comment he pushed past Derrymore and headed towards the garden, the sergeant at his heels. Today, the massed bushes hung even lower, heavy with water; great drops cascaded on their heads and shoulders as they forced their way under drooping branches to the stone wall. There was no obvious sign of Em's dog, only a patch of strangely flattened grass suggesting something heavy had rested there. When Reynolds saw the olearia bush nearby, its typical compact shape run mad and a few straggly clusters of white flowers still dangling from its overgrown branches, he

56

came to an abrupt halt.

'Look here,' he said. He pointed to the bush, tearing off some leaves so Derrymore could smell them for himself. 'A hybrid,' he explained. 'Discovered on Tresco in the Scilly Isles sometime in the early part of this century. Supposed to grow only a few feet high but double the size here. Usually flowers in late spring, so this must be a second growth. A rare enough combination to make it doubtful you'll find one like it anywhere else. And its flowers are caught in her hair.'

It was his turn to pause for effect.

'She was in the house when I arrived,' he went on, 'and stayed by the front gate until I left. She came into this part of the garden later. So for starters, I'd check that flattened grass if I were you. It may be where she was killed.'

Derrymore pursed his lips in a way he had when he didn't quite believe a witness. It made him look older. Before he could argue, Reynolds continued, 'Finally, while you're at it, check her fingernails and shoes.'

Without another word he retraced his steps to the front of the cottage. The gate had been blocked off with tape by now and the path swept clear by rain, but when he told Derrymore what to look for, under the rose bushes the sergeant discovered the little piles of crushed rosehips that Em had pulled off.

'I never went indoors, this was as far as I got,' Reynolds repeated. 'She dead-headed the roses while she was talking to me and then ground them in with her foot. Unless she had time to scrub her hands and nails or change her shoes, you should find the stains.'

He stared at Derrymore. 'And if the neighbour heard angry voices, she didn't hear mine. When Em got going I never opened my mouth. If I'm the only visitor who's been identified so far, what about someone else using a way in through the trees via the fields? That stone wall's no barrier. And the cottage walls shield this side from the attentions of any nosy neighbours.'

He had Derrymore's full interest; the sergeant was listening intently. 'Get the woman who saw me to list the exact times she heard the dog bark,' Reynolds went on. 'As far as I remember, I arrived about half past twelve or so. I left some twenty minutes later, say at the latest one o'clock.

Your witness should be able to corroborate those times.'

By now Derrymore had relaxed enough to nod in agreement. Reynolds pressed home his advantage. 'And if the dog didn't bark again, either it knew the later visitor, or it had already been silenced.'

He looked at Derrymore squarely. 'There has to be at least one subsequent visitor,' he added softly. 'Unless he was already in the house. I'm speaking of the person who killed her. Because, of course, I didn't.'

Letting Derrymore work on that, he went on, 'And now, if you'll excuse me, I'm off to see the Clitheros about their own private problems. And to tell them what I'm telling you: if anyone's missing they'd better contact *you*.

'As for a possible link between the missing man and this murder, I leave that in your hands. I've decided to bow out of the case.' He grinned, but didn't feel like smiling. 'You know where to find me if I'm needed,' he added. 'I shan't go far.'

To his relief Derrymore didn't quibble. He heard the sergeant giving instructions to his men to start searching the garden and the fields, while he went off to grill the neighbour whose damning statements had caused so much tension.

And all because I can't say no when I know I ought to, Reynolds thought, savagely gunning the motor as he backed down the lane. Now I've really got to make the Clitheros decide what they want to do, and persuade Newland's wife, whoever she is, to file an official report of her husband's disappearance, if she thinks it's necessary. Because if they don't, I'll look a right old fool. And if any of them has anything to do with Newland's vanishing, or, heaven forbid, with poor Em's murder, it won't help matters that I may be partly to blame. If I hadn't been so inquisitive and persisted in questioning her, none of her involvement with Newland would have come out, however innocent it may have been. It was a sobering thought.

Chapter 5

He found the Clitheros in a state of high excitement—or, to be precise, Marge was. Derek was nowhere in sight. At first he thought Marge must have heard of Em's

60

murder, but it was nothing to do with that. Marge's whole attention was riveted on number four caravan, where a small child could be heard crying and a boy's head could be seen rising and falling above the curtains as he leapt up and down on the sofa.

'Children aren't allowed.' Marge was almost in tears. 'Only with regular guests who know the rules. Look what she's letting them do.'

If his mission hadn't been so serious, Reynolds would have laughed. He'd already guessed the average Clithero guest was well past child-bearing age; it might do Marge good to deal with the real world for once.

'Have you heard the news?' he asked. And when Marge stopped her grumbling to echo him, 'Bad news,' he told her gravely. 'Em Tregurion's dead.'

He watched her carefully but her expression gave nothing away. Only her painted lips twitched. After a while she said with a sniff that could have been regret or disdain, 'She was quite shameless. Look what she let out yesterday. All untrue, of course. Ask anyone. They'll tell you how much I'm liked.'

Still unaware how completely self-centred she sounded, she added waspishly, 'I'm not surprised she's come to a sticky end. It's what she deserved.'

Realising too late that this remark could be construed badly, her face suddenly crumpled. Useless for Reynolds to tell her not to worry. 'It's your fault,' she whined, repeating a former argument. 'We relied on you, but you haven't located Mr Newland yet. Worse, you've plunged us into the thick of a murder case. You ought to be ashamed.'

Reynolds gave up. He was about to ask for Derek, when another burst of energy from number four diverted his attention.

There was a loud crash, the caravan actually seemed to rock and a woman's raised voice could be heard. 'They'll wreck it.' Marge started forward. 'Come on.'

Reversing his order of priorities, Reynolds followed as she burst in without even the courtesy of a knock. The caravan looked as if a whirlwind had struck it; clothes and toys were strewn from one end to the other and there was a distinct smell of burnt fat. Greasy plates littered the table where one of the vases had formerly held pride of place, and shards of pink pottery were scattered over the floor.

A wisp of a woman, her body and face all angles, stood in the bedroom doorway, a crying baby in her arms. By contrast the baby was so dimpled with fat Reynolds' immediate impression was that it must have literally drained its mother dry. The mother herself, presumably Mrs Newland, appeared unaware of the intrusion; all her attention was fixed on the boy, a skinny child of five or six, dressed only in bathing trunks, his face and chest liberally smeared with what looked like strawberry jam.

Having given up on using the sofa as a trampoline, he was now attempting to somersault over its sides. While his harassed mother tried to stop him, telling him he'd hurt himself, and Marge, equally distraught, screamed about damage to the furnishings, that vase alone cost a pretty penny, Reynolds scooped the boy up and placed him on his feet. 'Now, sonny,' he said mildly, 'I need to talk with your mum. Can you act like a proper big brother for a moment and keep an eye on your sister?'

His strategy worked. The boy stared with pale-grey eyes, then nodded, seized the baby in his arms and plumped it down in front of the window. Kneeling beside it, he piled toys and books around it until it was effectively cocooned from sight, all the while muttering to himself in a flat tone. Taking advantage of this respite, Reynolds introduced himself, without mentioning his former rank, and at Mrs Newland's nod when asked if she were indeed Paul Newland's wife, queried if she knew where her husband was.

'Here,' Mrs Newland said. She made a vague gesture to indicate the caravan in general. 'He's rented it, hasn't he?'

Reynolds shot a look at Marge, who was carefully avoiding his gaze. So Marge hadn't discussed the problem of where the husband was, probably hadn't even mentioned it. Crafty so and so; she left that to him, and he'd fallen into the trap. But with the wife here in person to take charge, Marge could no longer be held responsible for Newland's whereabouts.

As tactfully as he could in the circumstances, he indicated the possibility of Newland's disappearance, while Mrs Newland sank on the sofa as if exhausted, as well she might be. There were already signs that the baby-sitting process had lost its novelty, and the baby was beginning to grow restless under its brother's ill-timed ministrations.

When Reynolds had finished his explanations, Mrs Newland didn't speak. Her eyelids were lowered as she stared at the floor, and her hands, folded in her lap, gave the impression of meek patience, emphasised by the long grey dress she was wearing, its thin material clinging to her skinny frame. Her close-cropped hair, cut in a Quaker-like fringe, added to this impression, but when she eventually glanced up, her eyes were unexpectedly bright, fierce like a hawk's, and her reply was sharp. 'That's typical,' she said. 'Paul's always on the go, impossible to tie down, even for a moment.'

'So you see no cause for alarm?' Reynolds probed.

'Not in the least,' she countered. She looked at him, could it have been defiantly? He had the fleeting impression that given half a chance, under the exhaustion there was still a spark. 'I'm only surprised he didn't mention we were coming. Although if I'd known the drive was so long I'd have thought twice about doing it alone with the children.'

I bet, Reynolds thought drily as the

65

baby let out a squeal and she told its brother to give over his pinching; they'd exhaust me just taking them round the corner. Before he could ask where she'd come from, Marge interposed. 'I told her he'd booked it only for himself,' she said accusingly. 'He never said anything about the rest of the family.'

As Reynolds tried to come to the rescue, Mrs Newland surprised him again. 'We can sort that out when he returns,' she countered, equally sharply. 'Besides, he wouldn't want a great place like this just for one.'

She followed this telling shot with another. 'He often takes trips like this,' she told Reynolds, ignoring Marge. 'The difference is this time we planned to combine it with a summer holiday. The children need a change. We live in Birmingham.' And she rattled off an inner-city address so quickly that Reynolds had to ask her to repeat it before he could make a note of it.

All seemed in order—both she and the little boy spoke with Midlands accents—but Reynolds couldn't forget Em's description of Newland's excitement. 'Fond of old buildings and so on, is he?' he asked, to have Mrs Newland shake her head. 'I don't think so especially,' she said. Then, 'He's an antique dealer,' she added hastily, too hastily in Reynolds' estimation. 'I expect you know what they're like, in and out of all sorts of odd places. Whatever's old attracts them, it's like honey to bees.'

A strange analogy. Making one last effort, he asked again if she didn't think that the police should be informed; after all, her husband had been gone now for several days.

Marge must have let the rest of the conversation flow past her, but the word 'police' brought all her anxiety to the fore. 'There's no need for that,' she cried. 'I mean, we can rely on John.'

Reversing what she'd said earlier, an illogicality which never seemed to worry her, she added with a forced smile, 'John's a first-class detective, you know, now retired. He'll do what has to be done.'

'Not if it's a police matter already,' Reynolds contradicted her bleakly. 'There's been a murder,' he explained to Mrs Newland, speaking low so as not to scare the children. 'A young woman who worked here. They will probably be talking to everyone who knew or saw her ...'

Before he could elaborate, Marge turned on him. 'You've no call to talk about the police,' she positively frothed again. 'I specifically told you they weren't to be involved. And if Mrs Newland says there's no cause for alarm, then you'd better listen to her. It was only Mr Newland's welfare that interested us.'

Once more she seemed completely unaware of how illogical she sounded. Or of the effect her myopic view gave, as if a murder was of no consequence. Her unexpected attempt at alliance with Newland's wife was equally strange, matched only by Mrs Newland's reaction. During this exchange Mrs Newland's face had remained placid; in fact, with her dark head bowed and her hands still folded, she looked more than ever like some little Quaker busy at her prayers. Now she gave a laugh and shook her finger playfully.

'There you are, Inspector,' she said. 'We're both agreed. You're making a fuss over nothing. He'll turn up like always.'

Stalemate.

He was thinking up a new argument to make her see reason—after all, if somehow

Newland was involved with Em, the police would have to know—when the baby let out a squall. The stack of toys and books had collapsed as the little boy leaned on them. Mrs Newland moved to scoop her daughter up, while her son eyed the vacant couch as if contemplating another jumping session. There seemed nothing else to add, and even Marge was silenced. She withdrew in as dignified a manner as she could, leaving Reynolds to assure Mrs Newland that if she changed her mind he would do everything he could to help, an offer which she ignored.

Once outside the caravan, Marge reverted to her usual self. If looks could have killed, Reynolds would be drawing his last breath. 'I warned you,' she complained, her eyes narrowing. 'She's a mystery, that one. If her husband's disappeared I'll bet you anything she's to blame.'

Once more ignoring the fact of Em's murder, she added, 'I'm sure he didn't expect her to follow him. He never mentioned her or the children. What's more, I think he wanted to get away from them.'

'How can you say that?' Reynolds was angrier than he should have been. Her remark was typical of her, sheer fabrication, without any attempt at fact. 'You've no right to ...'

'Yes I have,' Marge fought back. He could tell from the way she licked her lips that she was considering her next remark. What she said was yet another surprise. For the first time she revealed the telephone conversation of the Wednesday evening. And it shed a very different light on matters.

The phone call was from Paul Newland's sister. Marge's voice was smug. Reynolds had to admire the way she now used this information to prove her point. The sister had rung specifically to check how her brother was. 'She was concerned,' Marge concluded virtuously. 'He was on the verge of a breakdown. Mainly family stress.'

She brought this out with a little smile, a gambler throwing down a trump card. 'I was only surprised about the car. His sister told me it was hers. Said she'd lent it him and was worried about it too. I would be myself, if I were in her position. Who knows where it is now?'

Not letting Reynolds answer, 'Newland certainly led me on,' she confided in

70

one of her now infamous *non sequiturs,* 'pretending it was his. Flashing all that money about as if he were rich.'

Her revelation put a different complexion on the investigation, partially explaining her fears for the missing man. Damn, Reynolds thought, stupid woman. 'Why didn't you tell me earlier?' he barked, to have Marge whine she hadn't known it was important, an obvious lie. But if it gave a plausible reason for her previous anxiety and justified her making Derek contact him, it still didn't satisfactorily explain her curious distinction between finding Paul Newland and knowing where he was.

Her concluding remarks left him in no doubt of her mood. 'I've done my best to hush things up,' she said virtuously, 'and if you hadn't mucked us about, I'd have succeeded. You wouldn't be so smug if you knew how much your mistakes are going to cost.'

And with that ambiguous remark she stalked across to her own caravan, went in and slammed the door.

Once inside, Marge's little moment of triumph faded. She sank down into a

71

chair, staring vacantly into space. She'd been stupid. Stupid to have told Reynolds too much about matters best kept quiet; stupid to have pretended to side with that hateful little wife. At least, she straightened up, she'd had the sense to hide the last part of the telephone conversation, the really important part. Wild horses wouldn't drag that out. And if she knew what was good for her she'd get rid of Mrs Newland and ex-Inspector Reynolds double quick.

Left to his own devices, Reynolds decided to allow his anger to cool before trying to figure out Marge's baffling behaviour, especially the story about the sister and her phone call. As for Mrs Newland, she certainly was a mystery. If he'd been in charge of an official investigation, her sudden bursts of energy and as sudden lapses into inertia would have raised all his professional antennae. He didn't envy Derrymore having to unravel the complexities of this case. But before he left, he'd one more part to clear up to satisfy himself. Turning his back on the Clithero caravan, he went in search of Derek.

Chapter 6

Derek was sitting behind a dilapidated garden shed, his shoulders hunched. A lawnmower stood nearby, and his sudden start at Reynolds' appearance made it clear that he was expecting his wife. Probably she took every opportunity to spy on him too.

When he saw who it was he hung his head, such a defeated, hangdog look that Reynolds felt another stab of pity. What he would give to have the old Clithero of army days back, with his cheeky northern wit and brash independence. He sat down on the bench beside his former comrade and waited. And presently it all came out, the sadness mixed with anger.

'Em was the best thing that happened since we settled here.' Derek was positive about that. 'In the first place, I never wanted to move south. Then Marge used all my army savings to buy this place. I never wanted to run a caravan park or wait on people, for God's sake.'

73

He'd been taken by Em from the start, he confided. She was independent, so obviously unafraid of Marge, he'd found her refreshing. Then, too, she was a worker. Like himself. Marge merely lolled about and gave orders.

In the few months Em had been employed at the caravan site, admiration had turned to affection, to love, yes, love, he repeated the word defiantly, although nothing he was ashamed of. He wasn't like his wife, vamping it up with every male she could get her hands on. They'd had no children; he wanted to help the younger woman. A familiar story, Reynolds thought. But again, the whole truth? Remembering the Derek of army days, he recollected another less attractive trait—the typical soldier's ability to turn an incident on its head when in a tight place. Derek might have been subdued by civilian life but that didn't mean he'd become hopelessly sentimental; there was surely still a streak of northern practicality, of northern realism, hidden under that passive veneer.

It was when he asked Derek if he'd known Em had met up with Newland 'after hours' that cracks began to appear. 'No,' Derek began, then, 'Well, yes. She'd mentioned it. We used to have a break for coffee about this time. Right here. Her chance to tell me what was on her mind, what she'd been up to, things of that sort.'

Keeping his voice deliberately neutral, Reynolds asked, 'And her outburst yesterday morning?' Derek's over-eager reply was that Em had obviously been joking. Perhaps, Reynolds thought wryly. But it didn't stop you having doubts when you heard what she said to Marge. And I bet it didn't stop you haring off after her, to have the facts out. He looked appraisingly at Derek, who in turn glanced up at him, his eyes watchful.

'And did you meet anywhere else?' he asked craftily, only to have Derek again answer both yes and no, with the added explanation that he meant that sometimes, when she'd had a particularly hard day, he'd driven her home. He'd use the excuse he had some repair to take care of, or some piece of equipment to buy; she'd ride off and wait for him to stow the bike in the back of the van.

'And did you go to her cottage yesterday?'

Derek shot him another of his terrier

looks. 'What if I did?' For the first time his answer was truculent. 'So did you.'

Touché. Especially when he went on to point out that he'd had the good sense not to park outside her gate. 'For all the world to see,' he added with a snort, reminding Reynolds of the old Derek.

He went on to elaborate how he himself never drove near Em's actual village. Instead, he usually followed the road past the turn-off for a couple of miles, leaving his van in a small layby. 'Cars are always parked there,' he told Reynolds. 'It's the start of a cross-country footpath. I follow it halfway along, cut across to her place and climb into her garden, no one the wiser.'

The vision of this ageing Romeo trudging through muddy fields and scrambling over walls had its amusing side. But Derek had also given away the fact that he'd used the route before.

As if guessing where Reynolds' thoughts had taken him, the older man blushed, as much as his grizzled cheeks would allow. 'No harm to it,' he insisted. 'Just didn't want to give the gossips grist for their mill, like you did. She told me you'd been, and to tell the truth, she didn't appreciate your visit.'

Touché again. 'What about the dog?' Reynolds' next question was mild.

'Old Kernow? That's what she called him, meaning Cornwall. Kern for short. He didn't bother me. And I didn't bother him.'

'Was he still there yesterday when you left?'

Derek looked puzzled. 'Of course,' he said, 'he always stuck to her like glue.'

'And you yourself stayed in the garden? You didn't go inside?' Reynolds insisted.

Derek asked why, then, as if answering his own question, added, 'I know she was found in the kitchen. It was on the news. But we sat on the grass. And she talked. Like she did to you. To get it out of her system. Marge was hard on her, that's why she made the story up to get her own back.'

Derek's version explained the flattened patch of grass, and was certainly feasible, Reynolds thought. It could probably be confirmed too if, like Em, Derek had olearia flowers or pollen on his hair and clothes. But, he couldn't stop his thoughts, all that may substantiate his claim he was in the garden; it won't prove one way or another what else he did. For one thing,

Derek had been trained in commando tactics. If anyone knew how to snap a neck bone, he did.

Repressing this thought, he harked back to the meeting between Newland and Em. 'And you accepted her story?' he asked. 'You believed their relationship was casual, nothing to it?'

Derek bristled. 'Of course,' he said. 'In any case, Em was always friendly like that with everyone. That's partly why I loved her.'

I wonder, Reynolds thought. She was pretty prickly with me. Or is love blind?

'Did she ever mention other friends?' His next question was more delicate, but Derek said aggressively, 'I suppose you mean boyfriends. No, she didn't. Not that I know of. She never mentioned any and I never asked. And since she started working here she was too busy to gad about much.' His head drooped again. 'Not that I don't think the lads might have been queuing up,' he added more softly. 'She was pretty enough. But when her father died, well, she turned to me, I suppose.'

All this had a familiar ring too, and substantiated Em's claims of being overworked. It also fitted Derek's own character that he would be the last to pry. But the Em who handed out leaflets and went off surfing must have had another life of her own at some time. About to hammer out this point, he saw the lines on Derek's face deepen. The older man began to sob, great dry, heaving sobs. When he'd recovered, 'She wasn't taken in by him, mind you,' he repeated, returning to the subject of Newland. 'Not like some. In spite of all that flashing of money and so on, she called him a faker, turning on the charm when it suited him. Coming down to Cornwall and pretending to enthuse over it.'

He sounded genuinely aggrieved, as if he himself wasn't part of the same pattern. Perhaps Em's ideas had rubbed off on him. And she'd more or less hinted the same thing.

Derek's final comment would have been funny if he hadn't been so serious. 'Besides, Newland's a married man. She wasn't likely to take up with him.'

Reynolds' last question was more direct. 'Does Marge know about these visits of yours?' he asked. 'They've been going on for quite a while, haven't they?'

Derek didn't reply. When he did, his

answer was even more truculent. 'Of course she doesn't know,' he growled. 'She never notices anything I do. Anyway, I've told you, there was nothing wrong in it. And no one can pin her death on me. I was there as her best friend. But,' here for the first time he looked worried, 'what if the police find out? That would be difficult.'

'Go to them immediately, now, and tell them what you've just told me.' Reynolds spoke forcefully. 'Ask for Sergeant Derrymore. He's an understanding man; he'll not make trouble for you with Marge unless it's really necessary, and it shouldn't come to that.'

He studied Derek's expression. 'You owe it to Em,' he said even more emphatically. 'In any case, the police are bound to question you and Marge, if only because Em worked here and you knew her. You can envisage for yourself how bad it'll sound if you wait until they get here to reveal what you know.'

He spoke from long experience, but his own predicament was also on his mind. And he couldn't help wondering about Derek's claim that his wife didn't know. He had heard that expression more times than he liked to count, and as far as he was concerned there wasn't a wife alive who wasn't aware, at some level, of her husband's possible infidelities. With a woman like Marge, he'd bet his boots she already had her suspicions. And a suspicious Marge was another loose cannon. Once more he repressed the thought.

'I'll come with you if you like,' he volunteered, but Derek refused, with another dogged look that suggested he would do what had to be done, in his own way. Reynolds was reluctant to leave him in this mood, because if Derek didn't 'confess', he would find himself in the unenviable position of having to do it for him, not a pleasant prospect.

After deciding that his talk with Derek had been as unsatisfactory as his talk with Marge and Mrs Newland, Reynolds did what he had originally threatened and took himself off home, out of immediate temptation, there to bury himself in work for the rest of the weekend. He had a new manuscript to proofread, but for once editing failed to hold his attention, and weeding the flowerbeds—his usual remedy for boredom—was cut short by heavy bursts of rain which drove him back indoors. By Monday he was desperate to know what headway Derrymore had made, yet too proud to make overtures or ask outright. Wandering about the house aimlessly and finally switching on the radio for something to do, he came upon a casual chat show that reversed all his previous resolutions.

It was the sort used to fill the airwaves in the doldrums of late summer, and wasn't in any way linked to the murder—which, having been hashed and rehashed in general terms over the past two days, had now been wrung out and left to dry; in fact, it revolved around environmental pollution, a theme dominating the local media for weeks.

'We've notice of another illegal dumping site,' the main speaker was intoning, 'an old eyesore that should have been shut down years ago.' He named it, in a small, obscure village in western Cornwall. 'Practically outside people's front doors. But no one in government pays attention, not even when, like last night, a car was set on fire and acrid smoke spread through the neighbourhood.'

A spate of angry voices from phone-in listeners supported this claim, among them one strident lady who kept protesting it wasn't just that the dump was an eyesore, it was also a danger to health, children's in particular. Reynolds thought she was probably right, but her manner irritated him. And he wasn't really interested in the failure to deal effectively with an illegal tip—it was mention of the burnt-out car that he'd latched on to.

Why on earth would anyone burn a car? His original thought was followed by another: what if the car's remains could be identified as a new blue BMW? And even more important, if it was the BMW, where was its driver, the elusive Paul Newland?

It was a long shot, one of his 'hunches', but cases had been solved before on such slender links. Trying to stop his imagination was like trying to dam a flood. Taking time only to change into hiking boots, he was out of the front door, heading towards the A30 and Land's End, all resolutions to stay at home and disengage himself happily forgotten in the excitement of the chase.

The village of Carnford lay inland, in a little valley between Hayle and St Ives. It had once been a mining village, before the closure of the tin mines in the 1920s had left the whole region deserted, like one of the gold-rush towns in California. As he drove past the crumbling chimneys and engine houses of these old mines, he was reminded again of the tenacity of the Cornish. They might have been ousted from their jobs here, but all over the world, wherever there were mines, 'Cornish Jacks' worked them. And, no matter where they settled, they never forgot their real inheritance, and when they could, came home again.

In the post-war years, however, the proximity to the coast, and a modern breed of tourist, had given new prosperity to the area, and Carnford had presumably enjoyed its share. Its row of miners' cottages had been renovated and the front gardens were bright with flowering bushes, a luxury mining families could never have afforded. Even the Methodist chapel, once the centre of village life, had been turned into a dwelling, with an attached garage and satellite TV dish.

As Reynolds approached on foot—mindful of Derek's criticism, he had found a place to park a mile or so off—he reminded himself that mine shafts probably ran under most of the cottages. They might look solid enough, but occasionally the ground subsided, taking down buildings and gardens with it, as he'd found to his cost in a previous investigation.

There was no sign of the offending dumping site, but it couldn't be far away. Not wanting to draw attention to himself by making enquiries, he stopped beside a stretch of rough pasture facing the main row of cottages, and consulted his map. In the old Cornish language, the first part of the village name meant a cairn, or pile of rocks, while the second suggested there must once have been water nearby; and sure enough, to the south, there was rising moorland of heather and gorse, capped by granite stones, with an old mine engine house and chimney still standing, whose run-off had probably swollen the moorland stream to larger dimensions than today.

Fortunately for the moment the rain had passed, although banked clouds suggested it might return. Better start moving, he thought, if I don't want to be soaked. Taking a chance, he headed south towards the higher ground, hoping that from the top he would get a better feel for the lie of the land.

His route crossed the open pasture,

where several boys, their faces and clothes liberally daubed with mud, were playing impromptu football among some grazing sheep. Their shouts, and the skill of one youngster in a striped jersey, kept him riveted until he remembered his objective. Skirting past the players, he strode on, only to have his way blocked by a gorse thicket, through which wide tracks had been cut as if by farm vehicles. When, curious, he followed, he found the illegal tip.

It lay at the foot of an unexpectedly steep escarpment, invisible until he reached its very edge. At its foot the stream ran sluggishly, its water still stained a dull red from mine waste. Strewn all along its banks and halfway up the steep incline, rubbish of all sorts had been scattered in grotesque heaps. Some of it must have been there for a long while; parts of old-fashioned farm machinery jostled with broken Cornish ranges, half buried under more recent garden waste and mountains of discarded tins. He looked around him, wrinkling his nose. And caught the fresh stench of a smouldering fire, coming from behind a rocky promontory.

Forcing a path through the mounds of festering rubbish, Reynolds cursed his lack of foresight in not changing his clothes. At least his boots did him yeoman service, gripping the side of rocks made slippery by the rain. And when he had eased round the corner, there lay the burnt-out skeleton of a car.

The fire must have been considerable, for there wasn't much left of the vehicle itself, just the bare frame, twisted out of recognition. Around it, the blackened heather and gorse was still hot, in spite of the rain. When he tried to walk across it, he felt it scorching his boots.

There was the distinct smell of rubber and plastic, which reminded him too vividly of burnt-out army lorries he'd seen in the desert around Aden. And there was another smell, he guessed petrol. From the empty tins scattered nearby, there had been plenty of it. So the fire had been set deliberately.

Approaching gingerly, he examined the debris from a safe distance. If there were the remains of a body buried under that mass of metal it would take an expert to find them, let alone determine what make the car was. But still ...' Thoughtfully he prowled about the wreckage, looking for clues, however small. And after finding nothing more incriminating than discarded petrol tins, and preferring a new route back, he clambered up the slope immediately behind him.

The gradient was steeper than he'd anticipated, and at the top a distinct overhang forced him to dangle uncomfortably into space while he heaved his body over. Scrambling ungracefully upright, he peered back, fighting for breath.

From this angle it was easy to see where the car had skidded and bounced before landing on its back. And when he looked behind him there were fresh wheel tracks in the wet grass and gorse. If someone had pushed the car over, there ought to be footprints. He was bending to search for them when his sixth sense warned him someone was moving stealthily through the bushes behind him, preparing to pounce. And he was perched above the overhang, on the lip of a precipice.

Instead of trying to stand up and maintain his balance, he acted instinctively, whipping round to face the prowler, and diving low at the legs. He brought the advancing figure down in a classical rugby tackle, but for a moment both slithered together over the grass towards the edge, until with a mighty heave he had gained the upper hand and was straining to hold them back.

When their forward roll had stopped, he clambered to his feet and stared at the man lying in front of him. To his surprise he was old, white-haired, with a wrinkled and weatherbeaten face out of which bright-blue eyes glared. Bunching a fistful of the man's jacket, he jerked him upright.

The figure came up surprisingly lightly, like a sack of bones, the clothes tied with string and reeking of the sour smell of stale dirt and unwashed flesh. 'What you do that fer?' the fellow snivelled, sleeving mud and blood from a cut lip, his chest rising and falling with his efforts. 'Never meant no harm.'

I bet, Reynolds thought grimly. Standing well back, he surveyed the man. 'And just what are you doing here?' he asked. 'Other than pushing people, or cars, over cliffs?'

The old man bristled. 'Never pushed no car,' he wheezed, ignoring the first part of the question. 'Saw it burning last night, that's all, and comed to look at what was left of it this morning. Just like you did.'

Doubled up with coughing, he tugged

at the string round his waist to produce a greasy piece of paper, yellowed with age. 'Got the right to look,' he announced proudly, between coughs. 'There's my licence, see. Trev Carthew. Rags and Bones. Not that they call it that nowadays; haulage merchants more like, and not much pickings for a small local man on his own when they've done with it.'

Recovering his breath, he began to brush himself down with long, dirty fingers. 'They'm all big upcountry people, like you.' His next comment was fierce. 'Not a Cornish man among 'em. And not a thought fer what's due real Cornish born and bred, bloody thieving beggars the lot. Ought to be banned. This here's Cornish land, and Cornish rubbish, and don't you deny it. And I don't need no competition.'

This last comment was accompanied by a threatening gesture. I presume he thinks I'm after his spoils, Reynolds thought. And he's obviously another mad nationalist; in a moment he'll be lecturing me about self-government.

'You're right that there's not much left.' He nodded in the direction of the car, his rejoinder brusque. 'But wrong that I want

90

it. All I want is to know who started the fire. Did you see that?'

The blue eyes stopped their blinking while Trev digested this information. Then, 'Never saw nothing,' he grunted. 'Nothing that anyone else wouldn't have seen if they cared to look. Which they don't. Good at making trouble from a safe distance. that's about their limit.'

He settled down to a steady grumble. 'Heard 'em on the wireless this morning, wanting to clear the site away. Doesn't make no difference, I suppose, that they puts a local man out of business. They'm upcountry too, these days.'

He blinked again. ' 'Spect you'm from the council, checking up,' he ventured, his voice wary. 'You tell 'em from me, if there's really nothing left, let me see what I can make of it when it cools down.'

He managed a watery wink. 'Waste not, want not, that's my motto.'

'I advise you to leave well alone.' Reynolds' voice had again hardened. 'This may be a police matter. You may be called as a witness.'

'Police?' Trev Carthew looked alarmed. 'I don't hold no truck with the police. I don't know nothing, I told you so.'

Another thought struck him. 'You bain't one of those plainclothes fellas, are you?' he asked, sounding even more alarmed. 'Now mind you say I was only protecting the evidence from what I took to be some good-fer-nothing snooper. That's what you look like, you know, in that grubby coat.'

And he gestured at Reynolds' dishevelled appearance.

Reynolds stifled a smile at the man's impudence. 'Where shall I find you?' he asked, to have Trev admit that he kipped rough when he was on the trawl, as he called it, but not so rough as all that; he'd a nice little shanty up on the moors, close to the stream, made from bits and pieces he'd garnered over the years. And as far as he was concerned these dumps, illegal or not, were meat and drink to him. Close them down, that'd be the end of him and no mistake.

Reynolds left him to his mutterings. He doubted if there was any real harm to Trev except an over-exuberant protection of his own, as it were, not likely to be repeated. Trev might be old but he had all his wits about him; he'd pay attention to Reynolds' warning. In any case the heat would keep any interlopers away from the car remains until Reynolds got back to civilisation and reported his find to Derrymore. And come to think of it, if it were the BMW, according to Newland's sister he didn't even own the ruddy thing! Reminding himself again to tell Derrymore that the sister, and her message to Marge Clithero, should be checked out as soon as possible, he made his way back through the gorse bushes towards the football field, while Trev limped off in the opposite direction.

The match seemed to have come to a standstill and the players were engaged in a brawl. Reynolds strolled closer. It occurred to him that small boys were noted for being curious; perhaps one of the group had noticed something more positive than Trev. He stopped to listen.

The focus of attention was the urchin in the striped jersey. Close up, he looked some eight or nine years old, although he might have been younger. He was short and stocky, dressed in what even Reynolds recognised as unfashionable clobber for a kid these days. The distinctive jersey of vivid colours, obviously hand-knitted, hung in folds over patched and torn grey shorts, also much too big, while the green wellies, not the best boots for playing football in, provided the final touch that set him apart from the others, with their Manchester United sweat suits and new Reeboks. But what he missed in stature and sartorial elegance he made up for in noise.

'I did, I did, I did,' he was shouting. 'And you can't say different. You were all tucked up in your beddybyes, too scared to poke your heads out and look.'

His voice, although raucous, had a soft Cornish lilt woven into it, and was different too from the others, who were sharp-vowelled and harsh. They closed on him, circling him like dogs around a cornered animal. Typical group bullying.

'Look at what?' Reynolds interrupted, in his mildest manner. And when collectively they spun round in alarm, 'Not the fire last night, by any chance? I'm interested if you did.'

Most of the boys shook their heads, and, as if afraid of being accused of some wrongdoing, picked up their coats and began to sidle off, until only the boy in the striped jersey and one older lad were left behind.

Striped Jersey broke the silence. 'What's in it, mister?' he asked. 'I mean,' and he made the age-old gesture of rubbing two fingers together, while looking hard at Reynolds. Under a thatch of brown hair, badly needing cutting, his grey-green eyes were appraising. A cool customer, Reynolds thought, amused.

The older boy pushed him aside. 'He doesn't know anything,' he insisted. 'But my mother does.'

His long face grew dour and he turned his mouth down disapprovingly, a veritable spokesman, Reynolds thought, a village elder in the making. But why the reaction? Just as Striped Jersey had done, he wondered, what's in it for him?

Before Reynolds could intervene, the older boy turned on the younger, seizing his arm. 'All you do is talk,' he shouted. 'You know you're lying.'

'Leave go of me.' Striped Jersey wasn't going to give up easily. 'He's only mad because I saw something he didn't.' The words, although muffled, were loud enough to reach Reynolds. 'Last night.'

Here another tussle silenced him for a moment and he was forced to harness all his energy into breaking free. Before Reynolds could come to his rescue, a solid kick doubled up his tormentor, after which

95

he took to his heels, a string of choice swear words floating behind him.

'He's a born liar.' When he'd recovered, the older boy's repetition merely sounded spiteful. He slicked back his hair. 'Last week it was his ma was a titled lady,' he confided, 'and the week before his grandma wasn't his grandma and he was adopted. And,' he looked more dour than ever, 'half the time he claims he's sick so he can skip school. My mother says he's just one of the local gyppos and we're not allowed to play with him.'

His expression grew cunning. 'But if you want to know about the fire, my mother is on the committee that made the complaints. You could talk to her.'

He preened himself expectantly. Not averse to a little self-publicity, Reynolds thought, irritated. Or perhaps a little reward on the sly. And that disparaging reference to the locals had an unpleasantly familiar ring.

'He's certainly your best striker,' he said coldly, turning away as if no longer interested. He didn't know what caused his reaction, but it put the older boy in his place. He too picked up his jacket and ran off, leaving Reynolds in the middle of the makeshift pitch.

Of all the courses now open to him, it seemed imperative he alert Derrymore to his suspicions about the car. And if indeed it turned out to be the one Paul Newland had been driving—he gave a silent whistle. That would mean I'd better get back on the case, he told himself as, after a vain attempt to clean the mud from his boots and clothes, he reached his car and unlocked the door.

He was about to accelerate forward when, as if by magic, Striped Jersey appeared in front of the windshield, causing him to jam on the brakes. The car shuddered to a halt. Rolling down the window, he let fly with some choice words of his own. 'It's all right, mister.' The boy's voice was calm. 'I bain't hurt and your car bain't either. But for a fiver I'll tell you what I saw.'

There were fresh bruises under the mud, but for one so young he seemed remarkably in control. As offers went, his was cheap. Reynolds would have paid a great deal more for information. He took out his wallet and laid it on the seat beside him. 'Let's have your version then,' he said. 'But first I need a name to call you by!'

The boy hesitated, looking from wallet to owner. A curious expression crossed his face, not greed but something more primitive—hunger, perhaps—that made him look much older. In which case, Reynolds guessed, the state of his clothes was probably indicative of something rare these days—real poverty. His interest intensified.

'I'm George,' the boy said at last. For the first time he looked down. A lie, Reynolds thought, not a good beginning. But deciding he had nothing to lose, he settled back. 'Shoot,' he said.

'Last night,' George said, 'I heard a car. It came up our lane. Without its lights. So I went to see what was up.'

Interpreting Reynolds' expression correctly as scepticism he added, 'Our place is back along, over there.' He made a vague gesture. 'Before you get to the Row.'

Presumably he meant the line of cottages facing the football field. 'The lane goes on past us so we'm closer to the dump than anyone else,' he continued. 'People use it when they chuck something away and don't want anyone to find out. And I can get out of the house easy, without disturbing anyone.'

That's no doubt true, Reynolds thought sardonically, as George went on to explain how he had crept stealthily through the gorse bushes towards the tip, just in time to see the car go over with an awful thud.

A man had pushed it over; he saw him clearly before he too disappeared down the precipice after the car. Just one man. And when George was sure he'd gone all the way down to the bottom too, he slithered like a Red Indian to the edge and saw him moving about by the car.

'It was on fire,' he ended triumphantly. 'He was pouring stuff on it to make it flare up. I thought that was weird. Because lots of people throw things over, like I said, but they don't bother to burn 'em afterwards.'

'Any idea of make or colour?'

George shook his head. 'Too dark to tell the colour,' he said, 'but it was a posh car, big like yourn. I could tell from the sound of the engine.'

The last comments were shrewd. 'So who was this man you say you saw?' Reynolds asked. 'Was it,' he tried a guess, 'Trev Carthew, perhaps?'

'No.' George was adamant. 'I know old Trev. He wouldn't be so stupid to burn

something before he'd had his pickings.
And Trev's a Methodist. He'd never work
on Sundays. This man was younger. About
your size. He wore an army coat and a
sort of woollen cap. Trev don't dress
like that.'

Reynolds tried another tack. 'You said
it was late, no one else was about. How
late?'

'After midnight.'

'And your family doesn't mind your
being out when you should be in bed?'

'No problem.'

'Doesn't your mother try to stop you—or
is it grandmother?'

'Haven't got a mother.' George sounded
sulky. 'And my gran was up late anyway.'

'Wouldn't she have heard the car too?'

'She was watching telly. Last week
someone gived her an old one and she'm
stuck on it. She's not used to it, so she
turns it up real loud.' A quick glance. 'Not
that I mind. It didn't keep me awake.'

This was said defensively. 'I was looking
out the bedroom window.'

'What at?'

'Stars,' the boy said smugly. 'It had been
raining but then the moon comed out. I
study stars.'

Reynolds gave up. But if there was a shred of truth to the story it would be a real find. 'Here,' he said. He held out the note, and as the child leaned across the window to take it, 'Next time,' he said in his ear, 'when I ask your name you give me it straight. And that goes for everything you tell me, understand?'

The boy drew back, as if affronted. 'I did,' he said. 'I always tell the truth.'

Reynolds left him clutching his five-pound note. But something in the boy's stance, and in that moment's involuntary defence of his grandmother, stuck in his mind.

Chapter 7

He drove straight back to Em's cottage, where, as he'd guessed, Derrymore was still busy. Taking advantage of the watery sun that had followed all the rain, a line of officers was halfway across the first field, still looking for clues, while others were continuing their systematic search of the garden. The flattened patch of grass

101

remained cordoned off, although the bush that had given such a vital clue had shed most of its flowers. Derrymore himself was in the sitting room, supervising a final search of the house.

Derrymore greeted Reynolds in his usual affable manner, immediately outlining his tactics as if he owed Reynolds an explanation. They'd already combed the place thoroughly, he said, but nothing seemed to have been disturbed, although it looked now as if Em had indeed been strangled in the garden and her body dragged indoors—muddy marks on her clothes suggested this. Time of death had also been established, about four o'clock on Friday afternoon. Here he looked down at his feet before sheepishly admitting that Em's shoes had also been examined and found stained green with rosehips, as were her fingernails.

When Reynolds made no comment Derrymore cheered up. He'd eliminated any possibility of robbery, he added, as Em's personal belongings and little bits of jewellery had not been touched, and even her books, of which she was so proud, were still in their usual place on the bookshelves. The only unusual thing they'd found so far was her financial records.

He showed these to Reynolds, standing back as if waiting for the older man to comment. They were contained in a clear plastic folder and although carefully organised to reveal how much money she'd saved for her university career—added up each month in her round handwriting, with almost childish glee at her miserliness—there were also several unaccounted for withdrawals.

'What do you make of them, sir?' Derrymore asked. 'At regular intervals. Cash only. As yet no idea what she used the money for. What about buying books?'

When Reynolds pointed out that Em had admitted most had been bought second-hand, 'for a song', the sergeant looked disappointed but not completely downcast, merely putting the folder aside to 'deal with later'.

One reason for his good spirits now became clear. Headquarters, swamped with other work, was leaving him in charge for the moment, he told Reynolds, although one of their inspectors would be down later to take over. In the past headquarters had not always been as appreciative as they should have been of Derrymore, or village policemen in general; this time, their keeping a distance, even temporarily, was not only a personal compliment, it was a distinct advantage to his and Reynolds' continuing partnership. He beamed.

'I was about to come and find you,' he went on eagerly. 'We've had a positive lead. We know who gave her the dog. An ex-boyfriend.'

As Reynolds stared at him, 'Ex,' he emphasised the word. 'We've talked with all the neighbours, and several mentioned him. Apparently he and Em parted company early this year. We've just identified the fellow. Ray Mabley. Lives on Sea Road. If he was anywhere near the house last Friday I think we'll book him. I'm off to interview him. Want to come?'

It was Derrymore's usual peace offering. When Reynolds, encouraged by this reception, proceeded with an outline of the morning's adventures—paraphrasing his interview with Striped Jersey and avoiding mentioning him outright, partly out of consideration for the boy's age but mainly because he still wasn't convinced the evidence should be taken seriously unless confirmed by more reliable witnesses—to his even greater satisfaction the sergeant immediately sent out instructions to deal with the burnt-out car, even suggesting to his colleagues further west that interviews with the Carnford villagers, and with Trev Carthew, were the highest priority.

All this entailed a rather more detailed account of the missing Newland than Reynolds had previously given, excluding Derek's testimony, again out of fairness, but including Marge's revelation about a strange phone call and reopening the importance of some possible meeting between Newland and Em Tregurion.

Derrymore listened gravely, nodding his head. 'We'd better get on to this Newland fellow then,' he said. 'Tackle his wife properly and so on, see what she knows. When we were there last Friday, neither she nor the Clitheros mentioned him except to say his so-called disappearance was a tempest in a teacup; he was expected back momentarily. I left it at that. I mean, there's enough to do as it is without organising a search for a man whose wife swears he isn't missing at all.'

He gave a grin. 'I suppose if Newland's wife wasn't worried, the Clitheros had no reason to be, especially as Derek was so forthcoming.'

He didn't dwell on what Derek had actually told him, but then that might have been his way of being tactful. Reynolds was doubly relieved. Mainly for his old friend's sake. But also because if Derek had admitted visiting Em after Reynolds had departed, the ex-inspector himself would be completely exonerated.

Yet as Reynolds squeezed into the official car, he was startled to hear the sergeant say almost triumphantly, 'They always say when a case breaks, it breaks fast. I think we'll find my idea about Mabley holds.' And he rammed the car into gear even more erratically than usual.

Reynolds made no reply. In the first place he didn't believe in the truism. And in the second, he was usually the theorist, whose flights of fancy sometimes paid off; Derrymore had always been the realist who kept his feet on the ground. He couldn't say why, but he didn't for a moment believe that Ray Mabley was their man.

The ex-boyfriend lived with a group of friends in a small semi-detached bungalow, badly needing painting. Leaving Derrymore hammering on the door, Reynolds wandered round the back. There were no traces of dog, or kennel, or run, only a collection of surfboards, some the worse for wear, and a line of scruffy beach towels flapping in the wind above a tangle of uncut grass and bushes that must have been the bane of neater neighbours.

After repeated knockings, a sleepy young fellow opened the door, looking as if he'd just got out of bed, although by now it was well after midday. 'Ray Mabley,' he yawned. 'What about him?' There was still no sign or sound of any dog, and their efforts seemed doomed to failure until another fellow stuck his head out of a bathroom down the hall, to shout that Ray had already left. 'Surf's up,' he added, slamming the door, as if that explained everything.

So Ray was a surfer. That tallied with the state of his living quarters, and with Em's account of her former hobby—possibly explaining the quarrel, if giving it up had included giving up Mabley as well. And incidentally added weight to the doctor's original gloomy predictions about the surfing community.

The beach where Ray had gone was

on the north Cornish coast, and was famous for its waves. Although in no way comparable with Hawaii, nevertheless world championships were sometimes held there, attracting an international crowd. Ray Mabley was presumably part of this group; the neighbours had all insisted he spoke with a 'funny' accent. 'Good-looking too, according to one.' Derrymore allowed himself a wink. 'I gather he didn't take kindly to being dumped. A new experience.'

They reached their destination along a small street lined with houses, passing a golf course and the entrance to a vast redbrick and stone hotel that dominated the headland. Finding a place to park close to a little beach café, Reynolds and the sergeant took a moment to survey the scene below them.

The tide was out, and the reefs at the right of the beach beneath the hotel stood in jagged lines against the swirling foam. To the left, in sharp contrast to those narrow streets, a vast expanse of sand stretched into the distance, obscured by a faint mist of spray drifting in the wind, while out to sea the water sparkled a vivid blue to the horizon's rim.

The beach was crowded with surfers and holiday-makers taking advantage of the sun after days of rain. Most of the visitors kept to the shallows, between the lifeguard flags, paddling in the surf that spun and eddied across the sand. Further out, where the line of waves broke in curling folds, clusters of serious surfers bobbed up and down, in their black wetsuits looking for all the world like seals. Occasionally, when an especially high wave approached, they would heave themselves up on their boards and ride to shore. The summer sounds of laughter, of children playing, even the shouts of the surfers to each other, came to them muted by the constant boom and suck of the surf.

'A right old job to find him among that lot.' Derrymore was pragmatic. 'But it's worth a try.'

As they picked their way among groups of sun-worshippers, most of them sheltering behind striped windbreaks, Reynolds thought ruefully that he and the sergeant made an odd pair, he in mud-stained clothes and boots, Derrymore in blue uniform. He was conscious of people's stares. But then he hated the sea and anything to do with it, so perhaps he was being oversensitive.

Luckily the surfers kept to themselves, the kings of the beach, the 'Malibu men', distinguished by their long boards as distinct from the shorter bogie-board riders. They'd set up base at the back of the beach, close to the lifeguard hut, surrounded by their boards and the usual outer fringe of admiring hangers-on, mostly female. They all knew Ray, a champion they said, trying to pick him out from among the bobbing heads, and then impulsively volunteering to go out to bring him in. And they all knew Em Tregurion, had actually been talking of her as the sergeant and his companion approached. Her death had come as a dreadful shock. She wasn't like most girls, one said with a wink, pretending to like the sea but really in love with the men who rode it—here the assorted females gave a shriek and threw sand at the speaker. They all agreed, however, that she'd been a surfer herself, a good one. She should never have given it up, she'd be missed.

Ray Mabley was tall and, Reynolds supposed, could be called good-looking, in a bronzed, blue-eyed Californian sort of way. When they came up to him as he emerged from the surf, he stood perfectly at ease, dripping with water, his board under his arm, smiling pleasantly while they, looking foolish in Reynolds' opinion, were forced to shift back out of the wet sand to dodge the incoming tide.

The effort of trying to hear, or make themselves heard, above the surf proved impossible. It was only when they had moved back up the beach that Mabley paid them any real attention, his interest only half focused, as shown by his frequent backward glances at the waves he was being forced to miss. But when he spoke, his accent proved he was Australian. And mention of Em Tregurion angered him.

Yes, he knew her, he said. Or had known her. He shifted the board. No, they hadn't been an item for a while. Not since she'd gone her own sweet way and he'd gone his, bad luck for her. He smiled again but his eyes didn't smile.

'You know she's been murdered?'

At Derrymore's blunt question, for the first time Ray looked uncomfortable, using his bare feet to stir up the sand. His eyes, reddened with salt, watered in the wind. When he admitted having heard it on the news, 'You were nowhere near her cottage last Friday, the day she was killed?' Derrymore repeated, to have him retort

111

that if he had been he wouldn't bloody likely admit it. He had been with his mates all day; they would vouch for him if the sergeant needed an alibi.

'We're trying to trace her dog.' Derrymore must have regretted his brusque opening, for he spoke soothingly. 'We gather you gave it to her and ...'

'Lent it more like.' Ray Mabley made no attempt now to conceal his anger. 'When her father died. She said she didn't like living on her own. But then I didn't expect ...'

He stopped himself in time from saying, 'I didn't expect her to break with me.'

'And you haven't seen it since her death? It's missing, and we wondered ... Dogs tend to make for an earlier master when they've been traumatised.' Derrymore still spoke soothingly, even flatteringly. Whether what he said was true, or whether he even knew much about dogs and their ways, he certainly made it sound convincing. And Derrymore had a disconcerting habit of coming out with odd facts which were often proved correct.

Mabley reacted to this information with unusual vehemence. He dropped his board and clenched his fists. 'Why didn't you say so first off?' he howled. 'That dog was a beaut. Cost me a packet. But she never thought of that. Took it, thanks very much, and when I go off to college I'll sell it. You can't treat dogs like that. Mind you,' he was already calming down, 'it homed in on her, you know. So if it's gone, someone must have pinched it.'

He picked up his board. 'I didn't,' he said in a flat voice. 'But when you find it I'll have it back. If she didn't spoil it for anyone else, that is. And now, if you gentlemen will excuse me, I'm off while the waves last.'

About to sprint back through the surf, he turned once more, this time with a smile that wasn't pleasant. 'If you're looking for a lead to who murdered her,' he said, 'why don't you try that couple she worked for? I gather the old man had the hots for her. At least that's what she said.'

Before Derrymore could finish thanking him—in a distinctly sarcastic way—or warn him that they might ask more questions later, he disappeared under the water in a shower of spray, leaving the sergeant staring at his disappearing back, as if fighting the temptation to go in after him. 'I certainly will check your alibi,' he growled to himself, trying to wipe the sand splatters off his tunic. 'Although no doubt your mates will swear blind you were with them even if you weren't.' He turned to Reynolds. 'What do you make of him?' he asked uneasily. 'By my book, a strange fellow. No reaction when I mentioned Em's murder, yet went all to pieces about the dog.'

As they retraced their steps, weaving their way through the hazards of sand-castles and recumbent bodies, he kept harping back to Mabley's detachment, as if a dog was more important than a former girlfriend, and what's more a dog he probably couldn't look after if he was out playing in the sea all day, and probably wouldn't take back with him when he returned to Australia.

'And how does he live? Where does his money come from? Perhaps that's where Em's spare cash went, subsidising him.' Derrymore's dislike of what he called 'layabouts' had never sounded more prejudicial. But Reynolds was piecing together a slightly different image, remembering the look in Mabley's eyes, watering in the wind. He wished now that he'd insisted on questioning Mabley himself.

It was not until they had reached the car that the sergeant came to the heart of the matter. 'And what on earth did he mean about Clithero? Derek never mentioned there was anything between him and Em.'

Reynolds stood still. Damn and blast, he thought, then what the hell *was* Derek so forthcoming about? Steeling himself for the worst, he asked exactly what Derek had said, to have his fears confirmed.

Derek had come up with a version of events that didn't gel at all with what he'd originally told Reynolds. Insisting he'd only given Em a lift home because she'd been upset by Reynolds' method of questioning, he'd specifically stressed that when he dropped Em off near the village, he'd seen Reynolds' parked car—meaning that Reynolds must have arrived before him and been waiting for her—while he himself hadn't been anywhere near her cottage. All this clearly suggested that he was in no way involved, yet gave weight to the idea that Reynolds was.

Although this revision was damaging to Reynolds to say the least, to be fair,

Derrymore didn't dwell on it. More to the point, it differed in so many essential details from the first version that Derek had to be lying deliberately. It was also inconsistent with other facts, such as Em's having time to change her clothes before Reynolds showed up—although there was only his word for that. Of course, if time of death was established at four he was well away from her cottage by then—still, it wasn't pleasant to be singled out as Derek seemed intent on doing.

This brought him to an even more sobering reflection: it was his version pitted against Derek's. Meaning that Derek, the honest, loyal, trustworthy old soldier, had implicated him without a qualm; or, to put it bluntly, had tried to save his own skin at Reynolds' expense.

Anger would get him nowhere. 'I think we'd better straighten these stories out,' he said calmly, although inwardly he was still seething. He let Derrymore drive back towards Rainbow Park in silence, until another thought struck him. 'Was Marge there when Clithero spun this yarn?' he asked, to have Derrymore admit that, as it'd turned out, he'd interviewed the Clitheros separately. He hadn't had a chance to ask Marge about her husband's testimony as he'd seen Derek after he'd talked to her. And his questions to Marge had all been routine ones, what she knew about Em and so forth.

'Don't trust her either,' he added thoughtfully. 'Had dealings with her in the past, once had a real run-in about their sewage pipes polluting the beach, but she would never admit it. Rumour has it she's up to her ears in debt. Rainbow Park's about to go under if what I hear is true.'

Mentally, Reynolds was going over the events of that Friday. Of course, if what Derek had told him about his feelings for Em was correct, as Ray Mabley now confirmed, the last thing he would mention in his wife's presence was driving Em anywhere, but as Derrymore had interviewed him alone, there had been no need for him to lie.

'All three of us watched Em pick up her bike and ride off,' he said at last. 'I left soon afterwards, to find her, but that took time. It could have been possible for Derek to drive off after I did, meet up with Em and take her home. But I'll swear that she was in the cottage when I arrived. Although,' here another thought

117

struck him, 'I suppose it's equally possible that Derek was inside too.'

As he was speaking he was remembering how Em had retreated to the porch and only later come down the garden path to talk. 'When she mentioned Derek specifically,' he concluded, 'I noticed she lowered her voice. I wondered why at the time.'

Derrymore concentrated on changing gears. 'But why did Derek alter his story?' he asked. Then, answering his own question, 'I imagine he'd be frightened of admitting he was there. On two counts. One, that his missus would find out. The other ...'

He pursed his lips as if to say, 'because he had something worse to hide'.

His next comment, 'I thought it odd you'd upset Em as he claimed,' confirmed that he accepted Reynolds' account without hesitation. 'You always handle witnesses with kid gloves,' he went on, again wrestling with the gears, 'and it was even odder that Derek vanished when I arrived at the site. Yet when I met him, he was loitering around the car as if he wanted to be seen.'

Another pursing of the lips. 'Seems to

me,' he said, 'that Derek and Marge Clithero have some explaining to do. And although so far we have two separate cases on our hands—a murdered woman and a missing man—the only link that I can see is that they were both connected in different ways with Rainbow Park. Any ideas?'

But for the moment, Reynolds had no theories left.

Chapter 8

In perfect accord now, the two working together in their customary partnership, they planned their strategy, a familiar routine. One of their objectives was to clarify Derek Clithero's testimony and determine, once and for all, why he had changed it. And this time Reynolds was in no mood to pander to him or Marge.

Another was to pin Mrs Newland down on what she knew about her husband's movements or whereabouts. Here they admitted they were on shaky ground. The possibility of Newland's being in some way involved with Em Tregurion at all seemed at best tenuous. It also came third hand, via Reynolds, through the dead girl, whose story of meeting him the night before he disappeared had likewise gone through a couple of revisions. If Newland were a possible link, an official search for him should be started, with or without his wife's permission. However, given the nature of the evidence so far, it would cause them a lot less hassle if she instigated the search herself.

It was late afternoon when they reached Rainbow Park and most of the caravans were deserted. A muddle of buckets, spades and damp towels heaped outside number four suggested the Newland family had returned from some seaside expedition, so they decided to speak to Mrs Newland first.

The car doors were open. What was Newland up to, Reynolds thought, borrowing a brand-new model when his wife and children had to cope with one this old? Looking in at the worn interior, even more dilapidated than the outside, he was amazed the car had even survived the journey from Birmingham.

Before they could knock, Mrs Newland

appeared in the doorway of the caravan, her arms filled with more beach clutter. The sight of a policeman in uniform came as a shock, but she covered her initial surprise well, with the, by-now familiar meek look, meant to elicit sympathy but which roused Reynolds' suspicions. When they went inside, however and Derrymore began the interview—not questions she might have expected about where her husband was, but focusing instead on his possible relationship with Em Tregurion—her expression altered.

He started quietly enough, asking if she had heard from her husband, going on to suggest it was quite a while now since the possibility of his being missing had first been raised. He was, after all, last heard of on the Tuesday night, almost a week ago, 'In Miss Tregurion's company.'

When she didn't reply, 'The murdered woman,' he pointed out.

Mrs Newland sank down in a heap, for once ignoring the children. 'I didn't know that,' was all she said. After a while she recovered. 'As far as I'm concerned,' she said, 'you've only got her word. He never mentioned her to me.'

A fair reply. But then he wasn't likely to if he'd really had an affair with Em, as

121

Em herself had first intimated.

Derrymore pretended to consult his notes, a trick he used when he wanted Reynolds' support. 'He was, I believe you said, an antique dealer,' Reynolds prompted, to have Derrymore continue, 'Would he have any reason to ask her for help, for example in finding some old building? Or some Cornish artefact in which he was interested?'

When Derrymore's use of grammar became pompous, the question was always loaded. Mrs Newland reacted violently. 'I don't know,' she said. 'And he,' she pointed at Reynolds, 'asked me similar questions. When he came last time. Masquerading as the Clitheros' friend.'

It was an underhand attack. 'Besides,' she was quick to follow up her advantage, 'Paul's the one to answer you. Why don't you wait until he returns.'

'Ah.' Derrymore looked grave. 'We can't do that; we need to find him right away. We would like your help in sending out a description, asking him to get in touch.'

An expression crossed that little Quaker face, and Reynolds wondered if it were fear. 'Why go on about it?' she cried. 'I've told you, there's no need.'

'Yes, madam.' Derrymore's interruption was polite. 'But if we can't persuade him to return, using an appeal over the media, for example, we may have to issue a warrant for his arrest. As a possible lead in a murder case.'

After a long silence her answer was so quiet they could hardly hear the words. 'Then send out one of those messages, you know, saying his wife and children want him back, he'll come running fast enough.'

It was a compromise, the sort they'd hoped for. But she'd agreed reluctantly, and when she'd recovered she told them so, with one of her quick flashes of energy, the gist being that when her husband showed up, 'You'll hear from our solicitors.'

'We are investigating a murder case.' Derrymore was stern. 'We have our duty to do. If he fails to appear voluntarily we'll have to use official means to make him do so.'

Letting that sink in, 'Now, let's start with the car.' he said. 'The one he apparently borrowed from his sister. A blue BMW, new registration. Is that correct?'

During this exchange the children for

once had remained quietly in the background. Now the little boy thrust up under his mother's arm. 'What are they saying my dad's done?' he protested. 'You leave my dad alone. Of course he's coming back. And our auntie's car is green.'

He turned to his mother. 'Isn't Aunt Izzie's car green, Mum? And didn't he promise to bring us prezzies when he came back? He said we'd be rich and ...'

'Be quiet.' His mother gave him a shake. 'Just mind your own business.'

The boy's thin face puckered. He turned away to sit by himself close to the window where he had previously buried his sister. Reynolds felt sorry for him. He was remembering how, as a child, his own father had made promises, never kept. And how when, in turn, his father had become rich, he'd loaded the young John with presents to compensate for all those previous non-appearances, presents that Reynolds by then no longer wanted or trusted. But he was also curious to know what else the child might have said before his mother prevented him. While Derrymore took down the description of the aunt's car, a green Cavalier, D registration, and details of the missing man, 'Tall, big, about Mr Reynolds' size, brown eyes, light-brown receding hair, forty-three years old,' and the type of clothes he might have been wearing—another suit, Reynolds noted—he knelt beside the boy. 'We'll find him,' he said. 'And then you'll have—what was it he promised?'

The completeness of the answer interested him. 'A toy car that works,' the boy said promptly. 'With a remote control. And an Alice in Wonderland doll for Jessie.'

He wrinkled his lip at the waste of opportunity, looking like his mother. 'She's just a girl,' he explained patronisingly. 'And a real car for us, a big one. New. A Mercedes.'

He brought out the word proudly, repeating it. A memorised word, Reynolds thought; like the rest of it remembered after many repetitions and retellings, the old fairy story with a modern twist. It left him even more puzzled. Why does a man with plenty of cash in his pocket have to wait to buy his children toys? More significant, if he isn't rich and has to borrow a car from his sister, and if the family car, driven by Mrs Newland, is an old banger, where is he going to get the money to buy a new Mercedes? And who's the Aunt Izzie who has the green car? As Alice in Wonderland would say, curiouser and curiouser.

Putting these questions on hold, he waited until Derrymore had finished with Mrs Newland. After warning her again that the enquiries into her husband's whereabouts were serious and that, if she heard from him, she must let them know immediately, they turned their attention to the Clitheros.

By now it was drawing on towards the sort of long, calm evening that Cornwall is famous for, when the air feels like silk and the shadows lengthen almost imperceptibly. Other caravaners were returning, like the Newlands loaded with beach gear. A smell of cooking began to waft across the site. In the Clithero caravan, Marge had already poured herself a drink, a large one, priming herself perhaps, as she must have seen them arrive.

She stood on the steps, ready for them as they approached, looking distinctly weary. Reynolds thought she seemed to have aged in the past few days and her colourful garments looked even less appropriate.

'What are you doing here?' she snapped at Derrymore. 'I thought I'd told you all I know. All these visits and questions, my guests are growing nervous. As for you,' she turned on Reynolds, 'I wish I'd never heard of you. Don't show your face again.'

'Ex-Inspector Reynolds is helping with our investigations.' Derrymore's tone was grim. 'And just for the moment, it's not you we want to speak to. It's your husband.'

Before she could stop him, he had brushed past her into the caravan. Derek was there, white about the gills. When Derrymore asked him if he would confirm his previous statement, after a few ineffective mumblings he crumbled.

'All right, I did get there before the captain.' He glanced at his wife furtively but didn't look at Reynolds. 'I saw the captain at the garden gate. I stayed inside until he left, then I left too. About three or thereabouts.'

His voice was calm but monotonous, as if he was reciting from memory. 'But I was home before four,' he insisted. Another furtive look at Marge seemed to summon up his courage. He shook his head and thrust out his chin, enhancing his terrier

127

image, ready to attack. 'And I admit I left after the captain, not before.'

This was said defiantly, but without any explanation of why he'd lied. 'It took me a while to get home,' he said instead. 'I had to walk back along the fields to my van just as I told him first off. Afterwards, I drove straight back here. I was that upset I didn't even go into the caravan but went round to the shed. So no one saw me even then.'

'Shut up.' Marge attempted to put an end to this confession. 'You don't know what you're saying.'

In the curious way she had of becoming her own worst enemy, revealing in her anger what was better left unsaid, she turned to the sergeant. 'Thought he could hide it from me,' she cried, misplaced glee almost showing. 'Thought I wouldn't find out. We wouldn't be in the mess we're in if it wasn't for his sordid little affair.'

Her voice had risen, her eyes flashed, affronted womanhood. So much for Derek's claim that she didn't know. She certainly knew now. So when exactly had she confronted Derek with his apparent marital infidelity? Reynolds wondered. He felt sure it had to have been recent for Marge to be speaking out now as she was.

'And what happened during those two hours or so, after Mr Reynolds left?' With admirable calm Derrymore tried to divert what looked like the start of a family row. 'Did you stay inside the house? Or did you go in the side garden, as you told Mr Reynolds you did?'

Derek glanced at Reynolds reproachfully, and shook his head. 'I had to go through the garden to climb the wall,' he explained. 'It was the route back to my van.'

'And before that?'

'I stayed indoors, most, some of the time.'

'With Miss Tregurion?'

'No, she was outside, but ...' Derek was beginning to sound flustered.

'You left her alone in the garden while you stayed indoors?'

Derrymore let his disbelief show, to have Derek protest he would have joined her, of course he meant to, but then he'd heard the gate creak open.

This was new. 'The front gate?' Derrymore asked.

Derek nodded, adding that he knew it was one of Em's friends because he heard her speak to him, and the dog didn't bark.

So he kept out of sight until the man went again.

'A man.' Derrymore pounced on the word. 'How do you know that? Did you recognise him?'

'I didn't know who it was. I only heard his voice.'

A second time Reynolds caught what appeared to be a furtive glance at his wife. 'I tried looking out of the window,' Derek was saying more confidentially now, as if on firmer ground. 'Everywhere's so overgrown you can't see a thing. I thought it might be the captain back again, that's partly why I said what I did to you.'

This last was addressed to Derrymore in a virtuous tone, as if again Derek had suddenly remembered a clue. 'But the voice wasn't the same. And then they were quarrelling.'

'About what?'

'I couldn't hear. When the gate banged I decided it was time to leave. So I did.'

'And Miss Tregurion?'

'She was alive, if that's what you mean.' Derek sounded relieved that the worst was over. 'We stood for a while talking, well, it was true what I said about her being upset. Then I got over the wall.'

'So, contrary to your statement of yesterday, you were in Em Tregurion's house and garden for several hours. And, again contrary to that same statement, you knew very well that Mr Reynolds had come and gone while you were in the house.'

Derrymore recited all this in a singsong tone. His, 'So why did you change your story?' came out like a pistol shot. 'You know the penalty for false information to the police. And now you expect us to believe that all the world was in and out of Em's garden that Friday afternoon.'

Derek hung his head but didn't reply. A thought suddenly struck Reynolds. 'When did Miss Tregurion usually get home?' he intervened.

It was Marge, who during this past exchange had remained conspicuously silent, who confirmed that Em usually stayed at the caravan site until five or so. 'She only left about midday that day in a fit of temper because she'd been questioned.'

'More like insulted. By you.' Derrymore put a stop to that line of possible complaint and followed up well on Reynolds' reasoning. 'So if some male friend came to see her specifically it must have been on the off chance; he wouldn't have expected her

131

to be at home. A pity, Mr Clithero, that you didn't make more of an effort to see who it was. Unless,' here he picked up his helmet which he had previously taken off, 'it was someone you recognised, and don't care to identify.' And he rammed the helmet back on his head.

Derek made no response.

'What jacket did you wear that day?' Derrymore's question had been well drilled into him by Reynolds, anxious that the importance of the olearia flowers and leaves shouldn't be forgotten.

Puzzled, Derek replied that it was the one he had on now, while his wife, in her usual unhelpful fashion, contradicted him by insisting he had been wearing his work one. And what a fright he'd looked, driving off in that state, not fit to be seen, what would her guests think?

Finally commandeering both coats, Derrymore warned Derek that he would have to come down to the station for further questioning. Before Marge could protest, 'And you too, Mrs Clithero,' he said. 'We'd like to know what you were doing that same afternoon. Just for the record,' he concluded over her protests of where the hell did he think she'd been, holding the fort like always while Derek waltzed about the countryside in the van. 'But I must warn you that any further outbursts will look bad. If anyone has shown a cause for grudge against Miss Tregurion, you have.'

That silenced Marge, but Derek watched with grave misgivings as the sergeant picked up his coats. 'What do you want them for?' he asked, then, as if he had made up his mind to a complete revelation, 'Mind, Em and I might have sat down on the grass for a bit, if that's what you're interested in.'

Derrymore and Reynolds exchanged glances. So finally Derek had admitted all he'd first told Reynolds, and more, although it had been tortuous, like pulling teeth. Marge, however, reared back, an outraged cat.

'Sat on the grass,' she spat. 'How dare you? Lay down more like. It's disgraceful, a man your age, you ought to be ashamed. And here am I, a good wife to you, trying to patch things up while we slide into ruin. If it hadn't been for ...'

She stopped, putting a handkerchief to her eyes and smudging the mascara. But Reynolds also noticed her calculated look at him and the sergeant. She might act stupid, she might act aggrieved, but he was sure she already knew all Derek had done that day. And she was still hiding something.

When, after an awkward wait for a larger police car, the Clitheros had gone, Derrymore let out his breath. 'Here's a complication,' he said. 'Which version do you believe?'

They had gone to stand on the steps, idly watching the other caravans while waiting for an officer with the appropriate warrant to complete his search. There were fewer people about than there should have been and several caravans were unoccupied. Derrymore, however, pointed out that as he'd already taken statements from the guests it would make little difference, and added that as soon as his officer was finished here he'd question those remaining, focusing this time on what they'd made of Paul Newland, and whether they knew about his possible involvement with Em Tregurion and so on. But it was the Clitheros, Derek in particular, who stuck in the sergeant's mind. He'd been sure Derek had told him the truth. Why, he asked again, had he been lying?

'Well,' Reynolds spoke abstractly, trying

134

to put his thoughts in order, 'we know that of his three versions, the second, to you, is all wrong—but I think that was when he tried his luck without Marge's help. Of the other two I would have said off hand that the first was nearer the truth. He'd just heard the girl he loved was dead; he was in no state to think clearly, let alone improvise. Now I think the third is the best we're likely to get, in strict adherence, of course, to the well-known adage that if you're going to lie, stick as close to the truth as possible. But for all that, it contains an important blunder.'

He looked hard at Derrymore. 'The substitution of a male visitor for a female one.'

Before Derrymore could interrupt, 'You must have realised that Marge had coached him what to say; he even kept looking at her as if afraid he'd muff his lines. They may loathe each other, Derek may be right she doesn't care two hoots whether he's faithful or not, but I've no doubt at all she's forced him to cover for her being there.'

Derrymore let out his breath again. 'Marge?' he questioned. 'Marge went to Em's cottage as well? How do you make

135

that out? If he used the van, how did she get there? And even if she did, how on earth are we to prove it?'

His spate of questions made Reynolds smile. 'To answer the last and most important one,' he said, 'the same way we'll prove Derek's presence. Examine her clothes, of course.'

He gave a short but accurate description of Marge's 'uniform', adding, as Derrymore looked at him strangely, 'If you'd once seen it it'd be etched on your memory too! As for how and why—let's wait until we ascertain we're right.'

When the results of the search produced better results than even he'd anticipated, Derry was impressed. The gaily coloured blouse, easily identified, actually showered small white particles as it was encased in plastic, and a cupboard full of identical sandals revealed one pair with green stains on the soles and heels, possibly from the roses. Most important of all, an eager young officer, rooting in a broom cupboard, discovered an unfashionable dark raincoat hanging at the back, possibly Marge's disguise, with a crumpled bus ticket in its pocket, the bus equally possibly her mode of transport. Optimism ran high.

136

Chapter 9

With something positive to go on at last, they worked late into the night. Back at an incident room established in the old Sunday school in St Breddaford, excitement mounted as urgent messages were sent to the media with descriptions of the missing Newland, and procedures for investigating Mabley's alibi were planned for the next day. The caravaners, those remaining on the site and those who'd already left, were contacted and questioned about Newland and any possible link between him and Em Tregurion—enquiries made possible thanks to Marge's efficient record-keeping; except in the one exception of Paul Newland, she'd kept a careful note of all her guests. Newland's sister, identified by Mrs Newland, was to be contacted and pressure increased to get the burnt car identified as soon as possible. These additional leads were followed up mainly at Reynolds' insistence. 'All very well to think you've got a case wrapped up,' he advised Derrymore, 'but always make room for the unexpected, even when you're sure.'

As for the Clitheros themselves, so far the evidence against them looked promising. A preliminary examination of Derek's work clothes, identified as a battered jacket and torn grey flannels—unsuitable garments for an ardent suitor; Marge had been quick to pick that up—proved them to be flecked with olearia Scilloniensis. More significantly, flowers and pollen from the same source were identified on Marge's scintillating blouse, and as a bonus the stains on her sandals turned out to be from rose petals and rosehips. These early results substantiated that both Clitheros had been in Em's garden—which, incidentally, was invisible from any window in the cottage; Reynolds and Derrymore had already checked that out, to find the view from upstairs and down effectively blocked by a mass of greenery resembling the canopy of a tropical forest. Still left open, of course, was the exact times when both had come and gone.

Equally, the finding of the ticket seemed to confirm that Marge had travelled by bus. The ticket bore Friday's date, the day in question, and immediately sparked off a search for the driver or any passenger who might remember her.

Throughout all this complicated business, even with fewer men than usual, Derrymore, still in charge of the case, remained his usual unflappable self, conscientious and patient, and much more efficient than Reynolds would have given him credit for. The ex-inspector was impressed. Now that the first flurry was over, he himself was not so sanguine. His reluctance to rely completely on forensic evidence or even on the bus ticket began to reveal itself ironically as Derrymore's optimism reached its peak.

'Always thought a love of gardening meant onions and cabbages.' The sergeant couldn't contain his pleasure. 'I'd best start swotting up on flowers and stuff, like you do, sir.' Happy as a schoolboy, he beamed. Not that he wished Marge ill, he went on more seriously, but if anyone deserved the full weight of the law upon them it was Marge Clithero. And if his first murder case was solved so quickly and easily, that was a piece of unexpected luck. His repetition of 'How did you ever latch on to her?' showed all the boyish enthusiasm of when he was younger and had first worked with what he had then thought of as 'the great man'.

Reynolds made a self-deprecating gesture. 'Your questioning helped,' he said. 'And she's her own worst enemy. I felt from the start that she was hiding something.'

He quickly outlined his original suspicions, adding 'It was really the way Derek's three statements came out. As I said, I was pretty sure the first was as close to the truth as he could bring himself, but I was obviously wrong. He had enough sense, if you like to call it that, to hold back the fact that there'd been someone else in the garden, someone he obviously didn't identify then as his wife.'

'But wouldn't it have been to his advantage to have mentioned it right away?'

'Not in his book.' Reynolds managed a grin. 'You've been a soldier yourself, ever heard of one who'd volunteer information if he didn't have to? He may be henpecked, but Derek's no fool.'

Derrymore grinned back as Reynolds continued, slower now, working things out. 'Yet I believe that underneath his tough exterior Derek's a secret romantic.

My guess is that after he'd found out about Marge, and she found out about him and Em, he came up with a second version, the one to you. A valiant attempt to protect Marge by throwing suspicion back on me. It was clumsily done, perhaps, and self-seeking in that he doubtless was still trying to protect himself at my expense, but I think his conscience drove him to it. In fact I'm willing to construe a scenario that goes something thing like this.

'Derek was inside the house, waiting for me to leave. He really didn't know at the time who the next visitor was. He may not even have tried to find out, he's strangely reserved in some ways and you know how overgrown the garden is and how thick the cottage walls. Marge showed up to have things out with Em after their last inconclusive encounter, when Em certainly got the better of her. She may have wanted merely to find out all she could about Paul Newland and learned more than she bargained for. Oh, she may have had her suspicions about Derek's goings-on before, but that's different from having the proof shoved under her nose, as I'm sure Em was quite capable of doing, given her mood at the time. Suppose Em taunted

Marge with Derek's infidelity; she might even have told Marge he was actually there at that very moment, although that would be over-doing it I suppose. Whatever was said, Marge didn't tackle Derek on the spot, probably not wanting to give Em that satisfaction. If she had, there'd really have been fireworks. The whole village would have heard. She returned to the caravan site and waited to confront him there.'

He glanced at Derrymore. 'You realise of course that at some point recently the Clitheros must have levelled with each other. Derek admits his love for Em (which may or may not have been consummated, but love is the term he used, and love is a more powerful force than lust, believe me); Marge reveals her presence in Em's garden. Both have too much to lose to let the other go under. So they join forces. Hence the third revision, pretty certainly Marge's work, a calculated attempt to do the same thing as the second, as far as protection goes I mean. They invent a mythical male visitor, a friend, who quarrels with Em and leaves.'

Again a glance at Derrymore. 'You noted too I'm sure, Marge's little displays of wifely outrage whenever Derek mentioned

Em. That also tipped me off. It was so out of place. And so artificial.'

'What of those nice touches about the dog not barking, and the visitor being a friend?'

Almost instinctively Derrymore was falling into his accustomed role of sounding board for Reynolds' theories.

Reynolds frowned. 'Marge's contribution, I suspect,' he said. 'Calculated to cause confusion. The dog couldn't have known Marge, therefore it should have barked. At the same time, if there'd been an argument between the two women—which I also suspect must have happened; Em was no shrinking violet and you've seen for yourself what a caustic tongue Marge has—that's probably the quarrel the neighbour heard, for all she claims it was earlier.

'As for said neighbour,' he went on, 'the most likely explanation is that she was already out in her own back garden, avidly trying to eavesdrop even if she couldn't actually see. Which probably explains why she didn't spot Marge arrive. If she'd stayed at her post in the front she couldn't have missed her.'

He took a breath. 'My main difficulty,' he went on, 'is Marge herself. I still can't accept her as a murderer. According to the doctor, Em was strangled by an especially strong person. Probably male. I see nothing to change that assessment. And Marge isn't that strong.'

Derrymore's face fell. 'But she's admitted she hated Em,' he pointed out. 'She had a motive.' His expression brightened. 'Suppose she set Derek up? We've accepted he'll do anything she says.'

'Perhaps. I thought of that myself. And I know he was trained in killing of that type. But breaking the neck of the woman he's admitted was the love of his life—I doubt it, no matter how much Marge pressed.'

'But suppose Em angered *him*—you've mentioned her claim to have had an affair with Newland ...'

'Contradicted immediately afterwards,' Reynolds interrupted. 'And when Derek followed her to find out, she had the chance to persuade him that she'd invented it, as she persuaded me. In any event, the important thing is that Derek believed her. At least he told me he did, and his reason, namely that she wanted to get her own back with Marge, was the same one Em herself gave. Although if you ask me, there're too many changes and alterations

144

in everyone's story for my taste.'

He stared through Derrymore into the distance. 'We may still have a case against Derek,' he said, 'but I'm beginning to be afraid that even with all the evidence, we're on the wrong track with Marge. I have a hunch that Marge may be a suspect, but not for killing Em.'

Reynolds' hunches were famous, or infamous, depending who worked with him. Derrymore listened respectfully while he outlined his arguments. 'I don't think she hated Em for having an affair with Derek; what she didn't like was the possibility of Em besting her with Newland. And I don't think that was only sexual rivalry. It may have played a part, but there was something more, something to do with Newland himself, where he's got to, what he's up to, things of that sort.'

Quickly he outlined Marge's strange distinction between finding Newland and knowing where he was, as well as her equally strange insistence that the phone call from Newland's sister was important. 'She may have thought Em could help,' he concluded. 'Come to it, I thought so myself, hence my own visit. In Marge's case I don't think the interest was altruistic.

And remember, my suspicions of her came from the very start—had nothing to do with Em originally, began before Em was even killed.'

His words were prophetic. When they met again after a few hours' sleep, dawn was breaking, another perfect day. But for them it brought more troubles—in the shape of several new clues which caused a major gap in the jigsaw they were trying to assemble.

The first concerned the phone call, supposedly made to Marge by Paul Newland's sister, the owner of the new BMW. Reluctantly, to be sure, Mrs Newland had been persuaded to give them her widowed sister-in-law's number, after assuring them that her husband had only the one living relative.

'Listen to this, Sarge.' An excited officer stuck his head into an inner room of the Sunday school, where Derrymore and Reynolds had retired to mull over the events of the previous day and try to reconcile their misgivings. He switched on the message he'd just recorded. It was abrupt, and not pleasant. Hardly had he asked the lady on the other end of the line if she were Mrs Elizabeth Worthington, of number 82, The Promenade, in a certain town in Dorset, when she burst out that she supposed they were ringing about Paul. Whatever he'd done now, she wasn't going to bail him out again, she'd given him enough money as it was.

'Did you recently lend him your car?' the officer's voice broke in. 'A new blue BMW?'

'What blue BMW?' The voice rose a notch. 'I don't own such a car. Mine's a green Cavalier. Years old. And I wouldn't lend it to him if he asked, I'd never see it back again. Like the hundreds of pounds he's already had to support him and his wretched family.'

This was bad enough. But when asked if she'd made a phone call to Rainbow Park on his behalf, professing to be worried about him and his relationship with his wife, her reply, when censored, boiled down to total denial. She had never heard of Rainbow Park, had never made a phone call to Marge Clithero, and far from being worried about her brother and his wife, she'd washed her hands of them long ago and hadn't spoken to them in months.

The slamming of the receiver ended the conversation. 'Of course we'll check it out again.' The officer was still shaken. 'We've put in a request to the local police to look into it. It should be easy to trace the call if it were made from her phone; for one thing it would be long-distance.'

About to add something unprofessional but accurate regarding Mrs Worthington's character, he withdrew, leaving Reynolds and Derrymore with another problem: namely, if Marge was so insistent she'd had a call, who else could have made it? And what had it been about to have her give it so much weight? Assuming, of course, it had been made and wasn't just her invention.

Hardly had they recovered from this setback when another piece of evidence, so commonplace as to be positively anti-climactic, scattered the jigsaw completely —but led to the final explanation of Marge's strange obsession with the missing Paul Newland, and her own bizarre behaviour.

It came from the driver of the bus that had taken Marge to Em's village. A stout man, receding into middle age, he volunteered the information so readily it was clear he was still smarting from the encounter. 'Remember her,' he growled.

'She wanted me to take her all the way and when I told her the lanes were too narrow acted as if she expected me to carry her there myself. Madame Superior wasn't in it. What a fright, tottering along in that mac and shoes.'

It wasn't her behaviour and appearance alone that caused the consternation. It was the driver's verification of the time. He'd dropped her off, he said, at quarter past twelve, at a stop midway between Em's village and one of the others, then picked her up again at the same place about quarter to four. Part of his regular run. He was never more than a few minutes late. It was a mile to Em's cottage, and a mile in high-heeled sandals made for slow going. Whichever way they took the evidence, if Marge was at the bus stop at three forty-five, then Em Tregurion must still have been alive when she and Marge had parted. Add that there was time enough for someone else to have paid a call at the cottage between Marge's leaving and Em's death, and the case against Marge was crumbling fast.

However unwelcome these revelations, the Clitheros were entitled to hear them.

But as there were still unanswered questions it was decided to try whatever else could be squeezed out first. On the strength of the earlier evidence against them, the Clitheros had been held overnight, pending further questions, Derek at his most hangdog, volunteering nothing; Marge for once also subdued, although apt to flash into temper if pushed too far.

When Derrymore and Reynolds confronted her first with the proof of her visit to the murdered woman's cottage, she finally admitted that yes, she had gone to have it out with Em, after their initial quarrel, but she hadn't killed Em, or even known she was dead until the next morning. And Newland's name hadn't even been mentioned between them.

'You never mentioned Newland? Even when talking to the woman who'd seen him the night before his disappearance?' Derrymore persisted. 'You didn't specifically ask her what she knew about him? After all, she'd just told you he'd spent the Tuesday evening with her. Wouldn't it have been sensible to follow that up?'

Faced with this barrage of questions, Marge again changed her tune and admitted that learning the whereabouts of Newland had been the reason for her visit.

'And what did you learn from Miss Tregurion?' It was an important question. Derrymore and Reynolds metaphorically held their breaths. Marge looked aggrieved and said, 'Not much. She merely mentioned he'd been interested in Cornish history and stuff. I mean, what would you make of that? I told her off though. Told her to leave my husband and guests alone. I was fierce, I can tell you, but she deserved all she got.'

Reynolds and Derrymore avoided looking at each other. She must have been fierce indeed for the neighbour to have heard. 'That's what I really needed to know,' Marge continued virtuously. 'I didn't care what she'd done with him, or my husband come to that.' Her eyelashes fluttered. 'All I wanted was to find out where he'd gone.'

'Because of the sister?'

Marge looked at him straight. 'Of course,' she said again. Asked next about the sister's phone call, even after learning of said sister's denial, 'But she did ring,' she insisted over and over, 'exactly as I've said. Told me who she was and why she was worried about him.'

'Nothing else?' Derrymore probed.

At last Marge confessed to the part of the message she'd hitherto kept hidden. The speaker, whoever she was—Marge was sure it was a woman—had offered a sum of money, a large but unspecified amount, if Marge would undertake to track down the missing Newland without involving the authorities. 'She didn't actually use the word "police",' Marge explained, 'but I knew that was what she meant. That's why I thought of John here. And I agreed because I needed the money.' Marge was now in tears. 'I didn't even tell Derek first off because he might have demanded his share. It was to pay off the debts, don't you see?'

They did see. But it took more careful probing to get the rest from Derek.

'What else did the caller say?'

When asked this question over and over. without Marge to back him, Derek broke. It was true Marge had kept the story of the phone call to herself, he insisted. He hadn't even known about it until their heart-to-heart—his choice of phrase—after the news of Em's death.

Insisting on starting at the beginning, once more he went over the story of his

152

going to see Em on that fateful Friday, the fourth and presumably last version. Patiently they listened until he came to the part they were now interested in.

He'd gone after Em, he explained, but not as soon as he'd intended. Marge had kept him busy clearing out number four; he'd had to hurry through the fields and reached the cottage just before Reynolds did. Then, after Reynolds' departure, when he was about to join Em in the garden, he'd heard the gate and decided to wait, not wanting to be seen himself.

At that point he'd no idea who this second visitor was, and when Em told him it was just a neighbour he'd believed her. It was Newland who *obsessed* him, he was wild with jealousy, but when at last he'd got Em by herself she had soon dispersed his doubts. He gulped.

That half-hour or so before he too had left had been the happiest of his life, he told them, his eyes suddenly brimming. Em had never been so sweet, so receptive. But that was what she was like, fire and passion, turning to gentle understanding. All innocent, he still persisted, nothing sexual at all, the sort of love that a daughter might have for a dearly beloved

153

father, and he doting on her as his own child.

They let that pass. And when he had recovered, 'You know the rest,' he said. When Reynolds had seen him the day after news of Em's murder had spread, all he could think of was that while he had been so happy, her last moments had been frightful. The idea tore him apart; he couldn't focus on anything else, had really almost forgotten the second visitor, the so-called neighbour, until Marge told him it was her.

When she confronted him later, screaming at him about his affair with Em, shouting that it would ruin them, he could have killed her—until she told him also about the phone call, and the threats it implied.

'There were threats?' Derrymore broke in. He'd been listening intently, but here was the actual lead he'd been waiting for. 'The phone caller not only offered money but threatened Marge as well?'

Derek nodded. 'She said Rainbow Park was an easy target. If we told anyone, she'd blacken our name so no one would dare stay here.'

He gulped again. 'She said either Marge

went along with her or ...' He made a chopping gesture.

'I couldn't bear it,' he said simply. 'First Em, then Marge. I felt as if it was all my fault. While I'd been fooling about, as Marge called it, she'd had the courage to keep all this to herself. It made me ashamed.'

Cut to the quick, he'd decided to do what he could to make amends, hence his second story to Derrymore, first making sure Marge wasn't about. It was the only thing he could think of on the spur of the moment, he felt he owed her that at least. But when Marge heard she became angry, called him a fool again, said he'd be the death of them. When she pointed out that his version was bound to be contradicted by Reynolds, he saw what a mistake he'd made. Then she came up with a new version ...

Bringing this maudlin explanation to an end, and showing by his expression that although Derek may have been bamboozled by Marge, he himself wasn't, Derrymore barked, 'You mean you allowed yourself to fabricate a story out of some sort of guilt?'

Derrymore's too young, Reynolds thought,

155

he can't sympathise with Derek. He's never been married; he can't begin to comprehend the twisted bond, the guilt-laden sense of responsibility, that connects man and wife even when love itself is gone. But Reynolds knew about all of that from experience—except it had been his wife who'd lied and cheated, and finally betrayed him with one of his own friends. Even so, he had never been able to leave her, had protected her; it was she who'd made the final break.

'And you stick now with your third revision: the visitor in fact was your wife?' Derrymore's next question was as sharp. When again Derek nodded, 'And you admit you tried to implicate Mr Reynolds, knowing that too was a lie?'

At that Derek had enough self-respect to defend himself. 'It was mainly true,' he protested. 'The visitor could have been a man.' Until that time he hadn't looked at Reynolds, and he didn't now, but he did go on to say. 'Marge expected the sister to ring back again that night like she said she would. But she didn't. If you ask me that's because she heard somehow that he,' jerking a thumb in Reynolds' direction. 'was involved and had let us down.'

The logic of this accusation couldn't hold, but he seemed to feel better having made it. His explanation left them with more new questions than the ones he'd answered, namely who'd threatened Marge Clithero and why it was so important to find out where Newland was.

Meanwhile, this version of events planted suspicion fair and square back on to Derek, who seemed unaware of the fact until it was pointed out to him. Even when he'd worked out that his confession placed him in the same quandary he'd tried to put Reynolds in, namely that he was the last known person to see Em alive, for all Derrymore's insistence he continued to maintain he'd only stayed for a short while after his wife's departure, during which time he and Em had lain innocently under the olearia bush.

He now pinned all his hopes of an alibi upon finding someone who'd seen his van. By his own earlier description, lots of people used the trail for walking their dogs, so 'Someone must have seen it,' he pleaded, as anxious to have it identified as previously he had tried to keep it hidden. But if Em's three known visitors that fatal afternoon had all left the cottage before or about three o'clock, one in his car, one along the lanes to her bus, one through the fields to his van, where had the last come from, the final visitor who'd killed her?

So far the only other male suspect was the surfing ex-boyfriend. But when the officers sent to round up and interview his friends arrived back with his alibi intact, Mabley looked in the clear. Even in their early-morning daze, his mates told the same story. According to them, they had all, including Mabley himself, spent the Friday milling about the beach café and the lifeguard huts. The weather hadn't been right for surfing, there'd been no waves to speak of. They'd hung around until early evening, then, when the pubs opened, had all drifted there.

The next news was equally unwelcome. The illegal dump was being searched for clues but so far there was no sign at all that Newland was involved with the burning of the car, still unidentified. Likewise, when the villagers were interviewed—Carnford was small enough for most to be contacted quickly—no one had anything to contribute; they hadn't bothered to investigate the car burning, although some had protested about it. Just as Reynolds had thought, sitting and complaining was what they knew best. Fortunately Striped Jersey hadn't been picked out—no doubt he was too young—although his gran, a Mrs Pascoe, had been, probably because of living so close to the tip. Reynolds identified her by the address, and by the fact that the interviewing officer had written the laconic message, 'Doesn't understand,' beside her name, confirming his suspicion that she wasn't mentally, and perhaps physically, capable of looking after a wayward grandson.

As for the other key witness, Trev Carthew, the rag-and-bone man, he seemed to have vanished. They'd found his shanty, and after having searched it discovered a good reason why he might have thought it politic to lie low somewhere else.

The shanty was on the far side of the hill from the mine, hidden from the village and tip, facing the distant sea. Quite apart from being illegally built on private land still owned by the mine, it was snug enough, roofed with galvanised sheeting purloined from the tip, and containing a fireplace with enough driftwood to keep a fire going day and night.

In a lean-to at one side several video players and TVs, a portable computer and three printers were lined up, still in plastic wrappers, as well as various boxes of expensive trinkets, including jewellery and silver of dubious origin. These were stacked in orderly fashion, placed on wooden planks to keep them off the damp. 'Looks as if he's a fence for stolen goods,' was the verdict, 'if he doesn't do the stealing himself. He's been scared off, and is on the run.'

With still no clues to where Paul Newland was, Trev Carthew made a second missing person in Cornwall. Two in the same small county was absurd. For one thing, it made the local police look incompetent; for another, headquarters had begun to breathe fire.

Derrymore had promised a quick solution—a rash promise, as it turned out. With all his and Reynolds' theories—or rather, to be bleakly accurate, Reynolds' theories—in tatters, he couldn't boast they'd advanced very far. Faced with more delays and expense he hadn't banked on, the possibility of having to hunt for Trev added to his problems. No wonder headquarters was beginning to favour someone with more experience. It was a bitter blow.

It wasn't that headquarters in its city environment had little time for rural policemen, although that was sometimes true. And it certainly wasn't because Derrymore couldn't or wouldn't work with headquarters; in the normal way of things he would have been glad of their support, might, as would be natural, be more than willing to let them shoulder the responsibility. The difficulty here was too deep-rooted for that, had overshadowed almost every case he and Reynolds had worked on.

It concerned a personal quarrel, a vendetta, between the ex-inspector and one of his former colleagues who'd assumed his rank and position after Reynolds had retired. The reasons behind this quarrel—not of Reynolds' making, it should be pointed out—were so complex they'd endured to this day, involving smear campaigns against the ex-inspector and seduction of his wife, fuelled by Reynolds' growing success in his new career, which added to his former colleague's jealousy.

This colleague now had the rank, and the power, to make his hatred felt, not merely by excluding Reynolds from any contact with the force, where hitherto he'd been respected and well liked, but by advancing anyone who supported himself and conversely, demoting anyone who disagreed, including Reynolds' supporters and friends. Derrymore fell into this last category.

Regarding his partnership with Derrymore, Reynolds had not always been wise or discreet enough to conceal it, as he might have done. Every time he 'interfered' or took some action, he put Derry in a difficult position. If headquarters had now become restive, chances were it was part of the same vendetta. It would not only automatically exclude Reynolds from the case but probably find some excuse to exclude Derrymore as well—the worst blow of all.

They had faced, and overcome, this threat before. But never when Derrymore had been nominally in charge. It was an unpleasant prospect; no wonder Derrymore was becoming depressed. The Clitheros' final story, Mabley's alibi, even Elizabeth Worthington's denial and Trev's disappearance, were all of a piece; headquarters' interference was the last straw although when the chips were down, as he would have put it, he knew where his loyalties lay. 'Even if things had gone our way,' he now told Reynolds, putting on a brave front, 'they'd probably find fault.' He stopped himself in time from saying it was unfair—and that they'd be left with nothing for their pains, no real clues, no actual evidence, all conjecture and theory, unless he could get hold of some proof fast.

For some reason Striped Jersey again came to Reynolds' mind; suppose he could be made to testify? Was he too young to be believed; would his testimony stand; could he be forced to speak? Reynolds was still reluctant to try.

For some reason he couldn't explain, he felt uneasy about Striped Jersey. It wasn't just that he wasn't sure of what he'd said; by and large he'd taken it with proverbial caution, but there was something about the boy that bothered him. In a funny sort of way it reminded him of Em herself.

In their brief meetings, Reynolds had liked Em and admired her enthusiasm. He couldn't forget that mixture of commitment and vulnerability which made her death so painful. It was the same mixture that he

163

sensed in the young boy.

He thought too of Newland's thin-faced son, with his touching insistence on his father's promises. What else might the child reveal? And what do I know, he chided himself, a childless divorcé who dislikes kids in general, suddenly surrounded by them and growing sentimental? It must be old age. But I wish Newland would reappear, put everyone's mind at rest, explain the mystery and provide the clue to Em's murder before headquarters claims all the credit. Wishful thinking. He was beginning to have serious doubts that Newland ever would show up. And barring a miracle, headquarters would be among them soon, bringing their investigations to a grinding halt.

Chapter 10

Next morning saw the third new clue that ended all their previous work before headquarters could do it for them. The weather continued fine, the sort of morning when the skies are so blue and the air so clear that visitors to Cornwall are lulled into thinking it will last for ever. High on his tractor, which he loved, Alfred Blunt surveyed his kingdom, stretching from the moors on the far side of the village of Carnford, down towards the sea.

Like his name, Alf was old-fashioned and dependable, a typical West Country farmer with his ruddy complexion, soft brown eyes and stocky build. Although the farm he'd inherited several years ago now was small, consisting mostly of moorland, rough grazing for cattle and sheep, he'd made the best of it. It was recent developments in the agricultural world which caused the frowns to develop and gave him grey hairs. The string of agricultural restrictions from Brussels, the reduction of dairy herds, the loss of compensation, and now, most recently, the BSE scare and the threat of falling sheep prices would drive any man to drink.

Yet on this August morning he felt almost happy. Thirty-nine, going on forty, with a nice little wife and two good kids, suddenly things didn't look so bad and his mounting debts lost their significance. Most important, in the field before him, the fresh cut of hay, the second crop this season, was already bagged for him to fork-lift away.

In his father's time, the field had been what was called a water meadow, prone to floods. His father, who was nearly sixty when Alfred was born, the only son in a litter of three older sisters, used to love explaining how as a young man himself he'd drained the field and dug the ditches and dykes and built the surrounding stone walls shutting off the moorland proper. He'd done it all, his father used to boast, in the traditional way, known to generations of Cornish farmers, none of the newfangled theories or contraptions, but with his own hands. Manual work, boy, blistering hard work, and proud of it.

The meadow was now his son's pride and joy, the one thing left on the farm that hadn't been spoiled by bureaucracy or over-modernisation. Its grass yield was phenomenal and always of the best quality, in striking contrast to the moorland's rough heather and scrub, and every time he looked at it or walked on it or, as now, drove his tractor across it, he remembered his father and felt the bond still strong between them.

Alf didn't like modern methods any

166

more than his father had. Take the system of hay-making, for example, silage they called it. For all that they said it was efficient, meaning it could be cut whatever the weather and stacked when wet, he didn't really like bundling all the fresh-cut grass into great plastic bags, which, when empty, littered the countryside. If given the choice he would have preferred traditional methods, even cutting with a scythe. One of his earliest childhood memories was hearing his father describe the old days, when workers used to cut and spread the grass to dry before piling it into stooks for the horse-drawn wagon to carry into the farmyard.

Sometimes now he couldn't even remember if these images were real or merely memories of someone else's memory. He only knew that thoughts of those times, the heat of the sun, the tickle of the drying grass, the smell of crushed wild flowers, were the closest he could come to sentiments of patriotism, to love of king and country, things no longer popular. He and his father between them spanned most of this century; sometimes he wondered what sort of world would be left for his own sons. He sighed, made sure the fork

167

to carry the bags was working properly, and started the tractor engine.

It was after he had fork-lifted and piled several lines of bags, dumping them together on higher ground in one corner where they would be easier to get at, that he saw something that shouldn't have been there. He switched off the engine and sat staring. Just for a moment he fancied he had returned to the past and had come upon a farm worker, up since dawn and at noon enjoying his traditional doze in the hay. But this was the present, and it wasn't noon, and anyway he couldn't afford help to have it laze about. And no man he knew could sprawl like that under suffocating black plastic with only an arm and leg stuck out to show where he was lying; no man could sleep so sound, with all that weight upon him.

'How are you so sure it isn't? You've never even seen him.'

On arriving at the scene in an official car, after being informed of the news, Derrymore's question was sharp, in answer to Reynolds' opening remark, 'Well, it isn't Newland.' Now, while local officers tried to drag the heavy bag from the body

168

without disturbing it, and others comforted the distraught Alf, who seemed more upset by some sort of violation of his property than the actual details of how a man came to be lying dead under one of his silage bags, Derry fretted uncharacteristically. A dead man was worse than a missing one, whoever it was. And if he had a choice he'd have preferred it to be Newland than Carthew.

Reynolds didn't bother to reply. He didn't have to say, 'But I have met Trev.' Several villagers who'd been attracted by the commotion had already identified the body by its clothes. And when it was exposed and the same doctor who had attended Em had arrived, he didn't have to add, 'Look at the way the neck is twisted.' They could see that for themselves.

Alf Blunt was protesting that he wasn't to blame. He'd cut the grass a day or so ago, then, with the help of a couple of chaps, had bagged it proper and left it lying where he'd found it today. There hadn't been another person in sight when he'd quitted the field on Saturday, and he hadn't seen a soul while he'd been here working today. It wasn't his responsibility if in the night someone came sneaking into his field to murder another someone and stuff the corpse clumsily under a silage bag, with arms and legs left sticking out as if it were a scarecrow. Here he began to sob, great heaving sobs, as if the heart was being torn out of him.

Reynolds surveyed him dispassionately. He'd seen murderers cry before and protest their innocence with even greater appearance of sincerity. But he didn't think Alf was a murderer. Not when the doctor, having finished his primary examination, pointed out morosely that in his opinion death had come to Trev in the same way it had come to Em; that is, by having his neck broken, possibly by the same pair of hands. There were certain marks he'd have to compare, he said, he'd like forensics to take a look; this was only his first opinion, mind, but—and he began to gather his things together—he was already pretty sure. He couldn't resist a quick smile of satisfaction which said as plain as words, 'Told you there'd be more trouble.'

When pressed for the time of death he suggested sometime last night; among other things there was fresh dew on the exposed limbs, in case they hadn't noticed. But if poor Trev had been killed in the

170

same way as Em Tregurion, presumably by the same person, that let the main suspects completely off the hook, since both were in custody when this happened. And, except for the method of killing, what in hell was the link connecting the two murders? The victims had nothing in common ...

The same thought had occurred to Derrymore. 'It seems to me,' he said slowly to the ex-inspector, his furrowed forehead suddenly giving him the appearance of an anxious bloodhound, 'that as well as being one of the last persons to see Em alive, you were also one of the last to see Trev. Could the link be you?'

Reynolds didn't hear him at first. He was gazing at Trev's body and his thoughts had gone far away. He'd liked the old man, with his testy ways and his feisty Cornish humour. Men like him were a dying breed; soon none of them would be left. It seemed a terrible waste to have him end like this. Derrymore was younger, he might not have the same feelings for the past, but he was Cornish. He should care for his heritage, even in the shape of one old man who had always been what was called a crafty dodger, and yet who stood for a way of life allied

171

to natural things like sun and wind and weather.

It wasn't until Derry had repeated his remark, adding sharply, a sign of the tension he was under, 'After all, you were the one who talked to them both about Paul Newland,' that the words rang a bell.

'My God,' he shouted to the startled Derrymore, 'you may be on to something. I certainly went to ask Em about Newland; although I never actually mentioned him by name, that's really what I was questioning Trev about, in connection with the burnt-out car.'

He gazed at Derrymore, not seeing him, but intent on working out some new idea of his own. 'Suppose Newland's the connection—why he's gone missing, for example, or possibly where he is. Or ...'

He felt the sergeant staring at him but had to keep on following his own logic even to its unwelcome conclusion. 'Or suppose he isn't really missing at all. Suppose he's the actual killer, for some reason finishing off anyone who had any dealings with him, or even possible sightings.'

It said a lot for Derrymore's faith in

Reynolds that he accepted this suggestion as more than a flight of fancy.

'Why?' His response was short but sensible.

Reynolds' answer was as quick. 'For the sake of argument, let's say to ensure no one can shed light on his movements. Which means that if they've talked, or he even suspects they've talked, to some representative of the law, they've got to be eliminated.'

He was convincing himself now as well as Derrymore. 'Come to think of it, remember how insistent the anonymous phone caller was that the police weren't to be involved,' he went on. 'Let's accept for the moment that unfortunately, I represented the law. So anyone talking with me specifically is therefore in danger. Meaning Em and Trev. And ...'

He suddenly stopped. If his idea was even part-way correct, there was someone else who had also talked to him. A child. Who hadn't named the man he'd seen and certainly couldn't have known Paul Newland personally. But if the burnt-out car or the man setting light to it were identified, his testimony would be of the utmost importance. 'George' could have been spotted speaking to Reynolds as easily as Trev had been. Or, another possibility, his childish boastings of what he'd witnessed may have spread—meaning he might be in as much danger as the other two victims.

On the spur of the moment he could think of only one way to prove if his theory was right, although he prayed it was wrong. He heard Derrymore shouting behind him as he ran towards where the police cars were parked, but he didn't stop. Shouldering his way past one officer, he wrenched at a car door and ordered the surprised driver to move out and leave him the key. Ramming the car in gear, he surged forward, turning towards Carnford on the other side of the hill. The thought uppermost in his mind was that he'd find George still on the football pitch in his absurd jersey and Wellington boots.

In the rear mirror he could see another car in pursuit, Derrymore probably. A bloody idiot I'll look, he was thinking as he tore through the village, where the football field was conspicuously deserted, and slowed down as he approached his former parking place, searching for the lane that George had vaguely indicated.

He almost missed it, a narrow opening between two ancient pillars that had once formed a gateway. But if a big BMW had driven this way, so could he. He manoeuvred through the gap, then gunned the motor down a rutted track that was wider than it first looked. It humped in a sweeping curve back towards the tip, passing on its way a huddle of buildings that might once have formed a prosperous farm.

Most looked derelict, roofs and windows gone, but the farmhouse proper was still inhabited; there were plants in window boxes and a hedge round a garden. He slammed on the brakes, and leaving the motor running, raced up the path.

The door was ajar, and he could hear the television. 'She'm stuck on it,' George had said. He shouted, and when no one answered, attempted to push the door open. Realising that something was blocking it, he squeezed past, to find himself looking at a body lying on the floor. An old woman. Dressed in a flannel nightgown under a man's jacket. She lay curled on her side, like a small stricken animal, her head still oozing blood where some weapon had struck it. He dropped to his knees, feeling for a heartbeat.

A noise at the door roused him. Derrymore, breathless but competent, was already speaking into his mobile phone, calling for police back-up and urgent ambulance assistance. Reynolds left him to it, and took the narrow stairs three at a time.

There were only two upstairs rooms. The first, the grandmother's bedroom, contained an antique four-poster bed with old-fashioned counterpane and neatly folded garments, and surprisingly in this once Methodist stronghold—a crucifix with a candle in front of it on a chest of drawers. Next came a boy's room, with unmade bed, a litter of wood and shells and a wide windowsill holding a telescope—but no sign of its owner, although the window was thrown open.

Reynolds leaned on the sill, noting the broken twigs and branches on the tree underneath. 'I can get out of the house easy,' the boy had said. Down the stairs again, out of the door, shouting instructions to Derrymore over his shoulder. Then, while Derrymore scoured the rest of the farmhouse and yard, he headed for the ruined outbuildings.

As he reached the first, he forced himself to a standstill, then moved forward stealthily. Already he was cursing his carelessness. With so much noise, so many cars and confusion, if the potential murderer were still on the premises he'd been given too much warning. And if he had caught the boy and was using him, as a hostage, say, he was likely to react with even more violence. Slow and steady, that was the way to handle a situation like this. He also cursed his lack of foresight in coming unarmed.

The first building was small, as was the second, both probably former cowsheds. Jagged timber showed against the blue of the sky and the floors, once flagstoned, were littered with debris that would have made good pickings for Trev but provided few hiding places. The third was larger, older than the rest, with trusses thicker than a man's arm and a tiled roof more or less intact. It backed on to moorland, a building once intended for protection in older, wilder days, its thick granite walls and great oak door studded with iron nails probably part of some medieval manor. More aware than ever of his own stupidity in coming unprepared, he slid into the semi-darkness, senses on full alert.

Inside, he paused to listen. There was no sound except his own rapid breathing, and, when he moved, the faint rustle of old straw. The dry smell made him want to sneeze. As he edged along, his eyes growing more accustomed to the dark, he immediately realised there was nothing suggesting a recent struggle, which raised his hopes again until it occurred to him that he was counting on George putting up a fight. The intruder could have grabbed the boy as he climbed down the tree and made off with him—if so, they might be miles away.

Nevertheless, just in case, he made himself quarter the whole barn, painstakingly clambering up a broken ladder to an upper floor where corn used to be stored in great wooden bins. And even when he had ascertained no one was lurking in the dim corners or hiding in the shadows of the rusting farm machinery, he still did not leave. The murderer may have got away, he may have taken George with him, but his own built-in caution, a sixth sense that had stood him in good stead so often in his former career, told him to keep searching.

Slamming the great door so that its timbers rattled, he tiptoed back to the ladder, where he waited, scarcely breathing —and after several moments was rewarded by a thread of sound, a mouse rustle, seemingly coming from behind the empty corn bins he'd just peered into. He steeled himself to patience, and after what seemed an age the sound came a second time.

In one swift lunge he was up the ladder, dragging the bins out. Behind the last one, in a narrow slit between the wooden struts, where the roof came down to the flooring, was the shape of a child's body, only partially dressed, pressed against the wall.

For a sickening moment he thought the boy was dead. Then, when he leaned down to touch the bare shoulder, the whole torso coiled as George kicked and fought, trying to scrabble back even further into his hiding place. Only gradually did he seem to recognise who Reynolds was. It was longer still before he could be persuaded to come out. When he did, his story confirmed Reynolds' worse fears.

By then the ambulance had come and gone; George's grandmother was alive and there was a chance, a small one, that she might survive—'She'm tough,' her grandson kept insisting, as if saying so could mend a fractured skull. While a fresh team of officers searched the farmhouse and outbuildings for clues, George himself, clothed once more in his striped jersey and torn shorts and wrapped in blankets, was taken to the local police station. There, speaking through teeth that chattered, he was remarkably precise about the details of what had happened, even giving his real name voluntarily before the duty sergeant identified him.

He was Nick Pascoe—grandson of Emily, the duty officer confirmed, the aged widow of a farmer whose family had owned land hereabouts for generations. This morning, his grandmother had got up early as she always did to make breakfast and to watch her new television. Here the boy gave the quick glance Reynolds remembered, as if expecting to be contradicted, and when the officer said nothing, continued more confidently. He'd been upstairs, dressing, he said, when he heard steps on the path and a knock at the door. He'd immediately stuck his head out of the window but the leaves blocked his view, so he'd gone to the top of the stairs, where for some reason, he didn't

180

know why, he'd stood still. He heard the knock again, louder, and before he could speak or perhaps warn his grandmother, he'd seen her heave herself up from her armchair and cross to the door.

'She's got rheumatism bad,' he explained, 'because of the damp when she was young and had all them cows to milk. She moves slowly at the best of times. And the door is never locked. Before she reached it, it opened and I saw him.'

He gulped, reliving the moment. 'A big man,' he said at last, 'tall, with a sort of woollen cap. He asked for me. "Where's Nicholas Pascoe?" he said. Nicholas Pascoe was my grandpaw's name, no one calls me anything but Nick. "Dead these thirty years," my gran said, "and off you go, my grandson's done nothing wrong." '

He scrubbed at his eyes. 'He tried to come in. I saw my grandmother put up her hands to push him out. There was a scuffle and a loud crash and I saw her falling. And then I didn't know what to do.'

For the second time he faltered. 'She blocked the door,' he said, 'and I heard him pulling her out of the way. I wanted

181

to go down but I didn't. I turned back again.'

Only after he had been reassured over and over that he'd done the right thing did he continue. As the man blundered through the living room before rushing up the stairs, Nick had gone head first out of the window, sliding down the tree faster than he'd ever done. He'd even heard the man shouting his name out of the window as he ran behind the cowsheds into the barn.

'I hid there,' he finished simply. 'I heard him coming after me. He must have guessed where I'd gone but he went slowly, searching every inch of the way. He'd just reached the barn when there was the sound of a car, and another, close behind it. Driving fast. There were shouts. I guessed he was standing by the barn door, listening. Then I didn't hear anything for a while. Until someone came to the barn and started hunting again and I thought it was him back.'

'Poor kid.' Derrymore's tone was thoughtful. 'Lots of boys his age would have panicked.' He and Reynolds watched Nick Pascoe from a distance as he began to recover enough to tuck into a slab of cake and drink the hot tea that was the duty sergeant's special. He sighed. 'Well,' he said heavily, 'that more or less confirms one part of your theory, doesn't it? I mean, somehow, anyone who's talked to you recently is in big trouble. And if the main subject was Paul Newland, I suppose that suggests he must be at the back of it. Although if the murderer is Newland, whatever he's afraid of beats me. What could a kid like Nick know?'

When Reynolds now revealed the extent of Nick's earlier evidence, explaining at the same time his own reluctance to implicate the child—after all, as with Em's story, it all came second-hand, he'd no proof at all that he'd been told the truth—to his relief, after a moment's reflection, Derrymore agreed. 'I'd have done the same,' he said magnanimously. 'But it makes identifying the man vital, doesn't it, along with the car itself.'

He looked even more harassed. 'Pity Nick didn't see enough today to make a real identification,' he added. 'I don't think we'll catch the fellow now, whoever he was. He must have taken to the moors behind the barn. If he'd headed for the tip we'd have spotted him when we arrived.

We'll put men out to hunt, of course, and set up road blocks, but I don't give much hope. This is really rough land round here. He could even circle about and come back when we've gone.'

His frown deepened. 'And we're still no closer to finding the real reason why no one must reveal anything about Newland,' he added. 'Or for that matter why some anonymous woman seems desperate to find him. What do you think he's up to? Something pretty big, wouldn't you say? Drugs, perhaps?'

'Perhaps.' But again Reynolds wasn't listening. He was still watching Nick Pascoe. 'What'll happen to the kid?' he asked abruptly. 'With his gran in hospital he can't be left on his own. And if the killer could come back he'll not be safe here anyway.'

He beckoned to the duty sergeant, who came over. 'Where will the boy go?' he asked.

The duty sergeant scratched his head and looked from Reynolds to Derrymore and back. 'Dunno really,' he said. 'Perhaps Social Services'll have a say. Mind you,' his face fell, and he spoke in a lower voice, 'they've had a right old tussle with

184

him in the past. Tried to put him in a home once before, suggested Mrs Pascoe wasn't up to keeping him in order and so on, but he wouldn't have any of it. She's getting on a bit, Mrs Pascoe, you know, senile I suppose they calls it.' He tapped his forehead significantly. 'But he insisted his gran and he do all right together, and to leave them alone. Said if anyone tried to separate them he'd make sure it didn't work, he'd run away and his grandma would die, and it'd be their fault. Myself, I'd say he's a bit of a handful, but his heart's in the right place.'

He leaned forward, speaking quickly now. 'The Pascoes had only one child, a daughter. Don't know the ins and outs, but when her first marriage failed, she didn't want the boy. Ran off abroad, I heard, with some titled gent, a foreign count or something like that, and left him with his dad. Then the dad remarries and his new wife doesn't want a ready-made kid either, so Mrs Pascoe ups and takes him in. Brave thing for her to do at her age. And since he's been four or so she's the only family he's had.'

Reynolds listened intently. 'I always tell

the truth,' the boy had said. In a way he had. He remembered the concern when there was any suggestion that his grandmother's abilities were failing, meaning he probably had all the work to do, such as it was, before he went to school, if he went at all. And meaning too that if they put him now in some sort of home, or even in foster care, he'd be out of the door or window before they could turn their backs. And that wouldn't keep him safe if someone was set to hunt him down. Already a new idea was beginning to form; Reynolds wanted none of it, but it had come into his head and wouldn't go away.

'He needs proper protection,' he said severely, 'at the minimum police surveillance until we solve this case. And even then he'll still need someone to keep an eye on him until his grandmother's on the mend—if she does mend, that is. She may be tough, but at her age ...'

He felt rather than saw both men watching him, heard his own voice, and was surprised at what it said. 'If it's all the same to you, I'll volunteer. In the first place I've a housekeeper at home who, as Derrymore will vouch, has nothing better to do but cook too much food and nag me to eat it. Together we'll have all the time in the world to look after one small boy. And when we need advice, at a pinch there's always Derrymore's mam. If Mazie could cope with bringing *him* up, she can cope with Master Nick.'

They laughed and he felt better. 'In the second place,' he went on, 'if anyone's been trained to act as bodyguard, I have.' And from their expressions he knew that they knew he was right, at least about being trained, and accepted what he said.

One problem solved, next came Nick's approval. At first the boy was confident that he could manage on his own. He'd made good his escape once, he'd be a match for anyone. Under the bluster Reynolds sensed fear, mainly about what would happen to his gran. He only agreed to Reynolds' suggestion after he'd been permitted to look at her through the glass of the intensive care unit where she'd been taken, and had seen the officer on guard for himself.

Which was why Reynolds found himself being driven home by Derrymore with a new companion beside him in the back, albeit at best a half-willing one, full of talk of what he'd do or not do when he caught the man who'd hurt his gran. It was rather like suddenly acquiring a boisterous puppy, Reynolds thought, letting the flow of words sweep over him, a flow that only stopped when they reached St Breddaford and Derrymore dropped them off. There, having explored Reynolds' house and introduced himself to the startled housekeeper, Nick unexpectedly fell asleep on the floor of the bedroom he'd selected for himself, next to Reynolds' own.

Worn out by the excitement, Reynolds thought, glancing in at the small curled figure that for a moment resembled the one he'd seen earlier on the farmhouse floor. He curbed an unexpected rush of sentiment. You've really gone too far this time, he warned himself, taken on more than you can handle, if not in the actual work of guarding the boy, certainly in the far more difficult task of ensuring that he stays around long enough to be guarded. He went downstairs to phone the incident room and discuss with Derrymore what their next move should be in this most puzzling case.

Chapter 11

If for the moment, Reynolds was taking his duties seriously and was unwilling to leave the child alone, talking over the phone suited Derrymore equally well. He had a mountain of paperwork to sort through, the sergeant said somewhat testily, all those depositions of last night, from the guests at the caravan site to say nothing of fresh ones from the inhabitants of Carnford, as well as from poor Alf Blunt. He needed to make sense of it all before concentrating on the new crimes. What he really meant was that he needed to be on his own.

Reynolds could understand why Derrymore was despondent. Today's events had thrown him off balance. Someone who didn't know him well might think he was disappointed that the case he'd been building had so suddenly collapsed, or even that he was nervous about being supplanted by a new man who might expose all his shortcomings—on their own, good enough reasons for anyone to show stress. Reynolds recognised that it wasn't the end of Derry's own hopes that had really upset him; it was the fact of murder, brutal murder, twice, so close to home.

Reynolds felt the same. Yet in his long career he'd encountered so many brutalities his only solution was to soldier on. One couldn't knuckle under, that meant the criminal had won. His tone was therefore particularly brusque when he pointed out that the first thing on the agenda was to let the Clitheros go. The bus driver's testimony put Marge in the clear; the doctor's initial report, reaffirmed quickly by forensics, suggesting both murders had been committed by the same person, eliminated Derek—although surprisingly no one as yet had come forward to identify his parked van.

The Clitheros' release incidentally had its lighter moments, as reported later. When the pair returned to Rainbow Park, they discovered that after the second round of questioning yesterday, and following their detention, the remainder of their guests had felt their loyalty was being strained too far. Overnight they'd decided to pack up and leave, a moonlight flit. Only Mrs Newland and her children remained, firmly established in number four, but whether the Clitheros merely endured her or were glad of her company, they never said. 'Rats, deserting what they take for a sinking ship.' Marge's assessment had been frosty. She was putting a brave face on things, but the truth was, Rainbow Park faced financial ruin. As Derrymore pointed out somewhat sourly, she'd brought it all on herself.

Nevertheless, the pair's release put an effective stop to Reynolds and Derrymore's main investigation. However, far from agreeing with Derry that the Clitheros had been 'real red herrings', Reynolds now reiterated his belief that, even involuntarily, they'd furnished several new clues. And new clues were what they desperately needed, since even he admitted the old ones had grown cold.

First, the Clitheros had more or less given them the means of clarifying the time of Em's death, although Derek's actual departure from the cottage was still open to question. Second, as far as could be ascertained at the moment. only three people had known that Em had gone home early on that Friday: Reynolds himself, Marge and Derek. Her friends would have expected her to be at work.

'So would practically everyone else!' Derrymore sounded sarcastic. Ignoring his objection, Reynolds persisted. What he meant, he explained, was that, apart from the attack being random, someone else, unbeknownst to the three, had the same information. Possibly someone connected with Rainbow Park. Newland himself, for example.

'She could have telephoned someone.' Derry was being stubborn. Good, Reynolds thought, better than depression. When he pointed out that she hadn't phoned from the site and didn't when she reached the cottage—her phone there having already been checked—and that moreover there were no phone boxes between the park and her cottage, Derrymore made an effort to be positive. 'I suppose,' he said reluctantly, 'if Derek drove her somewhere to find a kiosk, he'd have already mentioned it. We'll check on that. But,' he came to the essence of his objections, 'suppose we accept your reasoning, I'm still not happy about why you're so sure now the killer must be Newland.'

Reynolds heard him take a breath. 'We're expected to believe he killed Em simply because he's afraid she'll tell you something,' he went on in a rush. 'If so, explain how he knows of your involvement. Derek doesn't contact you until after Newland's gone missing.'

Back to his old role again, keeping Reynolds' flights of fancy under control, he went on to underline the fact that if Newland couldn't have recognised who Reynolds was, having never met him, it wasn't logical to suppose that Newland identified Reynolds as a police officer—a sensible conclusion that so pleased him he repeated it twice.

Concealing a smile at the sergeant's reviving interest, Reynolds retorted that Newland could have been hanging about at the caravan site that Friday morning. Suppose he'd spotted Reynolds earlier at Rainbow Park; wouldn't seeing him again immediately afterwards at Em's cottage make him nervous, especially if he'd followed her there as well? 'It certainly would me,' the ex-inspector added, 'if I were in his shoes.'

Continuing with his line of argument, he went on to suggest that, although Em had indicated she didn't much like Newland, that didn't preclude *his* liking her! 'She admitted finally that they only talked on the Tuesday,' he pointed out, 'but suppose the truth was somewhere in between. While they chat, Newland makes a pass; she gives him the brush-off; he wants to get even with her. Or again, she might have had something he was after. Those cash withdrawals for instance; it might be worth our while trying to trace them, although I know they'd been going on long before Newland arrived in Cornwall.'

After a moment's thought, he added speculatively, 'I suppose it's possible he might have wanted something from Trev too,' to have Derrymore retort that God knows what the old man had that anyone would want—except a pile of TVs and computers, which frankly he couldn't see tempting a so-called antique dealer into a killing frenzy.

Here Reynolds laughed, and was relieved to hear Derry laugh back. 'All the same,' Reynolds now added, 'we ought to check out Trev's contacts with the criminal world, although my guess is that he wasn't into anything big, surely not anything worth murdering for. I still put my money on the simple explanation that Trev may have been seen hanging around the tip, either while the car was being trashed, or later when I showed up. Trev's poked his nose in where he isn't wanted, so curtains for him. And the same for Nick Pascoe.'

He waited for Derrymore to speak and was relieved when the sergeant finally agreed that the sooner they found Paul Newland, or what had become of him, the better, even if that entailed tackling his wife again. 'She's a hard nut to crack,' he added, 'but I'll give it a try. I know we need to check everything about her, from where she lives to why she's here. She's surely got to know or suspect something. And,' with growing enthusiasm, 'of course there's always the sister.

'So far no hint that she's involved,' he added, 'no calls traced to her phone, and no reason to suspect her of anything except being dead set against her brother.'

Glad to have Derrymore functioning normally, Reynolds went over the various strands still left dangling, the main one being the identification of the car. Otherwise there were only two other clues, at best slender but under the circumstances worth pursuing.

'Keep on at Em's neighbour,' he now suggested. 'She may have noticed something she's forgotten. And keep trying to trace the dog. If it were killed or turned loose it should have surfaced somewhere by now. Unless,' another thought struck him, 'the murderer was also a dog-lover and managed to get it under control, presumably before he attacked Em. He might have taken it away with him—Mabley suggested it was valuable.'

Here he paused before mentioning the last thing, which he'd reserved for himself. 'And then there's Mabley,' he said. Even over the phone he felt Derrymore's dislike. 'I know his alibi puts him in the clear, and as one of Em's friends he should have been familiar with her working hours, but all the same my guess is he knows more about this case than anyone else. I'd like to tackle him again. First thing tomorrow. He may give us a fresh perspective. If that's all right with you,' he added, and again, to his satisfaction, he heard Derrymore agree.

These plans for the next day led to a peaceful night—ended in Old Forge Cottage by an early-morning fracas which brought Reynolds leaping out of bed. He'd been spelled about midnight by a young and eager constable who'd settled down comfortably in the kitchen, where presumably he'd experienced no difficulties—until day brought Nick and Mrs Stephens, Reynolds' housekeeper, into direct confrontation.

Reynolds found all three still in the kitchen. The smell of freshly roasted coffee and fried bacon and eggs wafted agreeably towards him, and the constable, somewhat shamefaced, was sitting at the breakfast table with a loaded plate in front of him. Mrs Stephens was guarding the fridge, arms akimbo, glaring at Nick, who, perched precariously on a stool, was attempting to reach a high cupboard where a new tin of coffee was kept, while a frying pan almost beneath his feet sizzled satisfactorily.

'Found him meddling with my supplies.' Mrs Stephens was outraged. 'And look what he's a-doing now, he'll fall in the fat if he isn't careful.'

Soothing her wounded feelings took all of Reynolds' skill and more of his time than he intended. It was not until she had been persuaded to get on with her other tasks that he joined the constable at the table and sampled the results of Nick's takeover. The coffee was surprisingly good, as were the bacon and eggs, a change from his usual tea and toast. It was only the general havoc that the young cook had created, a mess of dirty pots and dishes, which doubtless Mrs Stephens saw as more unnecessary work for her to clear up. He sipped his coffee reflectively.

Nick himself had recovered from his fright the day before. He was still dressed in his familiar grubby clothes, although Reynolds had taken pains to have fresh ones brought from the farmhouse, and when the constable had departed, he dragged up a chair and straddled it, watching Reynolds eat. Either Mrs Stephens' remark about her supplies had got to him, or he wasn't hungry, for he didn't eat himself and didn't say anything until Reynolds had finished. Then he stood up, picked up the plate and took it to the sink. Turning expectantly, he asked, 'When do we start?'

Reynolds was taken aback. 'Start what?' he said, to have Nick reply, 'Finding who attacked my gran, of course.'

He looked at Reynolds straight. 'That's why I came with you,' he said. 'They said you'd be in charge. They said you were a great copper and could track down anyone. So I'm counting on you to track down the man who tried to kill my gran.'

His faith was doubly touching, if

misplaced. First, Reynolds was no longer in charge of anything, and neither would Derrymore be for long. And secondly, whatever Reynolds did, he had no intention of involving the boy. In fact his whole aim was to keep Nick out of mischief and as far away from danger as possible. But that 'we' was a direct appeal that was hard to ignore.

'You and your gran,' he said, 'you get on pretty well, don't you?' Nick didn't say anything, but his face darkened.

'I mean,' Reynolds found himself speaking quickly, remembering the incident with the duty sergeant and making sense of Nick's claim that his gran made the breakfast, when it was obvious that he must have done so himself, 'you take care of her, don't you, do all the work and so on for her?'

Preventing Nick from speaking, he continued even more quickly, 'Good for you. You cook a mean egg.'

The compliment brought a painful flush to the boy's face. 'So she'll need you again when she comes out of hospital,' Reynolds went on, leaning forward persuasively. 'You'll be better staying here. We'll have another man round to keep an eye on things while I'm gone, and I'll stay in touch. Ring you if anything turns up. Later we might ...'

'I want to help.' Nick's tone hardened, no longer a boy's voice. 'If I hadn't gone to the tip I'd never have seen that man. Then someone wouldn't have come after me. And I shouldn't have blabbed about what I saw to anyone.'

It was a bleak but accurate assessment. Reynolds considered. The child barely reached to his armpit yet there was something about that level look that was daunting. No wonder the authorities in Carnford had been stumped how to manage him. After a while, 'OK,' he said. 'You can come this time. But we do things my way.'

He stood up. 'Clear up the kitchen double quick,' he said. 'Meanwhile I'll ring the hospital to find out about your gran.' He smiled. 'I'm sure the news is good. We'll go and see her later. Put on some clean clobber to do her proud. And keep behind me wherever we go, and stay quiet. No matter what you see or hear.'

He wasn't sure his strategy would work. But from his own boyhood experience he guessed that co-operation was better than coercion. When the boy presented himself, quicker than he'd have thought possible, still damp about the face and hair and wearing his best shirt and trousers, obviously hand-tailored from a larger suit, Reynolds was agreeably pleased.

He was also ready for Nick. He sat the boy down and had him repeat exactly what he'd seen of the man who came to the house, what identifying marks other than height and size and the cap or hat he'd been wearing. Try as he would, Nick could remember nothing new, but his description as far as it went corroborated his belief that he was the same as the man at the tip. If so, Reynolds wondered, what were the odds that he was also the same man who'd killed Trev Carthew, and therefore Em Tregurion? And now, in the cool light of a new day, what was the possibility that the murderer might really be Paul Newland, as he'd suggested yesterday?

There was no real proof. That was the problem. Nothing as yet to build a case that would stand up in court. But if size was anything to go by, at least it matched with what he knew about the missing man. Remembering how Newland's suit hanging in the caravan wardrobe had fitted, he told himself it couldn't surely just be coincidence that Nick had mentioned the man being 'as big as you are', or that Mrs Newland had made the same comparison. He made a mental note to get Mrs Newland to describe her husband again.

Meanwhile he was committed to finding Mabley and seeing what he could get from him. He felt Mabley had not been done justice to. If he could be pried away from his surfing companions, another side of the Australian might be revealed under that brassy exterior. An added inducement was that a surfing venue was the perfect place to keep a small boy busy while he himself did some investigating, as long as Nick didn't wander too far out of sight. Co-operation for the moment, he reminded himself; later comes the tightening of the screws. Once more securing a promise of Nick's non-interference, he backed the car out.

The morning was fresh, the surf was up. But Mabley was nowhere to be found. Reynolds and Nick discovered him finally in the beach café, holding court with a number of enthusiasts who, it turned out, were his pupils in the surfing school he ran. He didn't seem put out to be asked more questions and willingly accompanied Reynolds and Nick to Reynolds' car. The two men sat in the front seat and the boy, torn between wanting to run on the beach and afraid of missing something important, reluctantly remained in the back, soon losing interest in questions that appeared to have no meaning, and more curious about the surfers who came and went.

'I'm here unofficially,' Reynolds began. He had decided there was no point in pretending he was more than he was. 'It's about Em again.'

Watching closely, he sensed the stiffening of resistance. Co-operation, he advised himself, be careful. As Mabley started to protest, 'We accept you were nowhere near her house the day she died,' he added sympathetically. 'But you knew her well, better than most. Perhaps you can help us in a couple of other ways.

'We've some leads that might get us somewhere,' he went on, 'but we need some background info. For example,' he posed the question as if out of idle curiosity, although it was really of prime interest. 'did she ever mention what she was using her money for? Other than her planned university course, that is.'

When Mabley didn't answer, 'Did she give it to anyone?'

Mabley reacted quickly, but not as quickly as he might have if he thought he himself was being suspected as the recipient. 'Give her money away?' he brought out. He stared at Reynolds in disbelief. 'I only know about the damned university,' he said.

'And her planning to go away to university was what ended your relationship? That and abandoning her surfing?'

Reluctantly the Australian nodded.

'So when did you break up?'

'When she decided that work was all that mattered.' Mabley was growing angry. 'Said she owed it to her father, that sort of crap. Said she didn't have time for ...'

He stopped himself from saying, 'Time for me.'

'I wouldn't have minded if it was just going off to study,' he went on. 'I've no problem with that. It was the way she went at it, hammer and tongs. Made a clean sweep. Off with the old, on with the new. Know what I mean?'

Reynolds nodded understandingly. Better than most men he knew what it meant. It had been one of the causes of conflict with his ex-wife. Before Mabley could rehash all his grievances, Reynolds asked if he and Em had ever met since, 'For example, any time in the week before her death?'

It was a leading question and it struck home. 'How did you know ...' Mabley was startled. Then, 'All right,' he admitted surlily, 'I did see her once. A couple of nights before. She showed up at my house and said she was offering me the chance to buy old Kern back. My own dog. But I didn't go along with the idea, so don't come hunting for it again.'

'Right.' Reynolds copied Derrymore's tactics by opening a pad and pretending to make copious notes. 'And when exactly was this last meeting?'

Mabley considered. 'Tuesday,' he came out with. Before he could embark on another tirade about the real ownership of the Dobermann, 'What time on Tuesday?' Reynolds pressed, to have Mabley say latish, eight, perhaps quarter past, she said she'd been kept at work.

It was the same night she was supposed to have met Newland behind the hedge. Or had a liaison with him—and if she had, for the first time the question occurred to Reynolds, just where would that have taken place? Not in number four caravan, that was for sure, under Marge's eagle eye. But if Mabley were right—and again his story could be checked if she'd come to his house and his mates bore this out—Em's revised story of a simple meeting with Newland after work began to look more and more plausible.

The next question was delicate, but it was the one he'd been leading up to. 'That same night,' he said, 'did she mention seeing another man, specifically a big fellow about my size?'

Mabley's immediate answer was truculent. 'I've enough trouble managing my own affairs. I didn't keep tabs on her love life, if that's what you mean.'

'I didn't suppose you did.' Reynolds allowed himself a smile. 'But she may have made an off-hand remark about a friend that would give us a new lead. We've checked out Derek Clithero, by the by,' he added ingratiatingly, 'thanks to your tip.'

A silence. Then, 'I wouldn't say friend,' Mabley began slowly. 'And it only came out in a round-about way. That was all.'

Hiding his excitement, 'Who was he?' Reynolds asked.

'Couldn't put a name to him,' Mabley said, 'but I think he was someone at the caravan site.'

He too fell silent as if thinking, then, 'It was because of the books,' he admitted, 'the ones she'd collected, all those bloody books that changed her life and mine.'

He sounded disgusted. 'I told her if she needed money so badly, why didn't she sell her own belongings first, namely those books of hers. She was always on about how valuable they were.'

He paused, his blue eyes staring unseeingly out to sea. When Reynolds prompted, 'And then?' he gave himself a shake as if bringing himself back to the present. 'A big mistake. She got mad all over again. Said other people appreciated them even if I didn't. Like this fellow at the caravan site. He was keen to get his hands on one, she said, had told her it was a real gem. I could have warned him to save his breath to cool his porridge. She'd never sell.'

Paul Newland was an antique dealer. Reynolds felt a surge of adrenaline. 'Could you identify the book?' he asked more nonchalantly than he felt.

'Perhaps if I saw it. She told me its name but I don't remember it off-hand.'

'What about a little expedition then?' Reynolds looked at him expectantly. 'It would be doing me a favour,' he added persuasively. 'And her too.'

After all these questions Mabley appeared so lost in thought that he didn't seem to notice that Reynolds had started the car; at least, he didn't try to stop him.

'As far as I know, she saved every penny she could,' he said at last. 'She was like that, a bloody croc. Fixed on something, she'd never let go.'

He said suddenly in a different voice, the words forced out of him, 'I could have helped her, you see. Well, not me personally, I live on a shoestring here, but my dad's got the cash. If I'd asked he would have lent, or, damn it, given it her. He'd never have missed it and it would have taken the strain off. But she wouldn't have any of it. Her efforts alone. Even to selling a damn dog that she felt was hers. To tell the truth, I never met anyone like her before.'

He stared ahead unseeingly. 'I stayed on after last season just because of her. I don't suppose I'll ever find anyone like her again.'

It was a stark assessment, all the more real because it was so unexpected.

They made the drive in silence after that, even Nick saying nothing, although he watched Mabley carefully as if assessing him. When they drew up once more in front of Em's cottage, they found the police tapes still in place, but there was no sign of any duty officer. 'Damn,' Reynolds swore, the mildest in a series that soon attracted Nick's rapt interest. They walked up the path but the door was locked, as were all the downstairs windows.

Even in bright sunlight the cottage had a dejected look, its garden flattened by the tramp of feet and its rose bushes broken. 'Sorry about this,' Reynolds was just beginning when Mabley said abruptly, 'There's a way in through the bathroom upstairs. Via that tree.' He pointed to an ornamental cherry beside the wall. Like everything else it had grown out of all proportion and towered above the roof. 'The window's too small for us but the kid could do it easily,' he said.

Nick had been keeping in the background as he'd promised. Reynolds glanced at him. Instead of bursting with enthusiasm, his face had gone white. About to draw him aside and whisper that they would go back for a key, Reynolds was forestalled by Mabley. 'Up you go, mate,' said the Australian. He caught Nick by the shoulders and hoisted him unceremoniously into the tree. 'That's right, just shimmy on up to the window. Give it a jerk. And we're in.'

Nick glanced down, his face whiter than ever. 'It's important, isn't it?' he asked, then, as if answering his own question with another, 'You'll be there at the door?'

Quickly he scrabbled up the tree until he reached the window, which he struggled to push open. Reynolds watched more anxiously than he liked to admit, and when in turn he saw Mabley watching him curiously, explained the circumstances.

'Poor kid,' Mabley said, much as Derrymore had done. 'That takes some pluck. Wild horses wouldn't have got me up a tree or inside a house after an ordeal like that. Like running a video in reverse.'

When they heard the rattle of the window and saw Nick disappear, Mabley was the first to reach the door before it opened. 'Well done you,' he said, with a smile that showed how attractive he could be, while Reynolds contented himself with a thumbs-up sign. 'Now, where're the bloody books?'

They were still on the shelves, just as Reynolds had seen them last. If it was an ordeal too for Mabley to come back to Em's cottage he hid his feelings well. He knelt down and began to pull the books out, eventually hesitating over a slim red leather volume, frayed at the edges, its pages curled with damp. *'Churches of the West Country and Their Architecture.'* He read the title out. 'I think this is the one.' He weighed it in his hand. 'Not much to it, is there? But she said it was valuable. And old.'

If the book was a lead, Reynolds still wasn't sure in which direction it was going. Of itself it didn't seem to merit a killing. And if it were so valuable and Newland had been after it, why for God's sake hadn't he taken it when he'd had the chance? He'd have had plenty of time to search for it if he'd killed Em first.

As far as he could tell, it was the sort of tract that was common in the last century, a kind of hand-produced, amateurish item, written in his spare time by some clergyman, a Reverend

St John Hillard, MA (Oxon). It was divided simply by regions, and made no attempt to include every church as its title suggested, selecting apparently at random those that interested the author and giving a short history of each. What was unusual was that every church included was accompanied by a delicate line drawing, probably what made the book unique. But if the volume itself wasn't valuable, was it possibly the information it contained that had interested Newland? If so, which church, or churches?

The task seemed hopeless until Reynolds remembered Em's remark about Newland's plan to drive towards Land's End. If correct, that narrowed the search. In fact, only four churches in the far south-west of Cornwall were mentioned. He read out the names, but they meant nothing to Mabley and nothing to him. As for Nick, he knew enough to point out what was obvious: they were all close to Carnford, which had no church of its own.

Reynolds had thanked Mabley, promised to keep him informed and was about to deposit him back on the beach when a thought struck him. For a moment he hesitated, deciding that he was taking paranoia too far. Then, changing his mind, he suggested that the Australian watch his back, jerking a finger towards Nick to emphasise his remark.

'Right you are,' Mabley said, taking the warning in his stride but not making light of it. He leant against the rear window. 'And when you're off duty again, mate,' he said, 'come try a spin with me.'

He measured the delighted Nick with a professional look, as if the boy was one of his best customers, and said, 'Think we might have a board that'll fit,' before running lightly back towards the beach.

Nick watched him go enviously. Then, as if reminding himself of more important things, he dragged his gaze away, turned towards Reynolds and said, 'His voice is wrong. Besides, he's too thin. I don't think he'd hurt my gran, do you?'

Reynolds had to laugh. 'I don't suppose so,' he said. He started up the engine. 'But what's that about the voice?' he asked in a casual tone, and was intrigued by Nick's reply. 'It wasn't like the way I speak or you do neither,' the boy said. 'It was angry-sounding, sort of cruel.' He gave a little shiver.

He'd never mentioned the voice before.

It was an important clue.

'Well, Ray certainly helped us.' Reynolds changed the subject quickly. He tapped the book on the seat beside him. 'And this may give us a lead.'

'That little itty-bitty book?' Nick's reaction to remembered fear was truculence. Undoing his seat belt, he leaned over and picked it up, sinking back quickly as Reynolds bellowed at him to sit still. 'Make yourself useful,' the ex-inspector told him. 'Turn to the pages about those four churches and read me what it says.'

Glancing through the mirror he saw the boy leaf through the book, then, as if frustrated, throw it aside. 'Can't read in a car,' Nick said, 'it's too bumpy.' And that's a lie too, Reynolds thought. What you mean, my lad, is that you can't read. He gave a silent whistle. Here was another little problem needing solving when there was time.

After he had taken a roundabout route that brought them to the hospital, he took Nick to see Mrs Pascoe. She was still holding her own, had opened her eyes, but was too weak to be questioned. He might not have been able to drag Nick away except the sight of a policeman by her bed again convinced the boy that his gran was safe. He settled down then, and when dropped off at Old Forge Cottage appeared perfectly at home, left in the care of his own officer and Mrs Stephens—placated by the good job he'd made of the washing-up, as she herself told Reynolds. Meanwhile, again conferring with Derrymore, who agreed that it was better he went unofficially, no point in alarming people on what was after all a mere reconnaissance trip, Reynolds headed off west.

Chapter 12

The four churches he was interested in were grouped in a little cluster, several miles, as it turned out, from Nick's home, in an area not exactly popular with tourists, which was fortunate. A hot August afternoon was not the best time for sightseeing. The first three he visited were typically Cornish, with their square towers and shady cemeteries. When he had made the now customary application for the key to get inside, each in its way was attractive, although why more than others not included in Hillard's book was hard to say. However, each had some distinguishing feature that was made much of: a holy well nearby, a Celtic cross in one corner of the graveyard, a brass memorial in the church to some local dignitary. Even if none of these features was unique, the line drawings which accompanied the descriptions were very fine; perhaps it was these which made the Reverend Hillard originally decide to include them.

The fourth church was bigger, dedicated to a saint who must have originated in Byzantium. Unfortunately preparations for some village fête were in full swing—there were people everywhere, inside and outside the church, hurrying up and down with trays of food and bags of second-hand clothes and odds and ends that would have made Trev's eyes gleam. In an adjacent field, stalls were being erected, and after being mistaken for the man who did the tent, Reynolds went inside the church, where a harassed vicar told him to look around, he'd be with him in a moment.

Reynolds wandered up and down the aisles where only a few modern plaques attracted his attention. The floor was older, but the ceilings were Victorian, as were the light-wood pews replacing the medieval oak. He studied the book again. It puzzled him why this church was included, for in the Reverend Hillard's day it must have been new and had already lost most of its old charm. Perhaps it was just the fact of its having a spire, rare in Cornwall, that gave it any merit.

'Ah, Hillard.' The vicar joined him, looking even more harassed, a strand of tape caught on his jacket and his hair on end. He took the book and began to browse through it. 'Goes on about the spire, doesn't he, but doesn't include the main item,' he said. 'You know why? It happened after he was dead.' He gave a guffaw at his little joke, then, seeing the blank look on Reynolds' face, added, 'I'd show you myself but we've locked the hall up. The ladies are awfully keen on security and they've stored the auction items there. We always have a silent auction at our fête,' he went on to explain. 'That's where the money is these days. People are very generous. This year, for instance, we ...'

'What hall?' Reynolds cut him short.

The vicar raised his eyebrows. 'My dear fellow,' he exclaimed, as if shocked at Reynolds' ignorance. Reynolds almost expected him to say, 'Tut tut,' as if he were living in another age. 'The parish hall. It's actually built over the ruins of the original church. Or at least part of it.'

He gestured towards the rear of the main church, where, through a stand of trees, Reynolds could just make out a high roof. 'A very ancient church, very ancient,' the vicar was continuing enthusiastically. 'Virtually disappeared after a disastrous fire in the early eighteen hundreds. After which this church was built to take its place.'

He shook his head disapprovingly. 'Of course it too has been modernised since,' he explained. 'The Victorian renovators had a field day here. It was only later, in the nineteen twenties, long after Hillard's time, I'm afraid, while the site was being prepared for a Sunday school and parish hall, that workmen discovered the original foundations, virtually intact, absolutely primeval.'

He beamed and said in a lower voice, as if afraid of being overheard, 'Thank God, say I, that those nineteenth-century enthusiasts never knew about it or they'd have hacked it up. In my opinion they did more damage than Cromwell's men during the Reformation, but I don't say so in my parishioners' hearing. Some are descended from the worthy citizens who financed the so-called restorations here, and are, alas, very proud of their ancestors' work.'

He winked. 'Under that modern parish hall there's a perfect gem. Norman flooring, remains of twelfth-century wall paintings, even some Elizabethan tombstones, a right old architectural jumble that Hillard would have loved. Come back in a day or two and I'll show you round.'

And he was off, leaving Reynolds even more perplexed. Because if Newland had wanted the Reverend Hillard's book, what on earth was he looking for in St Theodosius' church, which wasn't really old in the first place and had been renovated less than a hundred years ago? Unless, of course, his mention of driving westward from Rainbow Park had been intended to mislead, another unwelcome possibility.

Dissatisfied with his day's work, Reynolds returned to St Breddaford to report back to Derrymore, who had been pressing forward with other lines of investigation without making much progress either. Still no news about the car, early days they said; still no leads in Trev's business affairs or his murder; no information about Newland, everything on hold. Newland's sister was proving very uncooperative, but since there was no proof she had rung Marge Clithero, there wasn't much to go on. As for the inhabitants of Rainbow Park, the Clitheros themselves might be off the hook and thus off their backs, as Derrymore put it, with fine disregard for mixed metaphor, but Mrs Newland was proving even more difficult than had been anticipated. Even the suggestion that she might be safer in a hotel, chosen so the police could keep an eye on her, had met with contemptuous refusal. Derrymore had used the words 'more comfortable' so as not to frighten her; she'd retorted that she was perfectly comfortable where she was. Besides, she, or rather her husband, had paid for another week's rental on the caravan; she wasn't throwing money away for nothing.

Her faith in her husband would have been commendable if it hadn't been so frustrating. Short of calling him a murderer, Derrymore had been unable to make a dent in her complacency. It took the events of the next morning to crack her resolve.

In the meanwhile, Reynolds, giving up for the moment on Hillard and St Theodosius', spent the rest of the day in various libraries, gathering all the information he could about other churches in western Cornwall. He limited his search to the west because that was the only clue he had—albeit one he was rapidly losing confidence in.

This work was tiresome, not his usual style, although he supposed if he'd settled to the subject he'd have gleaned enough information about church architecture, furnishings and surroundings to write a book himself. Nick was unimpressed. He kept coming to the door of the study where Reynolds sat surrounded by the volumes he'd borrowed, retreating after a while with a disapproving look. His original remark about that 'itty-bitty book' was repeated at regular intervals under his breath. And after he had asked for the umpteenth time why Reynolds hadn't found the murderer yet, the ex-inspector was ready to give him a good clout to shut him up.

Next morning, Nick had more than his fair share of excitement.

The first alarm came at daybreak. From Derrymore. 'A fire bomb. At Rainbow

221

Park. Chucked over the sea hedge early this morning. Considerable damage to the surrounding field and,' a significant pause, 'total destruction of number four caravan—burnt to the ground.'

Reynolds' pulse quickened. Before he could ask about casualties, the sergeant added, 'Would have been curtains for the Newlands, but as it happens they changed caravans last night. Marge's doing. She finally relented enough to let them stay on another week, but not in what she called a "prime property".'

'Coincidental or deliberate?'

'Oh, completely coincidental, I'd say. As you know, the regulars have left, so there're plenty of empty sites. And the Clitheros are so beside themselves as it is, I can't see them setting their own place alight. But it does seem ironic, doesn't it, given Marge's story? I mean, the possible threats from the anonymous phone caller.'

'Any clues?'

'Petrol. In cans. On the cliff path.' Derrymore sounded weary. 'We've had men out scouring the area since first light, but nothing else so far. Can you ...?'

'I'll be there.'

As he dressed, Reynolds' mind whirled.

This was becoming more serious than even he'd envisaged. Two deaths, two attempted killings, now what seemed like a premeditated attack on Newland's own family—and still no sensible reason why any of it was happening. Struggling into a jacket, he made for the door—to find his faithful shadow already dressed and waiting for him.

'I heard the phone.' Nick's voice was high, his eyes bright. 'It's the same man, isn't it? The one who burnt up the car, the one I saw that hurt my gran. We'll catch him now, won't we? He won't get away this time.'

'Hold your horses.' Reynolds bent down. Over the boy's head he saw the constable who had taken on the night shift standing by the living room door. 'You may be right,' he told the child, 'but it's no place for you. You can be more useful here, holding the fort and taking messages while I'm gone.'

He saw the disappointment, although Nick made no outward protest. 'Tell you what,' he compromised. He nodded to the constable who, immediately understanding, opened the front door and stood in the porch, blocking it while both men quickly

223

scanned the garden. All was serene. A few birds chirped noisily, a cat sat sunning itself on the wall, the dew on the grass was so thick it looked like glass. Not a blade out of place, no footprints on the gravel drive, no sign of disturbance, an ordinary summer morning in the heart of a peaceful village.

'Now then,' Reynolds said, relaxing, 'I left the car parked ready. But it's a devil to back into the road. You and the officer here nip ahead to open the gate and see me out.'

He unlocked the car door and slid into the driver's seat, smiling at Nick as he and the policeman came round the side. Rolling down the window as they passed, he said, 'We'll visit your gran later,' and turned the ignition key.

The engine coughed, stuttered to a halt. Usually it purred into instant action. Must be the weather, Reynolds thought, and then, 'My God!'

He was out of the door, bearing down on Nick, rolling with him clasped in his arms and shouting to the officer to run, the only cover too far away to be of any use. One second, two seconds, he had reached the edge of the lawn, had dived over the rockery into the shelter of the bushes by the flowerbed, heard the crash of the other man beside him. Another couple of seconds passed. Cautiously he lifted his head.

'What do you think, sir?' White as chalk, the officer lay beside him, while underneath him Nick wriggled and spluttered in the dirt. 'I think,' Reynolds said, 'we may have had a very lucky escape, Constable. Very lucky indeed.' He shifted carefully so that Nick could struggle free, and then, before the boy could protest, ran with him to the far side of the grass where again he dropped to the ground. He felt him over quickly to make sure he was all right and checked with the constable that he too was in one piece. His own ribs and shoulder were throbbing and there were scratches on his cheek. 'You stay here,' he said.

He worked his way back up the drive until he reached the car. It stood in the sun, its paintwork gleaming. Edging round it, he looked through the open door to where the key still dangled from the ignition.

Car devices had once been his speciality; this may have failed to go off but that meant it might be even more dangerous. Quickly he went over the procedures for finding and disabling it. A few moments later he'd located it, under the car, a package with wires connected, probably to the starter, large enough to blow car and cottage to kingdom come.

It had been the distinctive stutter that had put him on guard. Once heard, never forgotten. But who in this backwater had the experience to fix such a device? Or a reason? Against his will his own answer flashed into his head, 'To get rid of anyone on Newland's trail.'

Gesturing to the other two to leave the garden and keep clear, he decided this was a job for experts. Tiptoeing round the car, he went inside, locking the front door behind him and, before ringing the emergency number, persuading Mrs Stephens to leave the house via the back. Fortunately she was already dressed and on her way downstairs, so he was able to accomplish this with the minimum of resistance. Then, while his little group moved out of range and makeshift road blocks were set up to stop any passer-by wandering into danger, he and the constable alerted the neighbours to vacate their homes until the bomb disposal unit arrived.

They had come and gone and the crisis was over before he could interview the constable. Middle-aged, dependable, a local man, the fellow was adamant he'd not fallen asleep. He'd been in the sitting room all night, except for an occasional stroll through the house, checking doors and windows; he had gone outside once to have a look around, after midnight, when the whole place had been as silent as the grave. 'There was no one about, I swear,' he said, looking even paler than before, 'and I never heard anyone. He must have been walking on eggs to get so close.'

Reynolds believed him. The work had signs of a master touch, no fingerprints, of course, and the car door forced and relocked without a trace. But the experts in the bomb disposal unit had spotted flaws. Taking car and device away to study them more carefully, they left Reynolds with a list of several leading questions.

Derrymore was quickly on the scene, as soon as he could leave the caravan park. He was appalled by the two attacks in one night, at two different locations.

'Surely can't be the same person,' he kept exclaiming. Again Reynolds concurred, but with a different interpretation. 'Anyone can hurl a fire bomb,' he said. 'Along the coast road, at that time of night, or day rather, it'd be easy to park anywhere and take the cliff path to the site. My guess is that one person was responsible for both incidents, but after he'd made the bomb he delegated the task of throwing it to an accomplice while he himself came here. This is more specialised work.'

From his army days in Ireland, Derrymore also had experience of car bombs; he knew first hand the extent of the damage; he recognised the lucky escape. His own face paled.

'The experts claim this wasn't as clever as it seemed,' Reynolds went on soothingly. 'For one thing, there's enough explosive to blow up the whole neighbourhood. Meaning overkill. Then the device was rigged in an old-fashioned way, meaning not using what is thought of as modern equipment or techniques. No Semtex or stuff like that. And finally, lucky for us, it didn't go off.'

He managed a smile. 'So I'll lay a bet that we're looking for a one-time expert who's lost his touch. That narrows the field a bit.'

When Derrymore asked what he meant, 'Someone trained in bomb work several years ago. Not a young man. And possibly ex-army. Used to accepting authority, or more likely giving orders. To his assistant.'

Again a quick glance at Derrymore. 'They must have worked together,' he said. 'It can't be accidental that the two attacks were planned for the same time. They meant to finish me and the Newland family off at one go.'

'But who ...?' Derrymore began, to have Reynolds say grimly that that was for them to find out soon—before there was another attack that didn't fail. But he'd bank on it being an ex-soldier. Who'd been trained in sapper work. And that meant delving even further into Newland's background, although ... He bit off the end of his sentence. He was about to say that he had an idea Newland wasn't old enough to fit the sort of person he had in mind.

Meanwhile there was an immediate problem: what to do with Nick. The housekeeper, Mrs Stephens, took care of herself. She was out of St Breddaford by the first bus, shaking the dust literally from her feet. Nick was another matter, until Derrymore offered to take him during the day to his own house, along with the police guard. He'd been generous like this in the past when there were other victims needing protection. Or rather, he had turned the job over to his mam. And his mam was just what Nick needed at the moment.

Mazie met them at the door, a small, cheerful Cornish woman, a miniature Derrymore. Over the years, she'd become used to these intrusions into her calm life and her hospitality was proverbial. 'Come in, come in,' she cried, enveloping the boy in her arms and telling Derry he should be ashamed, letting Mr Reynolds go round without seeing to his cuts and bruises. She'd have warm water in a moment, the kettle was on, and would they like some currant cake?

There was no stopping her, and sheepishly Reynolds let himself be pushed into a chair and fed with tea and cake as if he was Nick's age. He and Derrymore left her listening with flattering attention to Nick while he explained about 'our narrow escape, very narrow indeed', in fair imitation of the ex-inspector, and she rolled out pastry and a new officer stood on watch with strict instructions not to let anyone in, or out.

After implementing the search of Old Forge Cottage and its grounds, Reynolds and Derrymore returned to Rainbow Park to oversee the investigation there. The stench of burning greeted them, along with a great patch of scorched tamarisk bushes and grass and at least two damaged caravans apart from number four, which was a wreck. The Clithero caravan was intact, but they were no longer in it, having asked for, and been removed to, some secure place. Only the Newland family car was left, in front of a smaller and, if anything, seedier caravan. Steeling themselves for a confrontation with the indomitable Mrs Newland, Reynolds and Derrymore approached the door.

Derrymore had already told Reynolds his other bad news—as he'd feared all along, headquarters was closing his operation down. He'd had word to expect a certain Inspector Upshaw; he was waiting in the wings, as it were, ready to take over, 'sharpening his claws', Derrymore said. This was their last chance to make a breakthrough. He shook his head. 'Not much hope,' he said. He was wrong.

Given the circumstances, Mrs Newland remained surprisingly calm. She was surely intelligent enough to realise that the attack had been aimed at her and her family, but she wouldn't admit it, even when it was pointed out. 'There're over twenty caravans altogether,' she retorted, 'and number four was closest to the cliffs. Stands to reason it was in the direct line of fire, that's how I see it.'

Unaware of her dreadful pun, and seemingly unaware of Reynolds and Derrymore's disbelief at her cheerfulness, she went on to say that it was lucky Mrs Clithero had persuaded her to move to this smaller caravan.

Her unfailing optimism, her regular Pollyanna-like attitude drove Reynolds wild. Only the presence of her children curbed his tongue. Derrymore was more patient. 'Yes, madam,' he said, 'but you know you had been occupying the caravan up to last night and the attack was aimed at it. For your children's sakes you should consider moving out.'

'But I don't want to contribute to

Marge and Derek's distress.' Mrs Newland smiled sweetly. 'Everyone else has gone. I don't have to follow their lead. Besides, how will Paul find us if we go into hiding?'

The argument was silly, but she'd made even more silly ones before. Reynolds' patience snapped. Usually he left the main questioning to Derrymore; now he took over. 'Why is it you persist in thinking he'll return?' he bellowed. 'I'd say the odds are fifty to one he won't. And if he does, it's because we've hauled him in with a list of charges a mile long dangling round his neck—unless you come clean and tell us what you know.'

For a second he thought he'd reached her. Her eyelids flickered and her mouth twitched. Before she could reply, her son did it for her. 'Mum,' he shrieked from the bedroom where he'd been banished, 'I don't want to be burnt. Tell them, tell them, tell them. Dad'll understand.'

Out of the mouths of babes and sucklings. There was a long silence, broken by his sniffling. Until Derrymore leaned towards her and said gently, 'And exactly what is it you have to tell?'

Chapter 13

Mrs Newland straightened her skirt and folded her arms. She might have been attending a prayer meeting. 'It's not what you think,' she told the two men, 'although you're ready to pounce. It's nothing to be ashamed of. He's overreacting, that's all,' as if her son's hysterical outburst was embarrassing.

'What he's referring to,' she went on, 'is something my husband and I decided a year or so ago. We changed our name. It's all legal,' she added, this time quick to notice their expressions. 'I'll show you the documents.'

She fumbled in her bag and produced a sheaf of papers, as if, Reynolds thought, she had them ready. Taking them, the two men read through them hastily, but it was as she'd said: Paul and Rachael and their two children had had their surname changed by deed poll to Newland. They had even been living in a different part of the country and moved to Birmingham later; they'd made a clean sweep of their old identity. The name Newland suddenly took on a special connotation.

Rachael Newland took the papers back and slipped them carefully into her bag, a faint smile flickering across her lips which she couldn't resist. 'I don't suppose even Paul's sister, Izzie Worthington, mentioned it,' she said after a moment. 'And if anyone would try to make trouble for us, she would.'

She looked at them calmly. 'You've noted, of course, that we kept our original first names. It was only the surname we changed. And what do you make of the previous one?'

Again the faint smile. 'Penderver. Nicely Cornish, don't you think? I suppose my husband's people came from here originally. But Timmy is convinced it's got something to do with his father's so-called disappearance. It's naughty of him, I know, but there you are.'

'Why did you change your name?' Again Reynolds took over the questioning. He couldn't explain why, but that little smirk made him even more uneasy than her pious self-righteousness, as if underneath her calm she was enjoying a joke at their expense.

She didn't answer immediately, then said, with a heightened colour in her cheeks, 'My husband thought Penderver was a difficult name to pronounce. In business, I mean. People were always getting it wrong and it caused, well, problems.'

Possibly financial ones, Reynolds thought. Bankruptcy high on the list. That tallies with Izzie Worthington's claim that you soaked her of money once too often. But why make a point of telling us all this now, unless your show of affability is concealing something else?

'What is your husband really doing in this part of the world?' he snapped.

When she hesitated, 'Or shall we have your boy in and see what he says?' It was an underhand trick, but it worked.

'No need for that.' Rachael spoke so quickly she became short of breath. 'He can't tell you. I can't myself. Paul is really secretive when he wants, he didn't confide in me. All I do know is he often goes on buying expeditions, so I imagine that's what he's doing here. He buys and sells old things, you see.'

Her eyes glinted. 'I told you, looking for them is normal for antique dealers.'

'Only if,' Reynolds permitted himself a brief but chill smile, 'what he's selling isn't some bit of old Cornwall that comes to hand easily, shall we say, to be flogged upcountry at bargain prices, no one the wiser.'

It was a guess only, but it caused a reaction. 'What do you mean?' She started to her feet. 'You can't know ...'

Recovering herself quickly, she sank back, saying, 'I mean, you don't know Paul. He's very law-abiding; he's not likely to take anything that doesn't belong to him, if that's what you're hinting ...'

'Timmy's let more cats out of bags than you realise,' Reynolds interrupted. 'At least that's what it looks like to me. Namely, that when your husband does return he hopes to come back rich.'

He looked at her. 'So where's that money coming from?' he asked. 'Not from touring local flea markets.'

'Timmy's just a child.' Once more her recovery was quick. 'I wouldn't put much stock in what he says. And come to that, don't you and the sergeant here expect to be paid for work you do, so why shouldn't my husband? In any case, you've no proof of anything wrong, no proof at all.'

It was impossible to penetrate that calm exterior. And what she said was not only shrewd, it underlined all the flaws in their own work so far.

'Agreed.' Reynolds stood up. 'But we give you fair warning that's what we're looking for. Proof. And we'll find it.'

Before she could answer, 'Meanwhile, you and your two children are clearly not safe here. So while you pack your bags we'll arrange for you to stay somewhere else. Under supervision.'

'At your expense?'

The question came out so pat it had to have been premeditated. Reynolds looked at Derrymore, who sighed. 'All right, madam,' he said, 'we'll worry about that later. But,' as once more she began to trot out the familiar excuses that she was perfectly satisfied where she was, and since her husband had already paid for a fortnight in full, she could get a discount here if she stayed longer, 'you can't stay here. Two murders already, two attacks involving an old woman and a boy not much older than your son; whoever is the perpetrator, he isn't playing games.'

'Mrs Newland had the best of that encounter.'

After they had arranged for a couple of officers to oversee Rachael Newland's removal, Derrymore and Reynolds roamed the deserted caravan site, ostensibly looking for clues, while the sergeant pointed out ruefully that whatever else the Newlands were up to, Rachael had done her damnedest to ensure the police paid for her new lodgings. Although what headquarters and Inspector Upshaw would have to say about that, God only knew.

Reynolds was only fitfully listening. He had already latched on to the one little hint she'd let inadvertently drop by her response to his remark about 'some bit of old Cornwall'. 'You can't know,' she'd started to say before she corrected herself. Can't know—what? That in fact he was after some old bit of Cornwall? If so, why not something in a Cornish church?

The rest of the day was uneventful. Once more they went over the statements, concentrating on any information linking Em Tregurion and Paul Newland. Reynolds had been right: as a newcomer Newland had roused curiosity, but most of the other caravanners were too engrossed in their own holidays to do more than notice him, merely confirming he'd left early each day and come back late. No one had bothered to speak with him, or find out anything about him—they left that sort of thing to Marge.

As for Em, the original statements taken on the day after her death had expressed regret and shock and spoke of her as being a hard worker, and always very pleasant, meaning people had taken her for granted. Added to these sentiments was the belief that as far as the guests were aware there was no involvement with anyone on the site, meaning that her relationship with Derek—and with Newland, if there were one—had been kept well hidden.

Out of this mountain of non-information only one small clue emerged. Asked explicitly if they'd spotted Em in Paul Newland's company, most of the caravanners said no. One couple thought they'd seen her talking with someone behind the hedge near number four. Questioned as to date, they couldn't say which day exactly. As for time, 'coming on towards evening' was the best they could manage. This sighting might have confirmed Em's second version of her meeting with Newland, but was so vague it would be useless in a court of law—especially when the wife, in a fit of enthusiasm, added that she liked Em better than the woman who'd cleaned for them last year—'all sulks and temper, very unhelpful'.

The repeated messages to Paul Newland on the media were continuing, with no response. They were still worded vaguely—there was no mention of Newland's being wanted for any crime—but as time passed it became more and more unlikely that his wife's faith, if genuine, in his speedy return would be justified. But without some concrete proof of his involvement, any concentrated search seemed unlikely at the moment, given the impending change over of regime.

The murders themselves were unfortunately given full coverage in the press, although as yet no formal police statement had made any connection between them. Officially, the death of young Em Tregurion from St Breddaford parish had nothing in common with the death of an old reprobate from Carnford. The other events were played down, and also not connected, the attack on Mrs Pascoe explained as the work of a sadist who had

241

some grudge against old women, while that on Nick Pascoe for the moment was kept under wraps, mainly for his own protection. As for the fire bomb at Rainbow Park, it was regarded as an act of random vandalism. If any commentator had doubts about just how random, or unusual, this spate of criminal activity was, he had the good sense—or had been given a forceful reminder—not to make his opinions public. What was remarkable was how all these crimes were accepted without surprise in a community where once stealing chicken eggs was considered a major offence and murder was so rare it happened only once in one's lifetime—a commentary on the extent of social change, even in this quiet backwater.

Strangely enough it was news of the car bomb that had the biggest effect. It could not be concealed, as too many people had known about it. When Reynolds and Derrymore returned to St Breddaford at the end of another frustrating day, they found a deputation of Reynolds' neighbours waiting for them.

Reynolds braced himself for more bad news. There had been times when he'd not been on good terms with the other villagers and his criminal investigations had been held against him. To his relief, now he became the object of sympathy. Colonel Philips offered condolences and help to 'catch the blighter'; even Miss Avery invited him to tea, 'and bring the little boy with you, so kind, and you a single man'.

Quaking at the thought of Nick set free among Miss Avery's precious family mementoes, Reynolds faced the last speaker, Mr Blewett. Blewett was a former gardener, now retired to St Breddaford to be near his daughter—and to make Reynolds' life a misery. Having once helped the ex-inspector in an investigation, he presumed upon their relationship to take over Reynolds' garden, and hardly a day passed when he didn't offer advice or criticism of a horticultural nature.

Bracing himself, to his surprise Reynolds heard the old man tell him to, 'Give it to 'em, maister, whosomever they be. Why should us be blowed out of our own houses like in those terrorist parts? You find 'em fer us, and good luck to 'ee.' This exhortation was only spoilt by his last comment, 'And while you'm at it, I'll just take a spray to them roses of yours, full of black spot when I last looked.'

After this encounter they returned to Mazie's house, to be fussed over and petted, a ritual Derrymore endured more stoically than Reynolds, who sometimes felt her mothering was more like smothering. More to stem the tide of hospitality, he asked her suddenly if she knew anything about the church he'd visited the previous day.

He didn't expect an answer. Mazie was a Methodist of long standing; it wasn't likely she'd be interested in churches anywhere, certainly not one several miles away. He was wrong. 'St Theodosius,' she sniffed, he guessed deliberately mispronouncing it so that it sounded like a sneeze. 'That's the most heathen name I've ever heard of. Whatever made anyone dedicate a Christian church to him, I ask you, when there're plenty of native Cornish saints? St Bredda's good enough for us, it should be good enough for them.'

She sniffed again. 'And not once but several times over,' she added, referring presumably to the rebuilding of the church. 'As for why that was, well, I thought everybody knew. It was on the news for ages.'

Giving him a look that, like the vicar's,

suggested his ignorance was surprising in a man of his age and standing, she launched into an explanation more or less similar to the vicar's—with one exception. She told them the name of the family that had financed the rebuilding of the second church after the nineteenth-century fire.

'Beggared themselves into the bargain,' she added sorrowfully, as if a lack of fiscal restraint was typical of all Anglican gentry. 'They held on for a while, mind you, but in the end it finished them. They'd once been wealthy landlords, but that was centuries ago. A great Cornish family, the Pendervers, but there you are, pride goeth before a fall.'

'What did you say the name was?' Reynolds was startled enough to leap to his feet, while Derrymore shouted, 'Run that past us again.'

Later, when they'd gathered every scrap that Mazie knew, the two men retired to the parlour to confer. This was Mazie's sanctum, seldom used except on Sundays and Christmas—Mazie kept to the old customs. In contrast to the warmth and cosy feel of the rest of the cottage, this room was dark and sombre, with stiff upright chairs covered in ruby velvet and even a horsehair sofa inherited from her mother. A locked bookcase housed religious tracts dating from the last century, along with her best cups and saucers, brought out only on solemn occasions. It was a room to intimidate the faint-hearted, but Reynolds and Derrymore paid it scant respect as they spread their papers out across the floor and concentrated on what to do next.

Both agreed it couldn't be coincidence that Paul Newland, born a Penderver, might have been interested in a church that had been his family place of worship for hundreds of years. But which of the two churches on the same site? And what had happened to the family since?

According to Mazie, the Penderver lands, the villages and farms they'd once owned, were all gone long ago, sold off to pay their debts. Their main residence, now torn down, lay somewhere in the west, she didn't know where, although another, at the opposite end of the county, nowhere near the church, now housed a theme park with a miniature railway running through the once-famous deer park.

A quick search of the telephone book revealed no entry under that name. Perhaps the Pendervers' ruin had been so complete they'd all died out or left the county under a cloud; perhaps Paul Newland was really the last of the line.

'It begins to fit together.' Reynolds felt the usual rush of adrenaline that accompanies a significant breakthrough. 'Suppose for a moment this is what happens. He comes to Cornwall to track down the family seat, perhaps in the beginning not even knowing where to start. He can't find any trace of them but learns there's a church they're connected with. Hunting for information about the church, as luck would have it, or bad luck, he latches on to Em Tregurion. She mentions Hillard's book—and from that stems all the rest.'

'But we've been over that before,' Derrymore protested. 'You said yourself if it had just been the book, he'd plenty of time to find it after her death—if he killed her. And if he relies on Hillard, he'll only learn that his family constructed a new church in the early nineteenth century, nothing about an earlier one.'

'You may be right. Or we may both be wrong, and he was looking for something completely different, say in the former deer park. We don't know for certain.

247

However, imagine this. Suppose while they're discussing Cornish history, she mentions Hillard; he becomes interested, and in turn mentions the Penderver family, without revealing his connection. She knows the true story and tells him—remember, she made a point of stressing that he was excited, and she didn't know why. In fact, he doesn't need Hillard; she's told him all he needs to know.'

It was an interesting idea. Pressing on, 'We do know Hillard's book's a clue,' he said. 'Even Mabley remembers her speaking about it. And Em suggested Newland meant to drive down to west Cornwall, and that's where St Theodosius' is. So until we get a better lead, for the moment we'll concentrate on what Hillard's book's about, that is, Cornish churches. If so, logic tells me it's the family church Newland's interested in, the one near the original main house, no matter how many other houses or estates they owned.'

He glanced at Derrymore, waiting for the sergeant to interrupt. 'Finally, since the present church apparently ruined his family, I'll lay odds that it's the original one

248

he's after. That's the church in full flower, as it were, when his family were at their peak. Stands to reason he'd be looking for something connected with fame and power rather than poverty and disgrace.'

'But even if it is,' not to be out-argued, Derrymore rose to the occasion with the main objection, 'I still don't see what he expects to find.'

'Treasure.' Unnoticed, Nick had squeezed his way behind the sofa and had been shamelessly listening to every word. Now he popped up like a rabbit. 'I bet it's buried gold. And if we dig ...'

'Get off with you.' Reynolds gave him a good-natured cuff. 'Time for bed. Presuming Mrs Derrymore'll have you, that is.'

For again an idea had come into his head, and when Nick, happily it seemed, had been packed off to spend the night in Derrymore's own bed, with yet another officer to keep watch, he told the sergeant what it was.

'If we're on the right track at last,' he said, 'one thing we can be sure of is that by now Paul Newland must be too. Even if he only learnt from Em where St Theodosius' is located, he's only to talk with anyone nearby to get the full story of the actual site of the original church under the present hall. And that's something to check out also,' he added, 'whether there've been any specific sightings of him in the neighbourhood. Even so, he can't have made many open enquiries or the vicar would certainly have mentioned them. Likewise, he can't actually have started a search, especially with the church jammed with people preparing for the fête.'

He looked at Derrymore meaningfully. 'Which suggests that we're still in with a chance of finding what he's looking for before he finds it himself. But only if we move first.'

He left the thought dangling. 'Before someone else upstages us.'

Derrymore caught on fast. In fact his first remark was unlike him in that it was more subtle than usual. 'Even if the church fête ties the place up for the next day or two,' he offered, 'it might not stop him. And I agree, it'd be a pity to let the opportunity slip.'

His next comment was more typically honest. 'So if there're things to be found, I'd rather we did the finding now before

250

Inspector Upshaw shows up to take the credit.'

Tacit understanding. Tacit approval. No need to dwell on what Reynolds was suggesting, especially as it was slanted to the shady side of the law. Not that there was anything specifically illegal about a visit to a country church; there was no rule that said he couldn't go into a churchyard late at night. But still ... When Reynolds added, 'I'd better go alone,' reluctantly Derrymore agreed. In the past it would have been the sort of covert operation the sergeant enjoyed and was good at; now, as official head of an official investigation, he had to be more circumspect.

'Right.' Reynolds stood up, and after phoning a garage he'd used before to hire a car, an unobtrusive one, announced he'd be leaving. But first he'd borrow a dark jacket and a torch.

'You be careful.' Mazie had the last word. 'I know when you and Derry are up to no good, don't tell me different.'

She's right about that, Reynolds thought after the car had been brought round and he'd squeezed his lanky frame inside. If I blow this, I blow Derry's reputation too. It was a dampening thought. On the other hand, he couldn't see that anything could go wrong. He'd no intention of being caught, and if Derry was good at covert manoeuvres, so was he. Although what the hell I'm hunting for I really don't know, he thought, as once more he headed off down the A30. Some family tombstone, perhaps, some Penderver relic that Newland thinks he can hack off and carry away.

He'd heard of vandals removing old Cornish crosses from the hedgerows; a few years ago there'd been a spate of such unlikely thefts, although he had no idea how much ancient monuments were worth. And then there were other ecclesiastical robberies: silver, rare books, even the contents of alms boxes, and recently, a precious casket had been stolen; most churches these days kept their doors locked. Remembering the austere Victorian interior of the new St Theodosius', he acknowledged it seemed an unlikely depository for Nick's treasure trove.

But perhaps Newland was in search of something more lucrative in today's market—drugs, for example, as Derry had suggested. The drug traffic in Cornwall was extensive; substantial hauls, each bigger than the last, were common. Yet choosing an inland church for a rendezvous or a drop didn't add up, with the longest coastline in England, and hundreds of secluded coves to chose from instead.

By now night had come. The long August twilight had given place to a sudden velvet black, lit only by stars far overhead and the promise of a later moon. Leaving the main road, Reynolds negotiated the winding lanes fast; there was little traffic, although occasionally he was surprised by an approaching car, speeding round the bends. Only once did he brake hard, when some furry animal scurried to the safety of a bank, and he felt rather than heard the bump of something heavy under the back seat. The torch; hope it hasn't smashed, he thought.

The lane narrowed again, the hedges here so high that the trees which crowned them made an arch. When he came to the village sign, he slowed to glance at his watch. Almost twelve, and another two hours at least before the moon rose. He had plenty of time. Switching off headlights and engine, he cruised gently to a standstill, and sat for a while listening. There was no unusual sound, only a dog howling on some distant farm and the small country noises of ditch and field. So far so good. He had suddenly been afraid that the village ladies might still be busy with their stalls and auction, but they had fortunately finished for the night.

The sleeping village lay round the corner. The church was close to where he was parked, but far enough away that there was no reason for anyone to associate it with the car or him. Carefully opening the door, he stepped into the road, zipping up Derry's jacket before leaning over to reach for the torch. As he groped on the floor for it, his hand lighted instead on something warm and alive.

The figure came up so easily he knew at once who it was. Holding him by his shirt front, he breathed furiously into the boy's ear, cursing him and at the same time threatening him not to make a sound. What to do now, he was thinking, little bugger. Take him back. I suppose, and miss the opportunity; I could throttle him. Struggling with the moral dilemma, he was about to thrust him inside and drive back the way he'd come when Nick recovered enough to offer a compromise.

'I know why you'm here.' The boy's voice came out in strangled gasps, but he hadn't lost his confidence. 'Looking for what I said. Buried treasure. But illegal, like. And suppose you can't get in?'

He gave an extra twist that freed his head, and said with a return of his old cockiness, 'I climbed in fer you at that other place. I could here. I'm not afraid.'

'The devil you aren't,' Reynolds hissed. He loosened the boy and stood staring down. What would Social Services say if they were to learn what I've led you into? he thought. And what will Mazie think when she finds you're gone?

'How the hell did you get out?' he asked, and in voicing the question aloud knew he was lost. He let Nick prattle on about how he'd opened the window and found a tree outside just like at home; it was so dark no one had seen him and the officer's back had been turned. 'Didn't mean to be left behind again,' was the final blow, 'and,' the child looked up, his face a pale blur, his voice at its most smug, 'you don't want to miss this chance.'

When Reynolds led the way down the church path, he didn't have to warn Nick to be quiet. Or to stay close. The boy became his silent shadow, moving more carefully than most grown men could.

255

When they passed the church and headed for the hall, he ducked when Reynolds ducked, stopped when he stopped, listened when he listened, a true professional.

As they approached the hall, Reynolds realised it was bigger than he'd thought, its steep roof giving the building an almost alpine look. A stretch of grass with a gravel path cut through it separated it from the modern church, a row of cedar trees edging the path like a line of sentinels. Even in the darkness the cedars seemed to cast a shadow turning the approach into the black opening to a tunnel. Walking on the grass to deaden their footsteps they came up to the main door.

This was one of two. The smaller, at the side, had a Yale lock and was clearly the one most in use. The main door, much bigger, studded with iron nails, a modern copy of an ancient one, had a big iron handle but was firmly bolted on the inside. Still treading carefully they circled the building while Reynolds studied it from all sides, but there were no other ways in; even the windows were high up and blocked with stout iron grilles. The ladies had chosen a safe place for their auction items.

'Let's call it a day,' Reynolds said, trying to hide his disappointment. Before he could add something fatuous about coming back another time, a tug on his arm stopped him.

Nick was kneeling, pointing to a narrow oblong opening that his sharp eyes had spotted cut in the base of the wall, at the opposite end of the building from the main door. Almost concealed by some low-growing bushes, it resembled a letter box, except much larger. Probably an old-fashioned coal chute, Reynolds thought, no longer in use. Before he could explain what it was, Nick had reached for the torch, stuck his head inside the opening and switched the light on. Reynolds had to grab his legs to stop him disappearing.

'Turn it off,' he hissed again. 'You'll have the village on us.' He felt tension mounting. 'We'll be in a real mess if you fall in.'

'Hold on a tick.'

Twisting expertly, Nick now hung upside down, pointing the torch below and round him, turning it off and on briefly. 'The ceiling's awfully high.' His voice came in a hollow whisper. 'And the floor's a long way down. Like in a pit. There are even steps leading up to the main door opposite.'

They've used the old foundations, Reynolds thought, as Nick continued, 'Along one wall, there're several tables, covered with white cloths, and ...'

There was a clatter as he dropped the torch. Reynolds heard his gasp of dismay. Then, 'It's all right,' the boy said, 'I'll go after it and unlock the main door.'

Resisting Reynolds' attempts to reel him back he gave a determined kick and vanished. There was a sliding sound, a bump, and then his voice came echoing softly, 'Not so bad, only ten feet or so. I'll meet you at the door.'

Scrambling back to his feet Reynolds gazed around him. Damn the boy, I'll have his hide, he thought. Probably planned it from the start. But without him I'd never have got this far. Running round to the door and again pausing to listen—they'd made too much noise as well as using the torch—he made the snap decision to take the opportunity now that it was offered. If luck were with them, and he thought it was, the churchyard was still dark and quiet, nothing moved, they might be in and out and away, no one the wiser.

The silence was complete, yet, and he

didn't know why, he had a feeling, an instinct, that made him uncomfortable, as if someone was watching. He listened again. Then, putting his fear down to nerves—after all he wasn't used to company on expeditions like this, certainly not interfering little boys—he let out his breath. Thank God the kid had immediately turned off the torch. Once the door was opened, he'd take one fast look round, then get them both out of there double quick. And if Nick knew what was good for him he'd turn over a new leaf even quicker, else he'd find himself out on his ear and in a reform school before he knew it.

It was then another worry struck him. Suppose the kid couldn't undo the bolts and remained stuck inside? The enormity overwhelmed him. How to get him out, what to do, try to haul up the way he'd got in, he supposed. How could a kid like this, one he didn't really know, a regular gad fly at that, make him so uptight that he felt the sweat break out? Even as these conflicting emotions framed themselves, he sensed the movement behind him, the first time ever he'd let himself be taken by surprise. Half turning to meet the blow, he took part of it on his arm, felt the rest fall dimly, as if it hit someone else. And then he didn't think at all.

Chapter 14

Inside the hall, Nick had already reached the other side and was about to turn on the torch again so he could see his way up some steps leading to the main door. He heard the dull thud of a blow, and then another, heavier, sound, like something falling. He stood poised, scarcely daring to breathe. There was a clink of metal against stone, as if a spade or perhaps a pickaxe had been dropped on the doorstep, followed by the sharper scraping noises of some heavy object being dragged across gravel. Then the dragging stopped, and a series of smothered curses erupted. There was a low whistle, running footsteps on the path, an interlude of short and furious whispers, after which the dragging sound began again. He couldn't tell who was speaking, but he knew the voices were masculine, two men at least; they must have been snooping round the hall and caught Mr Reynolds out.

It couldn't be the vicar or any of the villagers; for one thing, surely they wouldn't swear like that, even at a burglar, nor hit or hurt him or try to remove him unseen. From the way they were acting, he became convinced that they were there illegally, like Mr R and himself. And they were dangerous; perhaps one of them was the man who'd attacked his grandmother and come after him.

For what seemed a lifetime he remained pressed against the steps in the dark, listening to that awful dragging sound that seemed to go on for ages. Part of him hoped it was all a mistake and in a moment he'd hear Mr R telling him for God's sake buck up and get the bloody door opened. They didn't have all night, for God's sake—by now he knew that Reynolds' habit of swearing in emergencies was like a valve letting off steam. But part of him knew it wouldn't end like that, and if anyone returned it wouldn't be Mr Reynolds, and he would be next in line.

The realisation made him freeze. Fighting the impulse to rush up the steps, bang on the door and shout to them to stop, remembering what Mr Reynolds said when his gran was attacked, that he'd done the right thing by lying low and waiting, he slithered along the floor, moving slowly so no noise gave him away, and only pausing when he reached the tables that he'd spotted previously. Several of them were lined up against a wall; it took but a moment to duck under the white cloths, where he curled up in a ball, hugging his knees.

After a longer wait, he heard a car go slowly past the church, a four-wheel drive, he thought, followed by another which he recognised as the one Mr Reynolds had hired—it had a distinctive sound when the clutch went in. He began to breathe again; they can't have heard or seen me, perhaps don't even know I'm here. It's very dark and they can't have expected Mr R to be accompanied by a boy. By now he'd already calculated that as long as the door was bolted on the inside they couldn't get in at him. Mr Reynolds couldn't have fitted in that chute thing and they probably couldn't either. They wouldn't even have noticed it; it was low to the ground and although he himself had spotted it, Mr Reynolds hadn't.

After several moments' more hard thinking he realised something else, namely that
the two men must be looking for the same
thing he and Mr R were looking for. Why
else had they showed up armed with spade
and pickaxe? And what would they do
with Mr Reynolds now they'd got him?
he wondered. Take him to their hideout,
of course, where they'd tie him up to deal
with later, as they always did in James
Bond films. But before that happened,
Nick himself and Derrymore would burst
in to the rescue; he'd save Mr R like
he'd been saved himself, and Mr Reynolds
would be grateful and tell him ...

The image, comforting as it was, stopped
at that point. Because where were the men
while all this was happening? Returned
to this very hall, of course, it stood to
reason. They might have planned to start
looking in the graveyard, but—and the
thought made his blood run cold—seeing
Mr Reynolds by the door could give them
another idea where to dig. They could
easily hack down the door if they wanted
to. That brought him out of cover, starting
for the chute instead. But first he set his
jaw determinedly; he'd take a quick look
round.

The white tablecloths made a ghostly backdrop as he scrambled out, the tables themselves loaded with all sorts of strange objects. He'd no idea what they were and they seemed to glint menacingly at him, as did the walls, which he now saw were also white, covered with the same kind of paint they used at the farm. He checked the torch; it was still off, but there was light coming from somewhere and he felt panic again until he realised it was just the rising moon shining through the windows. Mr R had said there'd be moonlight later; it would make hiding difficult, but for them as well as him.

He also noticed again how deep down the floor was; that probably explained why a chute only a few inches above the ground on the outside dropped ten feet or more inside, and why the door had to have steps to get up to it. Moving even more stealthily, as if the light now streaking through the windows was a searchlight homing in on him, he made himself tour the whole building, running his hands over the walls as high as he could reach. Under the whitewash they were strangely rough; in some places there were projections as if stones had been put in at random, and once, where a shaft of moonlight caught it, he found a flattish one like he'd seen in graveyards, with funny stick-like writing which of course he couldn't read. When he reached the chute, there was just enough light to see that the wall below it was so uneven he could easily lever himself up. Stuffing the torch into his pocket, he began to climb.

He'd scarcely started when he realised that the unevenness of the wall was in fact caused by what he identified as a winding staircase, most of which had disappeared. If he followed along its natural curve it took him sideways, away from the chute—which even he could tell had been hacked clumsily out of the wall at a much later date—ending at a ledge. This looked as if it might have been the entrance to another room, or even the top of a window; he had the impression of a rounded arch and a series of fluted pillars growing out of the wall beneath him, but too low down to resemble other church windows he'd seen.

All this was very mysterious, and he could make nothing of it, so taking one more quick glance round in case he'd missed anything else important, he scrambled down the way he'd come and started up again. When he drew level with the chute he hesitated for a moment before screwing up his courage and pushing open the flap to peer outside.

This side of the building was still in darkness, and he could see nothing. But remembering how carefully Mr Reynolds had waited and listened, he made himself do the same. After a while, even more nervously, he levered himself head first through the gap, expecting any moment to feel a metal spade crash upon his neck, like one of those Frenchie guillotines. And when he was through and on his feet, he made himself steal carefully along the building until he could again see the gravel path leading between the rows of cedar trees.

It was deserted but there were marks along it, and when he came to the main door something dark and wet stained the threshold. His resolve broke. Not caring if he was heard or seen, he fled.

Crashing through the trees, he headed for the gate, only coming to a standstill when he reached the road. It too was empty, and when he ran to where they'd left the car, it was gone, the final proof that

266

he wasn't imagining things. But at least he was alive—if only, like in the stories his gran used to read him when he was small, he could live to tell the tale.

What would any hero do, Mr R say, if he were in this fix? The thought steadied him. He'd look for a phone, that's what, but not here. Everyone in this village could be in league with the enemy. Make for the main road, find an all-night garage where there're plenty of people about, dial 999. And, as he started along the way they'd come, keep off the road. If anyone sees you, and in this light they will, they'll stop and ask stupid questions. What's a boy like you doing out of bed so late, does anyone know where you are, things like that. Besides, if the men come back, the one who was hunting you will know who you are.

On that thought, he was over the hedge into the field, scrambling through the nettles to where he couldn't be seen and where he'd have plenty of time to hide if a car approached. As well as being high, the hedges were also wide, topped with bushes and trees. He had only to follow them on the inside to return eventually to the main road.

Easier said than done; several fields later he was so exhausted his legs felt like lead. He couldn't find any gates between the fields, so to make progress he had to scramble over the dividing hedge each time. Even walking was difficult, the ground closest to the road rutted and full of rabbit holes. Where there was grass the going was easier, but some fields had been tilled, and great clods of earth stuck to his shoes.

In one he came across a flock of sheep which scattered as he approached; in another he slid down almost on the back of a grazing bullock that snorted in alarm, almost as frightened as he was himself. Only one good thing happened, his caution rewarded when the sound of a car gave him enough warning to lie down and bury his face in the mud.

The car came fast, and when it had passed he jumped up to look at it. A four-wheel drive, a Land Rover, possibly like the first car that had gone by the hall when he was inside. It could be the same one. He plodded on.

He'd no idea how long it was since he'd started his trek, or how long since he'd first got out of the hall. The brilliant moon had faded, the night air was cold, and just before dawn a breeze sprang up. Sometimes now when he came to a crossroads, he had to climb out of the field to the road just to find which way to go, but all the lanes looked alike and the signposts were no help. It was probably sheer luck that while he was balanced on the top of a hedge he saw in the distance the lights from what must be a major road, and heard the occasional hum of a car.

Twenty minutes later he had reached the road. Here he moved more cautiously than ever, knowing now at least which direction he should take, to the east towards the rising sun still hidden beneath a bank of cloud, although the sky above it was already mottled red. His patience was again rewarded when he came upon the very thing he was looking for, a garage with its lights all on, and a couple of cars drawn up at the pumps. When he was sure there were plenty of people about, he ran the last few yards and burst through the doors. 'I need to make a telephone call,' he shouted to the startled customers inside and then, with one last attempt at cockiness, 'It's a question of life and death.'

The shrill sound of the telephone roused Derrymore from uneasy sleep. He rolled off the sofa where he'd spent an uncomfortable night and made his way in the semi-dark towards the phone. What he heard sent him crashing awake.

'How could he have got out?' His first question was echoed by the policeman who'd been on watch, and then, even more puzzled, by Mazie who, roused by the noise, came out of her room. In her dressing gown, her hair tied in pigtails, she looked like a small girl whose face had somehow aged. Adding, 'But he's still asleep. I checked before I went to bed,' her voice trailed away as Derry grimly pulled back the coverlet to reveal the heap of pillows and blankets carefully arranged. The oldest trick in the world, and they'd all fallen for it. But if Nick Pascoe had been out all night, after their united attempts to keep him out of harm, what of his story that Mr Reynolds was in danger too, had been hit on the head and captured by some enemy?

It sounded preposterous, a boy's invention, made up to hide what he'd been up to. Derrymore's anger mounted. Like Reynolds before him, he swore he'd give

Nick Pascoe what for—until all his attempts to rouse Old Forge Cottage got no response and he realised there was no sign of the hired car in the drive.

When he reached the garage the proprietor was waiting, with a jerk of his head and a wink that said, 'Over to you.' The boy was sitting on a bench, his head leaning on his arms, but when he roused himself at the sergeant's approach Derrymore was shocked. The child looked exhausted, his clothes ripped, his eyes dark-circled in a face streaked with blood and dirt. Great weals marked arms and legs that suddenly looked more stick-like than ever. The anger evaporated. Kneeling beside the boy, Derrymore listened anxiously while the owner of the garage and the curious customers tried to eavesdrop.

What Nick told him still sounded preposterous, but could be checked, and there was no doubt that the boy's anxiety was real. He clung to Derrymore's jacket, begging him to find where Reynolds was, and had to be prised away. Only after he was safely installed in a police car to be handed back to Mazie did Derrymore turn his attention to the church.

He knew he was in difficulties, of his

own making. True, he and Reynolds had already discussed their strategy if anything went wrong, meaning that Reynolds would take full responsibility for the outcome, without involving the sergeant in any way. At the time Derrymore had argued against this, but Reynolds had insisted; eventually Derrymore had assented, although reluctantly. He knew it was why Reynolds planned to go alone, and why he'd hired a car rather than use an official one.

In his own case, even the usual excuse, that he was acting in the line of duty, would scarcely cover him if there was a cock-up. At the time the worst he'd imagined was that Reynolds might be caught red-handed, as it were, by the vicar or one of his cohorts. A calamity of this magnitude hadn't occurred to him, although looking back at the way things had been managed, he wondered if perhaps Reynolds had taken it into consideration. As for Nick, the child was so upset he'd become almost incoherent about what he'd done; he repeated so often that it was all his fault that Derrymore felt sorry for him.

Now, as the implications became clear, the sergeant began to worry. It wasn't only that Reynolds would be revealed to be meddling in official police matters just as Inspector Upshaw came on board; it wasn't even that he'd had Derrymore's approval, although that too would have to come out eventually. The ex-inspector was apparently in real personal trouble, and, if Nick Pascoe hadn't exaggerated the situation, might be seriously hurt. It was with a sinking heart that Derrymore drew up in front of the church of St Theodosius and got out.

With his almost un-childlike attention to detail, Nick had described exactly where Reynolds' car had been parked, and it certainly wasn't there. In fact there were no cars at all in the road alongside the church, and at this early hour the village was deserted. A bad omen. Fearing the worst, Derrymore turned away from the church and decided to inform the vicar first, keeping strictly to the letter of the law—although, he admitted ruefully to himself, this was rather like locking the stable door after the horses had bolted.

The Vicarage was an imposing Victorian building, the same vintage as the restorations in the new church, much too big for the vicar in these days of small families and

273

no household help. The exterior hadn't been painted in a decade and the interior wasn't much better, and when Derrymore was ushered in by a small girl to see her father, the sergeant found him eating breakfast in his undershirt while his wife tried simultaneously to keep a baby quiet and do the household bills.

Seeing him, the vicar started up. 'Not the hall,' he shouted, 'not the bloody auction stuff.' And without waiting to put on a shirt, he bolted out of the door. Derrymore caught up with him as he reached the churchyard and, running now beside him, panted out that as far as he knew the auction things weren't the problem; it was the possibility of someone having been attacked in the churchyard the night before.

Hearing that, the vicar slowed down. 'Attacked?' he echoed, then, with an audible sigh of relief, 'Thank God. The ladies committee'd never forgive me if their precious items were damaged!' Proof, Derrymore thought, how small-minded some people are. He'd often noticed it in other cases he'd worked on, but never in a man of the Church, who might have been expected to have a broader view.

The vicar's relief was short-lived. They had come to the gravel path between the trees now and Derrymore was just in time to pull him off it before he obliterated the marks that Nick had described. They were still there, as were the red stains where the body must have rested; it looked as if Nick had not exaggerated after all. But it was the smashed main door that really brought home the extent of the damage.

'My God!' the vicar exclaimed, awe-struck. 'What's been going on? That looks like blood. Who did you say the victim was?' Derrymore could say nothing; he felt he'd been hit on the head himself.

Inside the hall the chaos was indescribable. The same pickaxe used to break through the door had hacked up sections of the flooring and pried some of the old stone monuments out of the walls. In the confusion the tables with the auction contents had been overturned and items were strewn about; some of the more delicate pieces had been ground like dust into the floor.

On seeing this destruction the vicar stood still, looking about him in bewilderment as if he couldn't take it in. 'This isn't an ordinary break-in, is it?' he said at last. 'This isn't a robbery. They've broken more than they've taken, if they've taken anything at all. Hooligans.' He was almost in tears. 'There goes our hope of any church repairs this year.'

Later, when he'd calmed down, and the church hall and yard had been sealed off for experts to search for clues, he went over the events of the day before. Yes, he remembered Reynolds, had shown him the new church—which hadn't been touched in any way, thank God for that. And yes, he had told him about the old church, whose foundations were used in the construction of the parish hall. But when asked if anyone else had been enquiring about it recently, he shook his head.

His wife had come up by now with a jersey, which he pulled on inside out so when he moved, the label at the back stood out like a ruff. She too was in a state of shock but unlike her husband remained articulate. Both doors were always kept locked, she said, the main one only opened for formal functions. Normally they used the small door; here she produced its key. As for the elaborate door itself, it had been purchased last year, for looks as well as security—but then they hadn't expected anyone to take a pickaxe to it.

She stressed that she'd heard nothing about strangers making enquiries; in fact, not many people even visited the church these days. She also confirmed that by the time Nick and Reynolds had reached the village, she and her husband were in bed. 'Early to bed, early to rise,' the vicar interposed with a nervous laugh. 'I mean, we sleep at the back of the vicarage, you know, the front is virtually uninhabitable. So we're not likely to hear much anyway, and I sleep very soundly when I do get off.'

Meanwhile officers had spread though the village and were taking statements. Unfortunately, like the vicar, most people went to bed early, and no unusual car activity had been spotted last night. Passing cars were so common no one paid any attention, the reason being that although the approach lanes were narrow, motorists often used them as a short cut to another major road, at times turning the village into a main thoroughfare. But if any strangers had been asking questions, they would have been noticed.

The only scrap of evidence was negative,

in that nobody in the village owned a four-wheel drive. If the Land Rover Nick had spotted from the field was indeed the same as the one he'd heard while inside the hall, it didn't come from nearby.

Derrymore was beginning to be seriously alarmed. Events may have suggested the ex-inspector must have been on the right track, but the sergeant still had no clues as to the attackers' identity, or even what they were looking for. He was at a loss where to start the search for the ex-inspector or his car, and the morning had gone by when Inspector Upshaw arrived to compound his difficulties.

Upshaw appeared at the church while Derrymore was still overseeing the search inside, and stood in the doorway, watching for a while before he made his presence known. One look at him and Derrymore's heart sank.

Through the network Derry had heard Upshaw was bad-tempered, and he looked it. Of medium build, almost as wide as Derrymore but not as tall, his small dark eyes behind gold-rimmed glasses already expressed disapproval. His very stance said that having come to deal with a simple murder case, almost wrapped up, he wasn't expecting all these new developments; this church diversion was as absurd as it was unnecessary.

He was also what Derry called 'one of the opposition', meaning his allegiance was to his boss, who hated Reynolds. He'd enjoy the chance to make the ex-inspector look foolish, and although he'd never met Derrymore and had nothing against him personally, being Reynolds' friend didn't add to his liking.

Nor was he stupid. When he'd calmed down he'd take the situation seriously, but just for the moment he couldn't resist a little fun at Reynolds' expense, using Derrymore as the butt of his humour. Unlike the vicar, who hadn't yet grasped all the complications, he went straight for the jugular.

'Are you telling me, Sergeant,' he asked sarcastically, his square jaw sticking out, 'that our ex-Inspector Reynolds has come all over religious, so much so he's taken to breaking and entering churches in the dead of night, along with some kid?'

Not waiting for Derrymore's mumbled reply, 'And what was he after exactly? Why are you so sure he's been hit on the head and carried off, kidnapped I think was the word used? I hear the boy suffered some minor injuries in his so-called escape—have you tested the bloodstains to see if they match? And finally, how do we know that the boy, aided and abetted by our valued ex-inspector, didn't hack down the door and cause the damage himself?'

The questions kept on coming and Derrymore had no answers. He stood stiffly at attention, feeling increasingly stupid, while Upshaw recovered from his bad-temper. The last questions, however, were more pointed; it was almost as if Derrymore's very reticence encouraged Upshaw.

'Was Reynolds there at your contrivance?' Upshaw asked, his eyes glinting behind the gold rims. 'And if so, as a private citizen, what right did he have to help you?'

It was the sort of distinction Derry had hoped would be glossed over. But Upshaw knew when he was on to a good thing; he didn't mean to give up easily.

'Was it part of the ongoing murder investigations?' he continued, gesturing to the hall, his words rattling out like machine-gun bullets. 'What's the justification? And do you have any idea how much this operation is costing the taxpayer?'

He moved closer to Derrymore, crowding him, his small eyes avid. 'What with police protection for half the county,' he sniffed, 'to say nothing of a wild-goose chase after a missing man whose wife says he isn't missing anyhow, it's already topped the national debt. Where's the money coming from? And who's to foot the bill?'

His final comment might not have been meant seriously, but he obviously couldn't resist the opportunity to make it. 'Isn't there evidence, somehow hushed up, that Reynolds was the last to see both murder victims alive?'

The double-barrelled innuendo caught Derry on the raw. 'That's absurd,' he exploded. 'A pack of lies and you know it. You also know what an asset Inspector Reynolds is. He's ...'

He bit his lip. No use praising the ex-inspector to one so firmly entrenched in the opposite camp. But still ...

'In the meanwhile,' he said defiantly, 'you're wasting time. Sir.'

The 'sir' was a tag-on, not the way to address a senior officer, and Upshaw let him know it. Perhaps he had been hoping to trick Derry into making a wrong move. 'In my opinion,' he said coldly, 'this whole case has been handled badly from the start, and I intend to say so in my official report. Not a shred of hard evidence so far, nothing that would stand up in court, all bloody theorising, the typical Reynolds trademark. It's time things were run properly and from now on I mean to do the running. You can spend your efforts searching for your Mr Reynolds if you want, but in the future keep off my patch. And that's an order, Sergeant, or I'll have your stripes.'

With that he stalked away to start the investigations all over again, leaving Derrymore with no option but to withdraw. For if it was mainly Reynolds' theories that had set the lines of their own enquiries, the only proof of these latest events came from a small boy who shouldn't have been there in the first place and whose testimony was at best flawed. No wonder that when, after a day of fruitless search, Derrymore arrived back at St Breddaford, his air of despair darkened the cottage. He, his mother and Nick sat round the kitchen table,

Mazie's pasties left untouched, while they racked their brains to discover what had happened to Reynolds and where he was.

Chapter 15

Reynolds was asking himself the same questions. He'd regained his senses with a throbbing head, in blackness, with no way of telling where that blackness was or, for a moment, how he came to be part of it. When he tried to move, fire burned before his eyes, streaking the dark with such vivid red that he shut them again. Only after what seemed an interminable period, when he forgot what he'd started to do, did he begin to explore his surroundings. He found he was lying on his side in a foetal position, arms and legs tied with cord in front of him. Thin lines of light appeared. Then his fingers brushed against metal on all sides. Box-like. Fighting horror, he lay still.

Ever since his imprisonment years ago, during his Army service, stuffed into a dried-up well, his worst nightmare was of restricted space where he couldn't move or breathe. Like now, he'd been tied up, left in the dark, no way out, facing certain death, slow and painful. His muscles tensed in anticipation.

After a while, more recent memories flooded back to counteract the panic. He remembered a blow and an impression of floating in and out of consciousness while a car bumped wildly over rough ground, and his head jerked off his shoulders, as if it didn't belong to him. This was immediately overshadowed by a vision of a narrow flap in a stone wall. He heard Nick's voice, saying, 'I'll unlock the main door.' My God, he thought, what's happened to him, is he here too?

Taking a couple of gasping breaths to reassure himself there was an air supply, he cautiously turned his head to try and measure the size of the metal box. And for the first time gathered he wasn't alone. Outside the box, men were talking.

At first the words were unintelligible, although he was sure he'd been hearing the dominant voice for a while now, a rough, harsh voice, insisting, 'Get rid of him,' while others, he couldn't tell how many, appeared to be resisting. Careful to make no noise, he strained to listen.

It was the same man talking. He was urging the others to wait for the tide. Almost at low now, it would be six hours at least before the water would be high enough, 'so they won't be discovered'.

'No point in muffing it like last time. Finish off both.'

The harsh voice laughed but there was no answering ripple of amusement. What was the second thing they must finish off? Again Reynolds fought panic. Surely they couldn't mean Nick?

He still found thinking difficult; before he could work the situation out clearly, a sudden noise warned him to lie still. The lid of the box lifted, then banged shut again. In that split second he sensed men staring down at him, and, as the lid lowered, through half closed eyes he managed to catch a glimpse of a tall broad man, larger than the rest, wearing a knitted cap on his head. It was this man's brutal voice which now said, 'Still out like a light. Makes things easier.'

Another man began to grumble. 'Enough's enough,' he was saying, or words to that effect. Then, clearly, 'It's got to be confirmed.' So the brutal-voiced man was having problems keeping control and there was some authority above him, able to override his orders. Dissent was good, it might help.

The argument continued; Reynolds couldn't make sense of the details. Suddenly the brutal voice shouted, 'Then I won't stay either. We'll go together, if that's what you bloody want. One for all and all for one, isn't that the motto?' The sneer behind the words suggested resentment. Violence might spill over at any moment. Another good sign.

After a pause there were clumping footsteps, a distant slam that could have been a door, and, further off, the sound of a car engine starting up. If he'd understood correctly, for some reason, probably mutual distrust, the whole group had gone together, stupidly—from their viewpoint—leaving him unguarded. His heart began to thump in anticipation.

The fleeting impression of the outside meant he knew now where he was imprisoned and that, strangely, made it easier: he was locked inside the boot of his hired car. He'd also had time to recognise that the car itself was parked inside some sort of shed. And, most importantly, although he was obviously destined for a sticky end if brutal voice had his way, there'd been no actual mention of Nick. Let's hope that's a good omen too he told himself, shutting down any other possibility, and forcing himself to focus on the work in hand. He couldn't afford a second lapse of concentration like the one that had put him in this situation in the first place. But ... His anxiety didn't diminish, only made him the more determined to escape.

After waiting and listening to be sure he was alone, finally he stretched, trying to bring life back to his cramped limbs. The throbbing in his head had lessened into a dull ache and his mind was now working almost to full capacity. He'd already decided that the big man in the cap with the harsh voice fitted Nick's description of his gran's attacker. If that was correct, according to his own theories, this was the man who'd murdered Em and Trev Carthew, and tried to kill Rachael Newland, and who he believed must be the missing Paul Newland. A major breakthrough—if he was right.

He'd also learned something else. They

were planning to wait for high tide, presumably to drive him and the car over some headland into the sea. That gave him a few hours' grace. But if the disagreement continued, or if there were a change of plan, his reprieve might be short. And if there was anything he disliked more than narrow spaces it was water. Get moving, he told himself, while you have the chance.

He was already fumbling for the metal edge of the lining, trying to find a place sharp enough to saw the cord around his wrists, difficult in the dark. Refusing to give way to despair, he persevered, to feel the first strand give.

With both hands free, he strained to push open the lid of the boot, exhausting himself in the process before he remembered another feature of the car. It was a hatchback, and the back seat folded forward. Bunching himself up as small as he could he forced himself against the fastenings until he heard them shift. Within moments he was crawling though the gap, out into comparative space. Another few seconds to become adjusted to the light and he was free to struggle out of the car and find some handy tool to cut through the cord about his feet.

He caught a glimpse of himself in the side mirror as he went. He looked a fright, his face smeared with caked blood and his jacket and shirt stiff with it. He fingered his head gingerly, to find a gash over one ear where they must have hit him hard with a blunt instrument; thank God it wasn't the sharp end he thought, wincing. And scalp wounds always bleed. If the headache didn't come back he'd manage. But what of Nick?

The shed was dimly lit and larger than he'd first thought, apparently used now by farmers; a couple of ancient tractors and a plough were stored at one side, while bales of fresh straw were stacked along another. Shuffling to the plough he used its cutting edge, still fairly sound, to get rid of the remaining fetters round his ankles, then, tearing off the loose strands, he began to search for the boy, scouring the shed from end to end. Only when he'd convinced himself that Nick was not there, and his heart had steadied, did he concentrate on his next move.

During the war the shed had been what was called a Nissen hut. Made of galvanised sheeting with a high curved roof, its purpose had been to store military equipment of various sorts. This one was so large it might even have been a hangar for small planes.

Its metal walls were still intact however, no way through them, and there were only a few dirty windows, too high up to be within reach. Concrete blocks filled what once had been open gaps at the hut's rounded ends, and in one a big wooden door had been recently installed, under which more light filtered. It was locked on the outside, and he concentrated on how to get through it.

His first thought was to rev up one of the old tractors, using it to force a way through, but they were both so dilapidated, their starting mechanisms were nonexistent. That left only the car. If he could get up speed, the hut door might give way sufficiently for him to break it open, but he doubted if he could drive the car out as well, or even if it would survive a headlong crash. Sparing a thought for the unfortunate rental company as well as himself, he buckled himself in, started the engine with a handy piece of wire and backed into position. Then, putting it into gear and bracing himself for the shock, he drove full-tilt ahead.

There was a horrid grinding sound and a splintering of timber. The car spluttered to a standstill in a cloud of steam, its radiator split and its whole front end caved in. But part of the door frame had buckled and the panels of the door itself had crashed against the car roof on the driver's side. Through shards of wood he glimpsed patches of sunlight, and when he had levered himself out of the passenger door, he was able to squeeze through a gap.

For a moment he drank in the freedom of light and air. Then, gazing round, he saw he'd been right about the hut being used as a hangar. It was one of several, forming a complex, from which traces of concrete runways radiated off into the distance. Although they were covered in places with weeds and short grass, the way the whole area had been levelled made him certain he was standing in an abandoned airfield, built towards the end of the war when bomber squadrons had been stationed in Cornwall.

The only road, adapted from one of the runways, stretched inland across a series of large, flat fields, dotted with a few grazing sheep. There were no visible signs of habitation, and no cover if he had to go on foot—and a cursory glance at the car was sufficient to prove it was damaged beyond repair.

Since his captors must have driven off along this road, they must perforce, return the same way. Even if they didn't immediately spot him, once they'd discovered he'd gone they would waste no time hunting him down. The thought of being apprehended in the open, especially after learning what was in store for him, wasn't pleasant. He made up his mind to head in the opposite direction, towards the coast, which he had also spotted to the rear of the hangars, not so far away.

Quickly he set off towards the faint blue line of the sea. If he were lucky, he might come across the cliff path, with its usual sprinkling of hikers, or even pass some cottage or house before he'd gone very far. The land he now ran across was also unusually flat and open, probably why this region had been chosen as an airfield in the first place. At least it helped his progress, although giving him no cover. He saw no one, and there was only one farmhouse, crouched down in the distance. Suddenly wary, he steered clear of it, and only paused to take stock when he reached the cliffs, by his reckoning a half-mile away.

He had come to a cleft between two headlands which reared up east and west on either side. More green fields led up to them; again, whichever way he went, he would instantly be visible. The only good thing was that he was beginning to get his bearings.

All this while he'd been puzzled about the exact location of the airfield; there were still several of them left in Cornwall and they'd been scattered up and down the length and breadth of the county, used for bomber raids over Europe. Now he was pretty sure he'd been brought a long way from St Theodosius' to a really isolated region in the east of the county on the northern coast.

Perhaps it was an area his attackers knew well, or equally possibly, it was so far removed from their usual haunts that they'd put people off their trail, but whatever the case, round the western headland was the only populated spot for miles, a scattering of houses and a small beach, mainly popular with surfers. The problem was, overland, even following the coastal path, it was several miles away.

By then he was more exhausted than he liked to admit. The headache hadn't improved, had degenerated into a flat, constant thudding, and his legs threatened to buckle. He wasn't sure how much longer he could keep up the pace. But suppose he could get down to the beach and round the reefs to the end of the headland before the tide came in, he didn't imagine anyone could catch him then, even if they tried. He peered over the edge of the cliffs.

They were steep, covered with heather and bracken and furze, a contrast with the fields themselves, and giving good cover. Even where he stood now, at the low point as it were, they were still high enough that if a car were pushed over there'd not be much left at the bottom. At their foot, a line of scattered rocks spread across pale wet sand to the reefs beneath the headland where waves curled lazily. Not much surf today, thank goodness.

There were probably similar reefs leading to the beach on the other side, and both beaches would be tidal, nothing of them left when the sea was full in. No doubt this was another reason why his captors had chosen this spot, hoping any remains would be washed away as the tide went out again. And it was the tide now became his problem; could he beat it round the reefs?

Once more he considered his options. In the open he'd be easy pickings, but if he could find a way down he stood a chance. For the first time since he'd left the hut he glanced at his watch and with trepidation saw how much time he'd wasted over his escape so far. Too long. His captors might already have returned—and the sea might already be coming in. Caught between the devil and the deep blue, he thought, make your choice.

Once having committed himself, there was no turning back. Walking and running in turn along the coastal path, he hunted for some gap where he could get down to the beach, finding it eventually in a bramble thicket, a small curling path like a sheep track, probably used for fishing off the rocks.

Without stopping to think, he plunged down, sliding at times, risking twisted ankles or broken bones. Again luck was with him; he reached the beach intact, closer to the headland than he'd dared hope, and in record time. Keeping close under the overhang of cliffs, he started off without a backward glance and came to the beginning of the reefs.

Here his troubles really started. The reefs were jagged, covered with sharp shells, and full of rock pools whose slippery sides rose high in the air only to plunge into crevasses on the other side. He started to tire. Furious, he forced himself to leap from rock to rock until he was dizzy. Once this would have been child's play, but not any more. Fool, he told himself, you're over-reacting, but he knew the truth was that he was too old for this sort of escapade.

All the while he studiously avoided looking back for signs of pursuit. Equally he refrained from glancing at his watch, or calculating the distance to the end of the reef, where the sea was lapping idly. He couldn't help noticing the ominous glimpses of the Atlantic swells further out in the bay, that constant great surge that eventually built up into the sort of waves surfers loved. At best, my lad, he told himself, it's going to be nip and tuck. He tried to redouble his efforts.

He was sweating heavily now, and his movements had slowed. Each rock pinnacle became an insurmountable obstacle. He had just scaled a particularly difficult one when he heard the first shout above the swirl and suck of the water. He turned. On the cliff, close to where he'd come down, there were three figures. Arguing with each other, pointing at him. They'd been quicker than he feared. He heard another shout. It made him speed up again.

He came to the outer point of the reef right beneath the headland, but it was already under water; he had to wade now, waist deep, long strands of kelp catching at his legs, the pull of the current catching him so he had to fight for balance. He could see the stretch of beach on the other side, with its little cluster of buildings behind, tantalisingly close and yet out of reach.

He reached a place where the sea was already too deep to wade across; he'd have to swim, but he didn't know how to. His only hope of survival was to turn back and trust he could get back round the point the way he'd come—into the hands of his pursuers, who might even now be making their way towards him. Gritting his teeth, he was about to edge into the water, trusting he would find sufficient hold to keep himself afloat, when he noticed the lone figure on the beach.

It was at the far end, looking out to sea, where already on flatter sand the surf was beginning to form with the incoming tide. Beside him was the long shape of his surfboard. Making one last desperate effort, Reynolds hauled himself upright and ripped off his jacket so he could get at his shirt, waving it wildly in one hand while he clung to the rocks with the other, all the while shouting until he was hoarse—and until his pursuers themselves rounded the headland, where they paused.

Ray Mabley had been taking time off to think; too much time, perhaps, but thinking was a new experience and it made him uncomfortable. Yet several things ex-Inspector Reynolds had said had stuck and he couldn't get rid of them.

He was not exactly what he looked like, the golden boy from down under, idling his life away; nor was he the wastrel Derrymore had dubbed him. In fact he was more a typical product of a wealthy and indulgent family, the oldest son, allowed time to find himself and see the world, as his mother called it, while his father kept the sheep ranch and other lucrative options open for him on his return. If he wasn't angered at the insinuation that Em Tregurion might have been supporting him, that was because he could have had more than enough money to support himself, and his mates come to that. And if he hadn't suddenly blurted out the truth about Em and the feelings he'd been trying to suppress, he might never have admitted even to himself how much he had, well, loved her, if that was the right word; enough at any rate to startle him into his present reflective mood.

He had also taken Reynolds' warnings to heart, sufficiently at least to cover his tracks when he went out, and avoid his usual haunts, where his movements were open to observation and where, he was cynical enough to admit, even his mates might be bought. The way the fire at the caravan site had been played down, to say nothing of the car bomb, didn't fool him. But if somehow Em Tregurion had been caught up in such a vicious web of murder and mayhem, he'd like to know why, before he too became embroiled.

It wasn't just idle curiosity. He felt the strange tug of obligation, duty perhaps. That too was a new concept. When Reynolds had suggested his help would be doing Em a favour it had gradually dawned on him that he did owe her that at least. Not that he wanted to become involved, not that he welcomed it, but for once the lifestyle he'd been following had lost its allure. Gilded youth searching for the perfect wave, the ephemeral summer sun, was only an illusion; there were other more important ideas.

It was also true he didn't have much to contribute to any investigation. Except he'd known Em well, perhaps as well as anyone. And he was observant. Somewhere out of his knowledge, fresh understanding of her death might come. If so, it behoved him to buckle down and offer his services; in other words, do something constructive that wasn't merely fun, face reality at last.

If Ray were asked, like Reynolds himself he would have said he didn't believe in fate. Fate sometimes plays tricks. It wasn't just coincidence that he had come by himself to a beach he didn't really know, a long way from his usual haunts; he wasn't there just because he'd heard someone mention it and its waves, said to be great when the tide came in. He was there because he wanted to be alone, because he needed time by himself to work out his position, because he felt at last he was being offered a chance to do something worthwhile. And when he plunged into the water on his board, he wasn't only helping a man he saw clinging to the rocks; by doing so he took the first real step towards helping solve Em's murder.

Not that he understood all this at that moment. His main concern was whether he could reach the man in time. If he noticed a group of people drawing back from the reef to the further side of the headland, he'd have assumed naturally enough that their efforts had failed and it was up to him. With long, flat strokes he paddled furiously, cutting through the water like a black shark, and plucking Reynolds from the sea just before the incoming waves drowned him.

Gasping and spluttering, Reynolds clung to the board while Mabley steered it back towards the sand. Spitting out a mouthful of weed, his first words, when he'd enough breath to speak, were, 'Did you see those men?' Followed by an impressive spate of curses when Mabley admitted he hadn't. It was not until he was safe on shore, wrapped in a towel that Mabley produced, that he had the grace to thank his rescuer, and, through wheezes, explain how he came to be in such a predicament.

Before he'd finished, another thought struck him. He started up, said abruptly, 'Have you heard about the boy? Nick. Any news of him?' And when the younger man admitted he'd heard nothing, 'Then he must be OK. And we've work to do. Quick, where's your car?' And without waiting for an answer he was heading across the beach before Ray could stop him.

It said much for Mabley's faith in the ex-inspector's judgement that he followed, although Reynolds' appearance had startled him. As well as losing shirt and jacket, Reynolds had no shoes, and although the water had washed away most of the blood, the wound on the side of his head was still visible. In Mabley's opinion he'd be better off in hospital rather than careering around the countryside. Convinced that the ex-inspector wasn't likely to listen to reason, not in his present state of mind, he paused merely to push his board into the back of his van before starting it up.

The van was of ancient vintage, the sort favoured by surfers, covered with stickers and graffiti and full of swimming gear. Eyeing it despondently, Reynolds urged Mabley to drive faster than was safe, while he drummed his fingers impatiently on the dashboard. As they careened away from the coast through twisting, narrow lanes until they came to a larger road, where they could make better speed, he explained what he was hoping for. 'They've got to get along the beach and up the cliffs,' he said. 'We may be lucky, and head them off.'

It seemed unlikely. In order to reach the former airfield, they had to drive inland before returning to the coast. They weren't sure which of several side roads to follow. When finally they reached the concrete road across the former airfield, it was clear they had lost too much time, and sure enough there was no sign of the men or their vehicle when they pulled up in front of the hangars. But the proof of Reynolds' story remained, in the smashed door, the wrecked car and, when they squeezed back inside, the strands of cut rope littering the floor.

'Missed 'em, by God!' For the first time since his reprieve Reynolds visibly sagged. He'd been hoping against hope to catch the men before they vanished again, guessing rightly, it seemed from the tracks in the grass, that when they'd returned to find him gone they'd driven immediately down to the cliffs and spotted him on the reefs. After his rescue, they must have retraced their steps and driven away.

This was a real setback. Although, on more sober reflection, it was perhaps just as well they'd gone before he could confront them. Mabley was strongly built and young, but even with his help, the two of them were no match for an undisclosed number of desperate opponents, probably armed. So he was back at the beginning, the last hope of actual identification lost and all the hunt to start afresh ... The willpower that had kept him going drooped, all he could think of was a quiet place to lie down and sleep. But first he must find Nick. Turning with a weary smile, he asked Mabley to take him home to St Breddaford.

He said little on the way, except to thank Mabley again and accept an offer of a thick pullover after he began to shake with cold. When they drew up in front of Mazie's cottage, he lumbered out, steeling himself for bad news, to be bowled over by a running figure that leapt into his arms. 'You'm safe,' Nick sobbed into the pullover. 'I thought you was dead.' Unable to move, his legs somehow entwined, Reynolds looked above the child's head to where Mazie and Derrymore came hurrying down the path, their relieved smiles as wide as the world.

Chapter 16

Forty-eight hours later, Reynolds was well into recovery, his head stitched, his bruises healing and his body no longer feeling it had been hit with lead piping. His emotions well under control, he was ready for action.

Unfortunately the same couldn't be said for Nick. For a while the boy wouldn't let him out of his sight. Alternately bossy and tearful, he hung round him with almost comical devotion, driving Reynolds wild, at every turn comparing his progress with that of his gran—also making a slow but sure recovery, without, unfortunately, any recollection of the events that had laid her low.

If he hadn't recognised the guilt behind the child's aggressive obsession, he'd have packed him off with Derrymore, or banished him into the kitchen with Mazie who, in the absence of the housekeeper, had come to take care of things at Old Forge Cottage. Understanding the fix Reynolds was now in, regarding keeping the child, and even more aware that if the authorities heard of his latest adventure they'd be very loath to leave Nick here, she and Derrymore moved in and took over without fuss or argument, and since it was the only place large enough for them all to bed down comfortably, they had jointly agreed this was the best move.

As it was, Reynolds put up with Nick more patiently than he gave himself credit for, even playing card games, which he hated, and occasionally letting the boy win. It's the other side of the coin, isn't it, he told himself ruefully, the downside perhaps that returns love for love so ardently it degenerates into greedy dependence. Like his ex-wife. But this was only a little boy starved for affection; the comparison was too harsh.

Mazie also played her part with gusto, feeding Reynolds hourly and giving him the impression he was a prime Strasburg goose. Meanwhile, the agency had retrieved its battered car and was muttering glumly about insurance, letting him know, in no uncertain terms, that they weren't about to rent him any more vehicles. At the back of his mind during this enforced convalescence was the fret of wasted time. The last thing he wanted was to allow evidence to grow cold.

He'd a hunch, backed by that disagreement he'd overheard, that the earlier spate of violence would be followed by a cooling off. 'Enough's enough,' someone had said. It would make sense in several ways. On the other hand, his escape would not only infuriate them, it would pose a real threat—hence the sensible suggestion that to be on the safe side, the two households combine under one roof where Derrymore, and eventually Reynolds himself, could keep an eye on things.

Meanwhile Derrymore had wasted no efforts in combing the region of the airfield, finding nothing suspicious. The farmer who owned the adjoining fields was clearly not involved, he and his wife having been seen in the closest market town during the time in question, as vouched for by the many friends they'd met. They lived in the isolated farmhouse Reynolds had spotted—he might have been safe there even though they weren't at home; there was at least one farm worker somewhere on the premises—but had no close neighbours. As for the hangars, as far as the farmer knew, they, along with the airfield itself, were still probably owned by the government, although from time to time the hangars were rented out. He himself used the large building to store unwanted machinery and to pen sheep during the lambing season, but for the moment had no special call for it and knew no one else who had ever gone there. As the door was always kept open and the key was left hanging on a hook, he admitted it would have been easy for unauthorised people to get in.

The exact identity of the men remained a mystery, except for Reynolds' fleeting glimpse of the tall man in the cap. Moreover, other scraps of conversation he'd overheard, such as the presumed reference to the burnt-out car, and the internal squabbling among the men, began to round out the picture of the main criminal, with some notable anomalies.

For one, who were his accomplices? If the man were Newland, and came from the Midlands, how had he rounded them up so quickly? If they had come with him, where had they been staying all this time? While at Rainbow Park, Newland's solitary habits had been noted; except for his overtures of friendship to Em Tregurion, he'd apparently spoken to no one. There had never been mention of any acquaintances coming to the caravan, so where had they met to make their plans?

Next, given the remoteness of the former airfield, someone among them must be local to have some knowledge of the countryside. The voices themselves gave no clue, added rather to the confusion. With time to analyse them more carefully, Reynolds had to agree that none sounded Cornish, or, come to that, what he called 'Middle English'; certainly none had an accent resembling that of Newland's son or wife.

Finally, the more he thought about the raucous quality of the main speaker, the more unlikely it seemed that it belonged to an antiques specialist, used to dealing with the public. There was something especially harsh about it, something almost habitually coarse and brutal that reminded him, of all things, of a sergeant on parade. An ex-soldier again.

'What we need,' he said, after he and Derrymore had rehashed these observations, 'is another go at Mrs Newland. Prise out more details about her husband's background, what he did before he became a dealer, was he ever in the army. And dig out a recent picture. If she refuses, get his sister to oblige. As for what he was after in the church, presuming he hasn't found it, so put the screws on the vicar ...'

His suggestions trailed off into silence. Neither he nor Derrymore was likely to get the chance to ask these questions, certainly not along the lines of investigation they'd been following. Inspector Upshaw, although grudgingly admitting he'd been over-hasty in his first reactions, had effectively put an end to that—another reason why the two households had combined; the last thing Upshaw was allowing was money for police protection. Mrs Newland being off bounds was bad enough; at the same time, doubtlessly influenced by Upshaw, the vicar was refusing to co-operate. In fact, as Derrymore now explained, thanks to Upshaw's rash accusations, he'd turned positively apoplectic whenever Reynolds' name was mentioned. He wasn't pressing charges, mind you, being a man of peace, and in spite of the major damage to the hall, as long as it could be tidied up for the church fête and auction he'd let things slide. He didn't want a continuing police investigation; like the Clitheros he didn't court adverse publicity. 'A no-go area,' Derrymore concluded gloomily.

Far worse, by taking Derrymore off the case and putting him on 'leave without pay', pending investigation, Upshaw had effectively blocked all lines of official information on his own progress. These were serious obstacles but ones they'd expected, having had to deal with similar situations before. There were ways round them, but they made things cumbersome. They also made them more convinced than ever that time was important.

They had one unexpected offer of help. 'I'm game to try.' Ray Mabley had become a frequent visitor to Old Forge Cottage, not at first to Derrymore's taste, although the sergeant was too thankful, and too polite, to show his dislike in a house where he was also a guest.

The Australian had stopped by naturally enough to see how Reynolds was but had returned later, partly to check up on his recovery—for which he apparently still felt personally responsible—partly to avoid Upshaw's searching questions.

Hardly had he reached home again, he told them, when Upshaw had descended with a squad of eager officers, combing house and garden, and challenging every alibi. They had only grudgingly resisted taking him off for further questioning when they could make no dent in his and his mates' original statements. In short, it was so obvious that Upshaw considered Mabley the main suspect, for Em's murder at least, that the pursuit and finding of any other suspect, namely Newland, would help clear the Australian's name. His genuine interest had finally convinced the sergeant of his change of heart; unwillingly at first, then with growing enthusiasm, he accepted him as part of the team.

According to Derrymore's buddies, who, although bowing to Upshaw's dictates, weren't averse to letting the sergeant know what was going on, Upshaw had put the search for Newland on hold, if not actually shovelled it out of the way. Thanks to

Mrs Newland's and Marge's insistence, he had been convinced that Newland couldn't be involved. It was still just a question of waiting for him to turn up. All the other evidence linking his disappearance with the burnt-out car and the death of poor Trev had been given short shrift. 'I know Reynolds' visionary approach,' Upshaw was supposed to have said. 'All froth without substance. I want proof that these events are linked.'

The surveillance of Mrs Newland and her children had been partially lifted. She had returned to Rainbow Park, where the Clitheros, faced with financial disaster, were actually glad to have her back. She was, however, still being watched, under the pretext of preventing another attack—despite Upshaw's grumbling at the unnecessary cost, off the record the inspector had conceded that he'd like to know when and how Newland made contact with his family, suggesting that his public scorn of Reynolds' theories sat uneasily with his private recollections of how often in the past they'd 'brought home the bacon', his phrase.

As a consequence of all these compli-cating factors, any hope of an interview with Mrs Newland looked remote, especially since officially she was in the clear. But, 'There's nothing to stop me rolling up at Rainbow Park,' Mabley was continuing enthusiastically. 'From what you say, in the old days they'd have dropped dead rather than cater for the likes of me, but beggars can't be choosers. While I'm looking at possible caravans I may have a chance to sound out Mrs Newland. No one could take exception to that. The Clitheros don't know me, certainly Derek doesn't. And if Upshaw gets wind of it, I'll tell him his constant harassment is bad for my health and I need a change of air.'

Derrymore and Reynolds exchanged familiar glances. On the face of it this was a good idea. And no danger to anyone. On the third morning after the abortive attempt to explore the church, Reynolds, Derrymore, Nick and Mabley set out in Mabley's van.

Reynolds had brought the child with him for several reasons, all of which made sense but none of which really explained the underlying one. Basically he was afraid to leave Nick on his own, even with Mazie. Not that he thought the child would get into mischief—he had more than learnt a lesson—and not that he thought there would be any further harm, but the effect of the night in the church had been great. Even a tough kid couldn't stand repeated trauma. He also had another motive, one he hadn't discussed, but which he hoped would help the child in other ways.

They used Mabley's van because Derrymore no longer had access to an official car and Reynolds' was still being held pending tests—Upshaw's orders, they gathered, although what he hoped to achieve other than annoyance to Reynolds was not clear. The Australian drove. Reynolds was grateful; with Derrymore at the wheel, his head would spin like a whirligig.

The three men sat in the front seat. Reynolds and Derrymore wore casual clothes but they certainly didn't look like Mabley's usual mates, although come to think of it, Derrymore wasn't much older. Nick, in the back, was happily engaged in rooting among surfing gear, trying on flipper feet and snorkel masks to his heart's content. When they approached within a mile or so of Rainbow Park, to ensure there were no slip-ups, Derrymore and Reynolds disembarked with Nick, leaving Mabley to drive on alone.

315

While Derrymore and Nick explored the surrounding hedges and ditches, Reynolds sat on a bank beside a gate, watching swallows from a neighbouring barn dart and swerve across the field where a small stream dipped under a bridge. It was a typical late-August day, part sun, part cloud, still warm. The few cars that passed were jammed with visitors making the most of the last of summer. But for all that holiday exuberance there was an underlying melancholy. The trees along the hedgerows had already lost their vibrant green; soon their leaves would curl and fall, the days would shorten and grow cooler, and like the swallows, the visitors would depart. And what shall I do then, Reynolds thought, what shall I become, growing older and more selfish, with no one to care for or to care for me? This morbid reflection, so unlike him, was startling, as if the effects of the last days had changed him too, more than he wanted to admit.

'I'm on to her.' Mabley's voice broke in on him as the van drew up in a spurt of gravel. 'Ma Clithero's out, but due back any moment, so I said I'd return in a quarter of an hour. The thing is, I've said I'll rent a caravan.'

He grinned. 'Anything for the cause,' he added cheerfully, 'and don't look so worried, Derry. I'll pay. But I've also seen Mrs Newland, at least I'm sure it's her. She's sitting on the caravan steps with an officer beside her, one kid on her lap, and another, a boy, playing ball by himself. If I can't chat her up sometime,' he grinned self-deprecatingly, not expecting for a moment that he couldn't—and remembering that secret spark in Mrs Newland's eyes, perhaps he's right at that, Reynolds thought—'let me take old Nick here and see what he gets out of a game of football now.'

Reynolds opened his mouth to refuse. It's not right, he wanted to say. I don't want him involved. I don't want my kid used to trap another kid. The impact of what he'd almost said aloud forced him quiet. He exchanged a look with the sergeant, hoping Derrymore would understand how he felt.

Derrymore rose to the occasion. The way his lip curled made him look like Mazie at her sternest, suggesting that he too didn't like that reference to chatting up; it only reinforced his original dislike of the Australian. But he appreciated, too, the need to move ahead while the trail was still hot.

'I don't think Ma Clithero takes kids,' he pointed out slowly, looking for difficulties. 'And you can bet your boots she won't welcome you. Surfers aren't her usual style.'

'She can't complain with two kids there now.' Mabley was still enthusiastic. 'And if she's in such a financial fix, she may be glad to give a notch or so. I'll say he's my nephew, just visiting, he won't be staying with me, something like that. In any case, it's too good a chance to miss.'

Before Reynolds could intervene, Mabley again bent down to Nick. 'Now listen here, old mate,' the Australian explained, quickly giving instructions, 'it's nothing complicated and I'll be there beside you anyway. When I start talking to his ma, stroll up to the boy, casual like, ask if you can play, just like you would anyone at home. Ask him his name, what's he doing here, things like that. If you can slip it in, ask him about his mum and dad. Can you do that?'

Nick was all agog; football was his game

he boasted, yes, he could. With only one quick backward look at Reynolds, as if searching for approval—and finding it in Reynolds' reluctant smile—he climbed back into the van, and the pair headed for the park.

Suddenly numb with anxiety, Reynolds strode up and down, Derrymore beside him. He didn't like this newcomer taking over; he didn't want Mabley so involved. Although he owed his life to him and should be full of gratitude, like Derrymore he distrusted his charm. My God, he thought, the idea bursting like a bomb, you're bloody well jealous of him. Over some kid who'll be off as soon as this case is solved and his grandma's well enough to have him back. 'My kid.' As Derrymore would have said, it made you think.

His anxiety was short-lived. Within a half-hour or so the van was back again, two faces beaming inside. When he and Derrymore climbed in, 'Bingo,' Mabley said. He started up the van. 'Old Ma Clithero fell for it hook, line and sinker. No wonder Em called her the cow.'

He brooded for a moment, then went on more soberly to recount how Marge, having

319

first looked dubiously at the van, eventually showed him various caravans, and in her anxiety to have him rent one left him to wander round alone. She would even have accepted Nick without reservation—as Mabley had pointed out, she could scarcely argue children weren't allowed with two there before him—although with a return of her old manner she did question if he was quiet and well behaved. 'Like some damn dog,' Mabley said, and he and Nick laughed.

'We convinced her that he was only with his uncle for the day, didn't we, mate?' Mabley allowed himself another laugh. 'Told her in any case that butter wouldn't melt, he was good as gold. Then while I paid my respects to Mrs Newland, asking what she thought about the site, was it quiet, blah, blah, blah, old Nick went off to tackle her kid.

'He's not a bad footballer, our Nick,' he added, 'and he did a great job. I didn't get much out myself, you see, not with Ma C watching out of the window and the officer cramping my style, but by God he did.'

Quickly explaining how Nick and the other boy had begun to fool around with the ball, he let Nick continue. 'His name's Tim,' Nick began 'and he's almost six, two years younger'n me, so he hadn't set up a goal or anything like that and couldn't kick the ball so good. And he couldn't stop it when I whammed it through, so we went off together to find it and chatted like you said. He told me about his dad being gone and all and how they were waiting for him. He even described his dad, said he was tall and bald.'

He paused to lick his lips, before asking hesitantly, 'Could his dad be the man I saw, the man who attacked us? I mean, perhaps his being bald is why he wears a cap. But I didn't tell Tim that. Not even when he said his mum was always crying when she was alone. And when he asked her why she wouldn't say. But he knows it's because she's afraid his dad isn't coming back.

'I think,' he added, as the men made no comment, 'he's probably right. When my mum went off, that's what my dad was like. Until he found someone else and sent me to my gran. But I didn't tell Tim that either.'

'Well done you.' Derrymore was loud

321

in his praise but Reynolds said nothing. He merely let his hand rest casually along the seat and felt Nick's slip under it and hold tight.

Well, he thought, forcing himself to concentrate, again out of the mouths of babes perhaps, but another clue. And if Mrs Newland's cheerful optimism is a front, and she knows her husband may not return, that suggests she's really afraid—of his involvement in all these crimes, perhaps? Of his being a murderer? Of his murdering her and her children? There's no end of reasons for her fears. It made interviewing her again a serious priority.

In the meanwhile they were on their way to their second objective, the one that Nick had no knowledge of but which was partially on his behalf. Their destination was a solemn-looking Victorian mansion, set in solitary splendour amid overgrown formal grounds, its owner a large and quite unsolemn former professor, who had come to Cornwall to find peace and quiet while continuing his studies in linguistics, at the moment Celtic languages in particular.

Reynolds knew him well; in the course of his professional career he'd consulted

Dr Howard several times, and had always admired his scholarship as well as his scholarly detachment. If anyone knew the history of a Cornish family like the Pendervers, or could find it quickly, he was the one to ask. He was also quick to find flaws in evidence, no matter how firm that evidence seemed, and Reynolds had often had good cause to thank his kindly criticisms.

Reynolds' faith in the professor's abilities was so great he admitted he should have come to him straight off rather than trying to solve the problem alone. But that wasn't the only virtue Dr Howard had. His love for children was equally well known. In fact, his early studies of children's language were the reason for his fame. Although he and his wife were childless, they'd made up for this by adopting several, and now, in retirement, still opened their home a number of times a year to children's groups, as well as playing host to various children's charities for fund-raising activities.

Reynolds had a special task for the kindly scholar. And when he'd telephoned in advance to spell out his own requirements, he'd explained it in full. Now, while Derrymore and Mabley took Nick on a tour of the grounds, he emphasised it again. 'The kid can't read,' he said. 'He's eight, going on nine, and won't or can't admit it, although he's as sharp as a tack in everything else. So I thought if he wants to help, and if finding what he chooses to call buried treasure means looking through books, perhaps seeing how you manage will give him a taste of what reading is all about.'

'And will help solve his problems at school.' Howard's eyes twinkled. 'And you'll be killing the proverbial two birds with one stone.'

The faded blue eyes opened wide, the wrinkled face looked more gnomelike than ever. 'Leave it to me, my dear fellow. Never knew a boy yet who didn't like a good adventure yarn. And once we've got him hooked, then you can check out obvious things like impaired vision and such. He'll let you know what he can or can't see.'

He patted Reynolds' shoulder. 'And don't take it so hard,' he said with one of his shrewd looks. 'I'll take care of him. If you're nervous, leave that good-looking young chap here. I'm fond of down under; we'll enjoy a chat. But for heaven's sake, leave his extraordinary vehicle behind. Borrow mine instead. Then go on about your own detecting business with that nice constable of yours.'

Another perceptive remark, since Reynolds hadn't introduced Derrymore formally as a police officer.

After a feast of sugar doughnuts and as much Coke as he could hold, Nick made no objections to being left for a few hours, not when he understood that Mabley would remain too. He'd already been shown Dr Howard's study, with its walls lined with strange artefacts and its chairs bulging with astronomical charts, and when Howard promised him a look through his telescope, the boy was won over.

Reynolds left the pair of them bent over a large book, and conferred with Mabley, who again raised no objections, his only concern being his van, which he confessed himself was tricky to drive. Thus freed, Reynolds and Derrymore set off.

Chapter 17

Their next move took them out of Cornwall, away from Upshaw's sphere of influence. What they intended wasn't exactly illegal, although it was true Derrymore was suspended and Reynolds wasn't officially on the case. They preferred to call what they intended 'private enterprise', a personal visit, in their opinion long overdue, to Newland's bad-tempered sister, Izzie Worthington. As his only surviving relative she might hold the key to the several confusing elements in his personality; if handled properly, she might be persuaded to reveal more details of his background. She might even know where he was!

Reynolds insisted he was well enough to drive, and at first devoted all his attention to the road, while Derrymore map read. But when over the border into Devon and on the new A30 heading for Exeter, Derrymore once more voiced the leading question that as yet had no answer. 'What's at the back of it all?' he asked.

It was the same question he'd asked many times and once more Reynolds had to confess he'd been puzzling over the same thing. But it suddenly irked him that, as usual, he was expected to come up with all the answers. Why doesn't Derry think for himself sometimes? he wondered.

'I mean,' Derrymore was insisting, 'there's got to be a reason. I can understand a man, any man, Newland or not, believing he's on to a fortune, and deciding he's got to clear away any opposition. But more than that ...'

His gesture was meant to take in all the horrors that had built up over the past weeks. 'One death, then another, the attack on Nick's gran,' he went on, 'you've called them part of a pattern, but what about the rest? What about the plan to kill you, even going so far as to chase you round the rocks? It isn't natural.'

'What you're saying is there's no sensible explanation for this last round of violence.' Reynolds kept his voice even, although his irritation was growing. He gunned the engine, then, remembering the car was borrowed, slowed down. Mind what you say, he told himself. We're all under strain at the moment, Derrymore most of all. But he couldn't help wishing that sometimes Derry would show more initiative. It's all very well to act as my sounding board, he thought; sometimes I'd like more than an echo back.

'In my opinion,' he went on, 'the fire at the caravan site and the bomb in my car are irrational. Nobody in his right mind would go to such lengths.'

He rounded a curve neatly, passed a large truck trundling along, opened up on the straight. 'I'm excluding what happened to me, you notice. I don't think it was planned. It happened because I made the mistake of showing up in the wrong place at the wrong time. And I'll exclude the destruction in the church hall, equally possibly by chance. Or out of frustration. But the rest of it—I admit, it doesn't fit.'

He passed another truck, and another. 'If it helps,' he admitted somewhat sourly, 'I'm coming to the same conclusion as you. And so perhaps are others, mainly those responsible.'

He repeated the words he'd overheard when tied up in the boot of the car. 'Enough's enough' and 'It's got to be confirmed.' Meaning, he suggested now, that someone in authority had to give approval to the carrying out of his death sentence.

'But who were the speakers appealing to?' Derrymore continued doggedly in his customary role. 'Who would overrule the man with the harsh voice?'

'Presumably someone with more clout.' Reynolds didn't mean to sound testy but the words came out that way. Seeing Derry's crestfallen look, he added quickly, 'I've been wondering about the woman who's supposed to have made the phone call to Ma Clithero. If it turns out that she isn't Newland's sister, we've no idea who she is. In any case, she could be part of the gang. Or even running it.'

Derrymore considered. 'Marge Clithero, still insists it was a woman's voice,' he pointed out. 'But there are signs, remember, that whoever did the two killings had to be a man.'

'Yet otherwise there's no reason to suppose we are dealing with an all-male group.' Again Reynolds found himself sounding irritable. He drove on for a while in silence, until he thought of something else. 'And then of course there're the regular cash payments Em was making;

we've never tracked them down either. But you'll have to accept we may be heading up the wrong path altogether, much as I hate to admit Upshaw is correct. Even our visit to Mrs Elizabeth Worthington may be non-productive. Because there'll be no motive, no logic to any of it, if, as we're now suggesting, we're dealing with a madman.'

This idea was so depressing that once more they drove on in silence.

They crossed into Dorset in record time, having probably broken enough speed limits to be caught on several police cameras, and came to the town where Mrs Worthington lived. It was a seaside resort, and her house was surprisingly close to the main beach, a newish semi-detached two-storey building, part of a long line, all alike. At least it was surprising to Reynolds. The impression he'd had of her was a middle-aged shrew, who lived somewhere grey and dull, with nothing much to be cheerful about. She didn't seem to fit this lively holiday bustle with, today, a fresh wind blowing the smell of seaweed and salt across the wide promenade which bordered her garden.

Someone was at home. They had decided

not to telephone in advance in case she refused to see them, and were encouraged by the sight of an old green Cavalier parked on the narrow gravel drive that led to a back alley. When she answered the door, her appearance caused a second surprise.

She was tall, handsome rather than attractive, broad-shouldered and vigorous. Her mannish look was emphasised by her cropped dark hair and her determined mouth. Even on this August day she was dressed in a severely cut trouser suit, grey striped, a blouse and tie and sensible low-heeled shoes, in marked contrast to her demure sister-in-law's long-skirted muslins.

Fortunately, she didn't ask to see their credentials, seemed to accept them for what they were, merely said, the third surprise, 'Well, it's about time. I'd been wondering when you'd come to your senses and get some real answers.'

After which she held the door open so they could enter, then led them through a narrow hall into her sitting room, with wide windows facing the sea and a collection of modern paintings on the wall, some of them good, Reynolds thought, snatching a look, with strong, vivid shapes and colours.

He almost asked, 'Who's the artist?' but thought better of it; the style suited her. It also complemented her brother's artistic interests, if he actually was an antiques dealer, one of the questions to which she now seemed willing to give 'real answers'.

She not only seemed willing; she was actually relaxed, as if it were true she'd been expecting them. Having settled them in front of the window with its superb view, she brought them coffee, and without waiting for them to begin, plunged into her story.

She and Paul were the only children in the family, she said; their father and mother had been Londoners, but she knew of some vague Cornish background, the name was a dead giveaway, wasn't it? She was older, had stayed at home after her mother died to keep house for her father and bring Paul up, had then married, she didn't say well, but they sensed it, and, being widowed, had come to live here; she had friends nearby, it was a well-known art centre. The one drawback to a comfortable existence was her younger brother.

He'd always been a problem, she said, never settled, one of those artistic misfits who had talent but couldn't bring it to bear on anything for long. 'If he'd wanted to paint he could have gone to art school,' she told them, 'but he never had the patience. No staying power. He dabbled with all sorts of things, none successful, then after his marriage,' her expression suggested disapproval, 'he decided to go into the antique trade, although he knew nothing about it. I lent him money to start off, but he soon squandered it in a succession of bad deals; he borrowed more, even changed his name,' here she did grimace, 'as if that would help.'

This was nothing new. Derrymore tried a direct tack. 'Was he ever in the army?' he asked, to have her look blank, and say, good heavens no, though the discipline might have made a man of him. Then what about his temper, was he ever violent?

Once more Mrs Worthington looked startled. 'He's a spendthrift,' she said finally. 'He's taken advantage of me time and time again, he and his wretched little wife, but violent? He's too lily-livered for that. Why, he's an innocent. That's why his business attempts always failed; people took advantage of him and he was too soft, or too naive, to stand up to them. In my opinion,' and here her dark eyes clouded, 'he was like a baby, he never grew up, needed looking after and expected me to do it as I used to when he was a child.' For a moment her expression softened. 'And of course,' she added, almost reluctantly, 'he always had charm. Could talk the hind leg off a donkey if he had to.'

It was a familiar theme. But not one that helped. Somewhat disgruntled, Reynolds asked for a photograph. Did she have a recent one? She did.

When she brought it back, he almost gave a shout. The man he was looking at had to be the same one he'd seen, in every detail a good match. Tall, broad-shouldered and square-jawed he resembled his sister even down to the eyes and the hair—in his case what was left of it. Rachael Newland had described her husband's hair-line as receding—perhaps that was just her euphemism. Nick, more practical, had suggested that that was why he wore a cap.

'Have you any idea where Paul might have gone?' Reynolds asked. And when Izzie Worthington shook her head, 'What about his state of mind? Could there be any truth in the suggestion that he was, well, disturbed?' It was the explanation that had come to him right at the beginning of the case. Having dismissed it out of hand then, funnily enough he was now coming back to it.

As he saw her expression stiffen, 'Even suicidal?' he ventured.

Her answer was slower this time. 'I'd say he was too selfish to do a good job of suicide.' she said with a sudden return to her bitchy telephone manner. 'Or too lazy. But disturbed, yes, I'd say that. It runs in the family, you know.'

And, more viciously, 'I saw you looking at my paintings, those bold, raucous colours, I can hear you saying, those awkward shapes. I'll have you know my work isn't just therapeutic, I've been in exhibitions, I'm a professional.'

'Ye gods,' Derrymore exclaimed once they were back outside. 'That was a rum conclusion. What did you make of it, sir? Was she just oversensitive? And what about her other information? Wasn't there something odd about it? Does ...'

'Does she have something to hide too?' Reynolds finished, cutting him short. Her vehemence had been the last surprise. 'In my opinion,' he said, 'we shouldn't take all she says at face value, but we shouldn't rule her out. That comment about mental instability running in the family was a real giveaway. Otherwise,' he shook his head, 'a very mixed bag. On one hand substantiating our suspicions, on the other cancelling them. To sum up, revealing more new problems than solving old ones. The only explanation I can think of is that some of Newland's cohorts are more practical, shall we say, than apparently he is—but that doesn't make sense either.' In a sombre mood they returned more sedately to find the old scholar and Nick still engrossed in chart-making, an historical one this time.

Mabley was helping them, both men encouraging the boy to help them find names in various books—thick, leather-backed, musty, not usual children's fare. Nick was then copying the names and dates laboriously on a long sheet of paper, much blotted and stained with crossing outs. He claimed this was a time-line concerning the fortunes of one family, Reynolds guessed the Pendervers. When Nick'd showed it off, and when Reynolds had complimented him warmly, Dr Howard drew the ex-inspector to one side.

'I can see you've not had much luck,' he said, listening patiently while Reynolds poured out his frustrations. 'An overprotective sister, eh?' he remarked at the end. 'Who's turned with a vengeance against her brother. And an overdefensive wife who may have every reason to fear her husband, if anyone has, and yet remains surprisingly loyal. Seems to me their roles are reversed. I'd reflect about that.'

He fingered his tie, a hand-knitted contraption fraying at the edges and already hanging askew under his baggy wool cardigan. 'To cheer you up,' he continued, after a tactful pause, 'we've made a diagnosis.' He nodded at Nick. 'Nothing really wrong with your little chap, I'd say, that a regular life and a challenging curriculum won't cure. I've some ideas on that. As for the Penderver family,' he picked up a pencil and began to play with it, tapping the pointed end on the desk, his habit when he was excited, 'I've some interesting things to show you after supper. You must be starving.'

With his usual patience, he waited until the travellers had been fed and watered, as he called it, his wife, a small, gentle lady, producing a gargantuan meal. Then, when Nick was once more engrossed with the telescope which Mabley had set up on the lawn for him to play with, he revealed what he'd found.

Actually, for non-historians like Derrymore and Reynolds, Nick's chart was very helpful, childlike as it was and full of corrections and misshapen lettering. It traced the growth of the Penderver family from their humble origins in the fifteenth century, when they first entered the records, to their demise in the mid nineteenth, 'A long innings,' as Dr Howard put it.

The pencil went pointing across the chart as he explained with all the enthusiasm of a born scholar how by the mid fifteen hundreds the family had doubled their holdings with the purchase of Church lands. 'After the dissolution of the monasteries by that great Tudor bully, Henry VIII,' he added. 'Making them typical of the new rich all over England, steering what had been yeoman farmers in a completely different direction.'

He tapped the chart again. 'Fourteen ninety, bested in an unsuccessful law suit with a nearby priory; fifteen thirty-seven, buy up the same priory, converting it into the family home; fifteen seventy-two, one of their sons is knighted. Not bad for an eighty-year span. And with a family coat of arms to prove it.'

His grin was almost boyish as he showed them the Penderver crest, some mythical heraldic beast complete with horns and claws, a larger version of which Nick had coloured in gaudy shades of purple and red.

'But the best's to come,' Howard added. 'Not only a nobleman in the greatest court of his time, but from the West Country, home of all Elizabeth's favourites. Hawkins, Drake, Raleigh, her sea dogs, her pirate adventurers. One of your Pendervers sailed with Drake to Spain, for the infamous singeing of the Spanish king's beard at Cadiz, returning reputedly rich with Spanish gold.'

He grinned again. 'Told you all small boys thrive on treasure trove,' he said.

'So what happened to it? Could someone today have an idea where it's gone? Has it been looked for before?' Derrymore couldn't prevent his questions spilling out.

Howard smiled. 'Ah,' he said, 'those are the leading questions. Unfortunately people have been asking them ever since. To no avail.'

He glanced at his listeners narrowly and noted their downcast expressions. 'My dear fellows,' he said severely, 'like the rest of England, Cornwall is crammed with old houses where hidden loot is supposedly waiting to be discovered. I know of no specific story concerning the Pendervers, but that doesn't mean there isn't one. A few years ago someone wanted to dig up the centre of Truro looking for King Arthur's grave. Of course his request was refused, but that doesn't prove it's not there. Or that it never existed. Legends can go either way. But for what it's worth, my opinion is that if the Penderver gold ever existed, they squandered it long ago. They helped King Charles' cause in the Civil War, you know, then made the mistake of supporting Monmouth's rebellion; that's what started them on the road to ruin long before they finished themselves off by rebuilding their family church.'

'But Nick says he saw all sorts of tombstones set in the walls of the hall. Couldn't their gold be buried there?' Derrymore argued.

340

The professor looked severe, his expression suggesting that although small boys might be forgiven for believing in hidden treasure, grown men couldn't. 'I expect there are old grave markers,' he told Derrymore sternly. 'I imagine they must have come from the original church. But if you remember how many other people have seen them since they were discovered, they're not likely to lead to anything new, are they?'

As if sorry now that he'd shattered their hopes, he added quickly, 'More to the point, I've found some other things that should interest you.'

He stabbed with his pencil again. 'The Pendervers, like all up-and-coming families, made suitable marriages,' he went on, indicating dates on Nick's chart. 'As good a way as any to substantiate their position. Soon they had holdings all over Cornwall. This one,' he tapped, 'gave them estates in east Cornwall, now the theme park. This, a year or so later, brought them a manor. The abandoned airfield you mentioned stands on manor lands!'

Before they could question him, he hurried on, 'Although the actual name apparently died out here in Cornwall in

341

the last century, there may be many lateral descendants through the female line. I took the liberty of ringing up the county records office to see if they could be traced. And,' here he gave an especially dramatic swipe, 'guess what? In the last week or so, someone else has been making similar enquiries.'

In the midst of darkness, a new spark.

'In order to use the records office facilities,' Howard now told them—they were familiar to him, he explained; in his line of work he often consulted them—'you have to make an appointment and then produce proof who you are. If your suspect was there he'll have had to produce some sort of identification. They house all kinds of Church records,' he went on, 'marriages, baptisms, deaths, back to the sixteen hundreds. I'm assuming of course that the Penderver family maintained its connection with the Church, seeing as they rebuilt one. If they converted to Methodism, say, the search unfortunately may be more complicated as we'll have to look elsewhere. We'll hope for the best on that.'

The process sounded time-consuming—and slow. Reynolds' misgivings were intensified when the old man went on to say that he'd only come by the main piece of information—indiscretion, more like—because he was so well known. No one wanted him to waste his time when research was already underway in the area he was interested in. If Reynolds and Derrymore tried to make similar enquiries they should expect delays.

Before they could rally from this second disappointment, or ask for advice, he volunteered his services. 'It'd be a pleasure. In fact,' and here his eyes twinkled, 'I've taken the liberty of making an appointment already. But I'm no policeman, you know. You'll have to make what you can of my discoveries. As for any truth in a rumour of buried treasure,' again his little twinkle, 'I suspect the best chance of finding it would have been when the main Penderver residence, once the priory, was pulled down. But that was over a century ago.'

With that gentle hint to leave well alone, he bent down to Nick, who'd returned from the garden and was standing listening. Nick was carrying a bag of books. 'Dr Howard's told me they're all about famous explorers,' he started to say, 'I'm going to read them aloud to you once a day,' when from behind his back the old man produced another parcel that his wife had prepared. Inside was a violently coloured yellow and black striped jersey, the Cornish rugby colours.

'You put this on when you do your reading,' he suggested. 'Then you can feel proud of being West Country yourself, like one of its great heroes. And when you have time off, come and help me again. I'll teach you how to say shove off in real Cornish.'

As the boy pulled his new garment on, the professor whispered in Reynolds' ear, 'I gather you've been impressing him with expressions he'd be better off not knowing, so he deserves to master a few in his own native language.'

A day of disappointment and discovery then, a time to rethink. At worst Upshaw might be right and the missing Newland had nothing to do with the case. Or was already dead himself, victim of his own depression, as Reynolds once had suspected and his sister partially confirmed today. With Dr Howard's help there was a last chance to test out their theories and find some actual proof. Because if Newland's involvement in Em's murder and in the subsequent acts of violence were mere inventions, the product of Reynolds' own desire to fabricate a solution, there wasn't much difference after all between his methods and those of headquarters in the person of Inspector Upshaw. Both would be guilty of pressing blindly ahead to gratify their own preconceptions.

As for Nick Pascoe and his reading— Reynolds groaned inwardly. It meant landing him with a new duty that made unfamiliar paternal activities suddenly sound more onerous than ever. I told myself I'd bitten off more than I could chew, Reynolds warned himself, as Mabley's van trundled off towards Rainbow Park, and he, Nick and Derry went up the drive to Old Forge Cottage. It needs someone younger, a Mabley or a Derrymore, to play the role of dad. I'm too old for it.

Chapter 18

The following morning Derrymore and Reynolds planned their next move, or rather Reynolds did, and as usual Derry went along with his ideas. They decided to leave Mrs Newland completely to Mabley, perforce, as she was still off limits to them. As Derry remarked morosely, 'I hope to God he doesn't blow it. One false move and Marge'll have him out on his ear, if Mrs Newland and her official guard don't first.'

'Mabley knows what he's after,' Reynolds retorted. 'Leave him to plot ways and means. We've warned him that if Upshaw grows suspicious, he's on his own, and God help us all.'

The immediate objective was the records office; not to collect details about Penderver relations—wisely they left that to the expertise of Dr Howard. With the help of Mrs Worthington's photograph, they were after some sort of positive identification of the person who'd been interested in the same family connections. Although Upshaw's writ didn't run there yet—and given his lack of interest in Newland he had no reason to turn attention in that direction—nevertheless they felt uneasy at trying to obtain information unofficially.

'It's like going round naked,' Derrymore somewhat shamefacedly confessed. 'I miss the uniform.'

I know what he means, Reynolds

thought, in my way I miss it too. It doesn't matter if we call it uniform or training or experience, once we've had it, it never leaves us. And it's a protection, a cover for what we do. On our own, we're walking blind.

Again they had to rent a car—'I'm running out of dealers fast,' Reynolds joked—a protracted business as they didn't want to use another local agency, setting village gossipmongers agog. As they drove along, Reynolds fingered the photograph in his coat pocket. Dr Howard had warned him that the records were carefully controlled, as indeed they should be, and without police backing, he doubted if the routine could be broken. He planned to try. Once more, on his own. 'I've landed you in a mess once,' he told Derrymore sternly. 'I'll go it alone.'

It might be regarded as a noble gesture, but after the last disastrous effort, Derrymore could have retorted, Reynolds should have learnt a lesson too. Or so Reynolds told himself as he strode up to the doors of the imposing building where the records were kept. He didn't mean to mention the Penderver family, nor did he mean to say outright that he was part of an ongoing police investigation; he wasn't going to be drawn into bold-faced lies. But he didn't want to give the impression that he was just an ordinary citizen either, wandering off the streets on the off chance. He hadn't yet decided how he was to strike a balance between these two extremes; he felt that was best left to a spur-of-the-moment decision, depending on his reception. But he was confident he would come away with something. Again he fingered the photograph, his trump card.

Meanwhile Derrymore was left to his own devices, meaning, of all things, trailing round the shops with his mother! At the last moment Mazie had begged a lift, citing Nick's urgent need for new clothes, and it would have been churlish to refuse. Another result, Derrymore thought grumpily, of being out of uniform. If he'd been officially on duty Mazie wouldn't have dreamed of taking advantage; it was the rented car, the quick spin to a well-known shopping centre without all the hassle of public transport, perhaps even the summer gear he was wearing, that gave her the impression of a general holiday; she'd settled herself and Nick firmly in the back seat without any idea she wasn't wanted. Or rather, Derrymore hadn't wanted her to come; he didn't know how Reynolds felt about it and didn't ask.

Now she was having the boy try on clothes, not that Nick was enjoying it much. From his position at the shop doorway Derrymore could read rebellion in the way the child pulled his new black and yellow jersey off and on. Striped Jersey, he thought, that was Reynolds' name for him. He's led to a lot of trouble. And he'll lead to more. Mr Reynolds is getting too involved with the boy. When the gran recovers there'll come a reckoning. And for the boy as well; he's too attached. It's like love affairs in general, he thought even more gloomily, for he knew the feeling. Either one side or the other grows over-fond, the balance tips and then everything goes wrong.

Not that he minded baby-sitting; he liked kids—and here he glanced quickly at the two figures glimpsed dimly through the open doors among the trouser racks—but it had dawned on him that he was slipping too easily into that role, while the main line of investigation moved away from him. Upshaw, Howard, Reynolds himself,

349

even, for God's sake, Mabley, had all been assigned parts; he had become superfluous.

Derry wasn't particularly introspective. If asked, he would have called himself an average sort of fellow, easy-going and fair-minded. He knew he didn't take umbrage often. But now he felt, if not angry, at least uncomfortable, that he had been demoted from his position of control—which frankly, to his surprise, he had enjoyed—left instead to lounge about on a regular working day without anything to do. It wasn't right.

In justice to himself, he knew his investigation had been thorough; head-quarters couldn't fault him on that. Upshaw might not agree with his findings, might ignore them, but Derry was confident he hadn't overlooked anything. When Em's body had been discovered, he'd taken statements from all her neighbours—that was how he'd latched on to Mabley. He'd collected statements from the owners and guests at Rainbow Park; it wasn't his fault that they weren't helpful or that Derek Clithero had lied; in any event the lies had been discovered soon enough and satisfactorily explained. Equally the statements taken after Trev's murder, including ones from all the villagers in

Carnford as well as from Alfred Blunt, were all in order; his men hadn't skimped or omitted anything; headquarters itself couldn't have done a better job. So why didn't any of that evidence add up to a breakthrough like he'd hoped?

True, the burnt-out car still hadn't been identified, or at least he didn't know if any findings had come in and Upshaw probably wouldn't tell him if they had. And true, Newland hadn't showed up and in his opinion too never would. After the abortive trashing of the church hall—if that were indeed Newland's work—and after finding Reynolds gone—again, if he were the one who'd taken him—Newland and his gang had probably fled the county. Derry couldn't help thinking that if Reynolds hadn't been somewhere he shouldn't, all this would never have happened.

So it was no use moaning to himself and asking why in devil's name headquarters felt it had to come bustling in and rearranging everything. He knew where he'd gone wrong—letting, or being persuaded to let, Mr Reynolds, and in consequence the boy, go off half cocked.

No point shedding tears over spilt milk, Mazie would have said. Fair enough.

But Derry hadn't done the spilling, thus blotting his own copybook. And if Em's dog was still missing, its dead body probably tossed somewhere long ago, and if all his efforts to trace Em's unknown payments had discovered nothing new—two items Reynolds had picked out yesterday—it wasn't for lack of trying on his part. 'You can't trace cash unless you use numbered notes,' the bank manager had explained smugly, unnecessarily patronising.

Deep in thought now, Derrymore leaned back against the glass door, oblivious to the shoppers milling round him, and went over the evidence that he and Reynolds had discussed a hundred times. As he did so, the yellow and black colours caught his eye, another flurry of activity as rugby jersey came off and a new set of shirts was tried on. Everyone was using Cornish colours nowadays, he thought idly. Black and yellow shirts, black and white St Piran flags ... not to mention bonfires on Cornish beacons, marches on London to save the countryside, even schoolchildren protesting about lack of jobs. This wasn't the Cornwall he loved, with its wild moors and headlands, its lonely beaches. And in his Cornwall, murder didn't happen ... although to be fair, it was the awfulness of it that attracted attention, not the prurient interest in gruesome detail. As for all this talk about an independent Cornwall, he didn't believe in it. Cornish nationalism was all very well, but where did it lead you—

Suddenly startled, he repeated the words aloud. Because where had it led poor Em except to a tragic death? And for the first time he made a connection that hadn't occurred to anyone.

Derrymore would have been the first to admit he wasn't one of the force's great innovators. He wasn't known for the speed of his thinking in either his personal life or his official capacity. In all his dealings with ex-Inspector Reynolds he'd happily left that side of things to the older man. Ideas were Reynolds' speciality. But that didn't mean Derrymore wasn't capable of independent thought himself. People who considered him the village plod didn't see half of it.

Snatching another quick look to make sure his mam and Nick were still busy, he hurried down the street, looking for the information he was now anxious to track down. He found it in a tourist centre where, among advertisements for theme parks and hotel special offers, he picked up a leaflet—detailing the next meeting of the Cornish nationalists.

Part of the pamphlet was written in what he supposed was old Cornish. 'What's this all about then?' he asked the pretty girl behind the counter, to have her shrug and say in a Welsh accent that she didn't know, but it wasn't like Wales, where poets in white robes chanted verses and such. She'd heard they were a political group, very serious. If he was interested, why didn't he go along? The meeting was tonight in an arts centre, look, and before he could stop her she was giving him a map, and marking where the meeting was to be held.

He emerged somewhat dazed at being taken for a tourist in his own county, but with the fixed determination of following the information up. He returned to his post and was deep in perusal of the leaflet—it mentioned several well-known figures among its members, so it must be respectable—when Reynolds rejoined him. The ex-inspector was smiling, a smile Derrymore knew well. 'Cracked

354

it,' Reynolds said. He tapped his pocket containing the photograph. 'I asked if anyone had seen him, and someone has. She didn't say it in so many words, but I could tell from her expression. And her actions gave her away. Very properly she asked why I was interested, and would I wait a moment. When she went to fetch her supervisor I was off.'

He looked at Derrymore and grinned. 'Don't ask me how I got that far,' he said. 'You wouldn't like it. But it means if Newland was there and was looking through those Penderver records, we'll have some firmer evidence. We have only to get official confirmation at a later date to make a case that will stand up in court.'

He was so full of confidence again that Derrymore felt a qualm. But when his mam emerged with an equal triumphant smile, she and Nick trotting off to the car with their bulging carrier bags swinging, his own sense of underachievement strengthened his resolve. He'd go to the meeting on his own, by gum he would. No harm in that. Off duty, he could be as ardent a Cornishman as anyone. And if Striped Jersey had inadvertently turned up trumps again, for the moment he'd keep that knowledge to himself, thanks very much. He'd let Reynolds in on it if, and when, it paid off.

It wasn't as easy to achieve as it should have been. A chap who lives with a doting mam has to manoeuvre more than other chaps for a bit of space. Fortunately Reynolds was busy planning his next move. Having turned his house into a hostel, he'd equally happily adapted his study into a makeshift control room by the simple expedient of clearing his desk and bundling the proofs of his new book into a cupboard, to be retrieved later. While he sat there making lists, the sort that Derrymore knew were one of his specialities—lines of names with the evidence building against them compiled into neat columns—Derrymore slipped off before his mam could ask where he was going, and what was he a-doing of, borrowing Mr Reynolds' hired car.

He knew the site of the meeting well, a small village in the heart of clay-mining country, not far from St Breddaford; not the most likely birthplace for sedition and rebellion. And 'arts centre' was the village hall gone upmarket since the days when he'd played football and its main use was by local lads to change in. When he arrived, several people were there before him, the numbers increasing dramatically when the speakers climbed on to the makeshift platform.

And what speeches. He'd expected the usual humdrum approach typical, say, of parish councils. These were all buzz and fizz. Plans for rallies here and there, calls for financial help from Europe if the government wouldn't cough up, and protests, always protests from the floor about the lack of government support. With the slowing down of clay mining, what were men to do—and where were their children to find work if the clay industry didn't offer the jobs it used to? It made you think. But it was not until the end that he had the chance to make real contact.

After an impassioned plea to save a local hospital from closure, another genuine concern, the audience dispersed, to mill around in the foyer—previously the away team's changing room—drinking milky tea and discussing their grievances all over again. Derrymore stayed too, looking carefully for anyone he knew; he had a good eye for faces and had been well trained to remember them.

The bulk of the audience were local people, many of them dark-eyed and short, typical mining stock, but there were several farmers and a few outsiders like himself. When he spotted an acquaintance he made a line for him, and with his help was soon introduced to the secretary, a beefy farmer with a red face.

He was in fact a member of the local hunt, his particular interest in Cornish independence being that he wanted fox hunting left alone; the countryside was best managed by those who knew it best, genuine country folk. When he could stem the fury, Derrymore managed to slip in the questions he was interested in—could anyone become a member, was there a fee for membership, and who, if anyone, actually ran the club?

The hunting farmer was interested in new membership, and suspected nothing. He cheerfully gave Derrymore the information he wanted, even taking the time to write down the chairman's name and telephone number on the back of the map. Yes, there was a fee—he named a nominal sum—but of course larger contributions were always welcome. He laughed, but his eyes looked expectant.

Derrymore had one last question. 'Did you know Em Tregurion?' he asked. The man's expression changed. For a moment his cheeks paled. 'Why ...' he began, then recovering, 'How do you know her?'

'She was a friend.' Derrymore stressed the word 'was', to have the man relax and say heavily, 'For a moment I thought ... Yes, I knew her. We all did. Dreadful, dreadful,' and he shook his head. 'One of our leading lights. Sorely missed.'

That's what the surfers said too, Derrymore thought, pretending to drink his tea but still keeping his eyes open; it might mean something. And the farmer was obviously worried when I mentioned Em. Perhaps it doesn't add up to much, but Reynolds builds mountains out of such little clues. And I've got a name. Carefully folding the map, he put it in his wallet and, feeling pleased with his first private expedition, returned to Old Forge Cottage, there to field his mother's questions with unaccustomed aplomb.

Next morning, the breaks they had been hoping for for so long suddenly

359

materialised, coming in a rush as Derrymore had so cheerfully, and erroneously, predicted in the early days. The first was via one of Derry's colleagues. He'd slipped out, he confided in a low voice, as if even in a pay phone he was afraid of being discovered. The reports had just come in. There'd been a muddle somewhere, that was why they'd taken so long. The burnt-out car had been identified. A BMW, colour and date still unknown, but possibly blue. No trace of any human remains. Upshaw hadn't made much of it yet, but when the penny dropped he would. He'd be off to interview Newland's wife, that was what, like Derrymore had said he should. So ...

He rang off before they could ask more. But they'd heard enough. It put their theories back on line again. And it left Mabley in a fix.

No one at the caravan park could have linked Mabley with the investigation; he'd never met the Clitheros or Rachael Newland, and when Reynolds had specifically asked about Em's previous boyfriends, although Ray had heard of Derek, Derek, who might have had the most reason to have heard of Ray, had been adamant that he and Em had never discussed her past love life. Only Upshaw knew who Mabley was. At best he'd think it odd, at worst his suspicions would be roused, if he saw Mabley consorting with the wife of the other main suspect. But before they could decide what to do, the second break occurred.

Like the first, it brought good news and bad. Dr Howard must have worked hard; with the help of his wife—who once, many years ago, had been his student and his partner in many joint ventures—he'd spent the entire day in the records office and sent his findings by special delivery. First, he established that there were no true Pendervers left in Cornwall at the present, and Newland actually might be the only true heir to the name. His great-grandfather, born in the ancestral home and christened in the new St Theodosius' church, had left Cornwall at the end of the nineteenth century and never returned.

He had been an only son, but had had several sisters. And his father in turn, although also an only son, had had sisters in plenty, like many old Cornish families the line ending with few or no male heirs. From these females came the present Penderver relatives, descendants of cousins and second cousins, half cousins even, all the branches through the female relationship.

It was a tribute to Dr Howard's staying power that he'd worked this out so quickly, to say nothing of his skill. The bad news was that there were so many names.

Looking at the hand-written lists with their careful notations and additions, Reynolds couldn't help thinking how pitiful his own looked beside them. And what a loss these two well-honed minds were to the legal world. If he or Derrymore had tried their hand at getting the information, they'd still be struggling. True, the professor's accompanying letter pointed out that the starting date had been chosen arbitrarily, and, for the moment, only major descendants were included, with lesser ones weeded out. All those connected with Newland's own family were omitted, as were those of dubious or possibly misleading origin—namely people who liked to give themselves airs by assuming fictitious names relating to great families in the past.

Even with the omissions, it would need an army to tackle the lists. Or the support of an enquiry team, at the moment probably twiddling their thumbs as Upshaw hared off in the wrong direction. Thoughts of Upshaw brought the problem of Mabley once more to the fore.

Reynolds and Derrymore knew they couldn't appear in person at Rainbow Park. If anyone was unwelcome they were. They also ran the risk of meeting Inspector Upshaw. In the end, for lack of anything better, they decided on a phone call to Rainbow Park, and as luck would have it, reached Marge.

Her suspicions were immediately roused, perhaps justifiably so after all the troubles of the past weeks. 'Who's speaking?' she insisted. 'What do you want Mr Mabley for?' It was not until Mazie rose to the occasion and said in her firmest voice that she must speak to Ray that Marge relented.

They heard her shout to Derek to fetch number ten, and when Mabley came at a run, Reynolds managed to make him understand the possible danger before Marge could be alerted. Mabley caught on quickly. 'Right,' he said, and then, 'Right again.' As he put down the phone they heard Marge protesting that that couldn't possibly be his mother ...

'She said the voice was local,' Mabley told them when he joined them at Old Forge Cottage. 'I never mentioned who it was, she just assumed. Typical, I'd say. So I explained my mother came from Cornwall originally. Which happens to be true. That's why I showed up here in the first place.'

He hadn't had a chance to make much headway with Rachael, he explained, although they were already on first-name terms. His real find was Derek, who had taken to sitting behind his garden shed, not doing anything but, Ray thought, drinking heavily. When he'd seen Ray he'd invited him over and offered him a beer. In a drunken sort of way he'd begun to talk of the tragedy that had happened, the loss of the park, he was sure it would never recover, the loss of his wife—she'd never forgive him—the loss of his beloved.

Here Mabley stopped, coughed, and said in quite a different voice, 'It wasn't pleasant hearing him speak of her. I mean,' he coughed again, 'he didn't know I knew her. And in his way I think he really felt what he was saying was true.'

After a pause he continued, 'He also

spoke of you.' He looked at Reynolds. 'He talked about a friend he'd betrayed. Said he regretted it, went on and on about old days. But he also said he regretted lying.'

'Lying?' Reynolds pounced, to have Mabley say, 'He suggested that he'd concocted some story to try to save himself. But he now knew that what he'd said finally wasn't true at all.'

'Hell's teeth.' Reynolds and Derrymore looked at each other in dismay. 'He gave us several versions,' Reynolds explained, 'but damn me if I didn't think we'd peeled him down to the truth at last. If what you're saying means what I think it does, old Derek's held out on us again.'

It too was a lead, albeit an unwelcome one. To be left for the moment while they concentrated on the work in hand. Mabley gave a whistle of disbelief when he saw the lists. 'My God, there must be over a hundred names there,' he said, only half jokingly.

They were soon at work, even Mazie playing a part by looking up addresses and phone numbers. Trying to make sense of the lists, at Reynolds' suggestion they divided them by area, then, wherever possible, by profession. Single women, for example, were excluded, as were town-dwellers. Their prime targets were country folk, farmers, even fishermen, the sort of people likely to live away from others and thus be freer to come and go by night, or to harbour unidentified guests. Among these they then targeted those who lived near either St Theodosius' church or the disused airfield.

The distinctions were rough and ready, at best based on equally rough attempts to understand the psychology of the criminal mind. It still left them with too many names. Besides, as Reynolds was the first now to stress, there was no reason to consider farmers more suspicious than town-dwellers. As for eliminating women, a woman had been responsible for that original threatening phone call ... It was at this stage that Derrymore finally spoke up.

All this while it had been taken as an unspoken fact that their haste was in part to forestall Upshaw. The memory of all the times headquarters had thwarted them in the past motivated their desire to best Upshaw as its representative. Although they had not admitted this aloud, it ran like an undercurrent, giving urgency to their cause. Derrymore understood this.

He had not deliberately withheld the name he'd been given the night before. In fact he'd been wondering how to introduce it without sounding officious. Hearing Mabley's confident account had given him courage. Nor had he seen all the names on Dr Howard's long list; each had been given a section to work on, a division of labour which had only just been made.

When he saw the name there, he told himself it must be a mistake. And then that it was only a coincidence, there must be several people with the same name. He knew Reynolds didn't believe in coincidences, and for the most part neither did he. But ...

Taking a deep breath, he pulled out his wallet, unfolded the map and laid it on the table. 'I got this yesterday,' he said as the others stared at it. 'That's where I went last night. To a meeting. This is the chairman's name.'

He read it aloud, 'Reginald Burley, of Tregarth Manor Farm.' Then, checking against Howard's list, 'Descended through the female line from the sister of the last heir. A distant cousin therefore to Paul

367

Newland, formerly Paul Penderver.'

And his nervousness made him sound as if he were reading out a charge in court.

Chapter 19

Hesitantly, but with growing confidence, he explained how it'd suddenly dawned on him that the one aspect of Em's life never thoroughly explored was the one dearest to her before she died—a free Cornwall. Perhaps that was where her money had vanished, to support it. Yesterday in Truro he'd gone off to make enquiries as to whether there were a special club or society, had attended a meeting and been given the chairman's name—one which had now emerged so conspicuously on Dr Howard's list. Tregarth Manor Farm was very close to St Theodosius' church, he went on, and the lead with Cornish Nationalism had never been followed. He'd like to get on to it straight away. 'It can't be coincidence,' he said.

The reception his news received was

368

most gratifying. Mabley was sufficiently impressed to slap him on the back, telling him he was a cool customer, my word, wasn't he the one. Nick jumped up and down, shouting, 'We've caught him,' while Mazie, torn between pride and anxiety, alternately hugged him and told him off. Only Reynolds said nothing.

The truth was, the ex-inspector was dumbfounded. Like Derry, he had instantly identified where the farm was, not five miles from St Theodosius', close to the site of the former Penderver mansion. He'd never visited it, of course, nor met its owner, but although instinct told him the evidence couldn't be mere coincidence, he wasn't sure. For one thing, although Derry's assumption made sense on several levels, such as explanation of the cash payments, the dog's failure to bark—presuming the murderer was one of the members of the society and was familiar with it—and finally the link with Paul Newland's family, in his opinion, at this late stage, it was too much to expect that Derrymore had uncovered a whole new track.

For another thing, what the others were accepting as a little masterpiece of police work really consisted of nothing more than an unrelated fact, previously overlooked, followed by a hasty connection. No hard evidence; no confirmation that Em'd paid the money to the organisation; no evidence that Tregarth Manor Farm had any links with Paul Newland, except through this one tenuous suggestion of a remote family tie. In short, it was the sort of wild leap of imagination, or sheer fantasy, that was his own trademark—he couldn't have done better himself.

Nevertheless, Derry had made the connection. And the fact had been overlooked. In retrospect, his own bad-tempered carpings at Derry's pedestrian approach to detection looked incredibly petty, unexpectedly so out of line that he felt a fool. He wanted to apologise, but on second thoughts decided not to. Derry was probably unaware of his feelings; let the ghost of them lie.

He was too big-hearted to deny Derrymore any of the credit, or to dampen his enthusiasm. 'Well done,' he said eventually, and meant it. Then, with a grin, 'Carry on. This is your show,' for the first time ever deferring to the younger man. In the long run, what harm could it do to interview

Reginald Burley; at the moment, they had no one else. And—here, even his senses began to stir—it was just possible Derry might have made a breakthrough.

From Derry's expression, Reynolds guessed the sergeant hadn't got much further in his thinking than how to reveal his discovery. He hadn't expected it to end so dramatically and for a second was tongue-tied. Then, thankfully, common sense took over.

Derry took time to rehearse the next move, first going over the procedures for apprehension and arrest. His final decision came out defiantly. 'Upshaw be damned. We'll go official. I'll wear uniform. We'll use your car; I'll drive.'

Apart from the bit about the car, the choice was bravely uncompromising, Reynolds thought. And typical. If the attempt failed or went wrong, Derry would rather go down with flying colours. In spite of himself, he was impressed. Derrymore's come of age, he thought. The idea didn't exactly bother him but again it did make him feel old.

It was then that Mabley intervened. 'If you're off and running,' he said, 'don't forget I'm with you.' Sensing opposition,

371

he laughed. 'After all the dirty work I've done, that's only fair.' He didn't actually say, 'Remember, without me, Reynolds wouldn't be here at all,' but he must have been thinking it.

The ex-inspector left this and all other decisions to Derrymore, but he hoped the sergeant would be fair. At this point, the question of Mabley's unofficial status seemed irrelevant; Reynolds too had finally been reduced to the status of private citizen. Nevertheless, he was relieved for several reasons that Derrymore accepted Mabley's offer; chief among them was the fact that they might be glad of an extra body to give them weight. If his previous assessment of the men was correct, they'd need all the help they could get.

The drive down the now-familiar road west was not without its complications. Firstly, before they left, Mazie insisted that Derrymore's uniform needed pressing. They hadn't explained what they intended, but she sensed the tension. Her determined mouth said plainly as words, 'If he's going to make a big arrest, he's got to look proper.'

Then, just as they were leaving, Nick became hysterical. Informed he couldn't be included, and convinced they'd all be killed, he clung to Reynolds. His final outburst, 'You don't even have guns,' echoed in their ears for a long while, seconded by Mabley, who said, 'I never thought you guys wouldn't be armed.'

Asked if he wanted to withdraw, he shook his head. But the way he eyed Derrymore made Reynolds suspect that the Australian was reassessing his opinion of the sergeant too, presumably favourably.

They didn't say much as they drove along, each lost in his own thoughts. When they approached the turn-off, Derry roused himself to ask Reynolds for advice on how to conduct the interview, and they rehearsed their tactics quickly and efficiently. Finally, just before they reached the farm, they warned Mabley that if there was trouble, meaning danger, he was to lie low and leave it up to them. Looking at his grim expression, Reynolds had the feeling Mabley wasn't listening. He too had come of age.

Tregarth Manor Farm was more secluded than they'd anticipated; they might never have found it except for a faded sign which carried the name, along with that of its owner, Major R. Burley. The military title raised their hopes. Reynolds had been so sure a former soldier must be involved.

Derrymore steered the car more carefully than usual up the overgrown track where pot-holes full of mud made the going treacherous. A scattering of farm debris, from old machine parts to broken buckets and troughs and discarded plastic bags, emphasised the general impression of decay, intensified when they reached the manor house proper, its once attractive façade smothered in ivy and what should have been the garden turned into a slurry pit. On one side was the customary scattering of outbuildings, most crumbling into bits, along with a paddock where one old grey horse was standing, looking as dejected as its surroundings. As they got out of the car, they heard dogs howling in the distance, the usual farm guard dogs, hopefully tied up.

Gingerly wading through the slurry, the three arrived at the house and knocked at the door. They caught only a brief glimpse of the man who answered before the door slammed shut again and they heard him shouting, 'It's the police,' his voice tailing away into the distance.

After a wait, the door opened again. 'Roger Burley,' said the man, holding out his hand and trying to look friendly. He must have been close to fifty, and in spite of his torn jacket, dirty trousers and muddy boots, typical farm labourers' wear, he spoke in educated if surly tones, inviting them to come in, they'd find Major Burley—he emphasised the rank—in the lounge.

The word conjured up a modern sitting area, with modern conveniences, not the greasy, smoke-filled room where Roger led them to meet his father. Major Burley was seated behind a large deal table, dominated incongruously by a big brass bell and strewn with papers and plates of congealed food. A large cigar smouldered in an ash tray in front of him, and he didn't bother to get up. Only after his son left did he gesture to them to sit down.

In spite of his age—he must have been well over seventy—he had a military look, his grey hair cropped short and his voice authoritative. The family likeness to his son—both big, with heavy jowls and short grey hair—was complemented by his way of speaking; he too had a neutral accent, without the lovely Cornish lilt that

Reynolds liked so much.

'What can I do for you, gentlemen?' he began, with a disparaging smile. 'It must be serious to have two plain-clothes detectives supporting our sergeant here. Have the sheep got out, or is it the cattle this time round?'

On the surface his tone was good-natured, but Reynolds wasn't sure. He sounded reasonable but he might also have been sarcastic.

As planned, Derrymore opened the questioning. Was Mr—he excused himself —*Major* Burley in charge of a Cornish nationalist club? They were interested in the membership—how many members, what was the annual subscription and so on. While Burley answered in a languid drawl, Reynolds glanced about him, trying to fathom the nature of the man from his living quarters. No women about, he guessed immediately, and at least the one middle-aged son at home. And impoverished. The major's air of self-importance couldn't hide the fact that his style of living was certainly not luxurious, in spite of the cigar; and his clothes, now there was time to examine them carefully, were almost as threadbare as his son's. But once there had been wealth. Like the Penderver family this was a riches-to-rags decline.

When asked who the actual members of the club were, for the first time Burley's composure stiffened. 'Why all these questions?' he now queried. 'Is something wrong? I had the impression this was still a free country, however much the nanny state threatens control.'

'We're making enquiries about one of the members.' Derrymore didn't back down. 'A certain Em Tregurion.'

The three waited expectantly for a reaction, but were disappointed. Major Burley shrugged. 'Should I know her?' he asked. 'What's she done?'

'Nothing.' Derrymore was firm. Resisting the temptation to retort, 'It's what's been done to her,' he said. 'We've reason to believe she was a member of your organisation. We're checking out regular cash payments, substantial sums.'

Instead of denying or confirming this Burley latched on to the word 'was'. 'You mean she's left us,' he said quickly, 'abandoned the cause perhaps? How inconsiderate. We expect better staying power from our friends.' Only when Derrymore

377

told him bluntly that Em was dead did his expression change.

'Dead,' he repeated, with a frown. 'Well, I never. And just how did she die?' Then, before Derry could answer, 'I hope you're not blaming me,' he added, reverting to his superficially joking way. He put his hands on the table and gave a push, to reveal that he was sitting in a wheelchair.

He must have noticed their consternation, for a grin formed. 'Wounded in the war,' he said, 'not up to much since. So if you're trying to involve me, you're barking up the wrong tree. I don't get out and about these days.'

The realisation that Burley was an invalid, incapable of murder or violent attack, possibly even of moving far from his home, was so unexpected that the three men were completely taken aback. Reynolds recovered first. Burley might not be capable of murder, but that didn't mean he couldn't plan or implement it.

More than that, the major's tone in speaking of Em caught him on the raw. If Burley hadn't heard that Em was dead he must be the only person in Cornwall. And if he'd killed or had a hand in her killing, his question as to how she'd died was an affront.

He and Derrymore had already rehearsed the way they would attack if they met with opposition, turn by turn, each probing, then withdrawing to let the other advance. The technique had worked for them in the past, it was time to try it again here. Reynolds began the attack.

'Your son, Roger Burley,' he began coldly, 'lives here. Just the pair of you?'

'No.' The major was making no attempt now to hide his amusement. 'I've two other sons, Inspector. Or should I say ex-Inspector. Only one other actually lives with me. Nigel. My second.'

The use of that expression, 'Or should I say ex-Inspector?', spoken in the semi-mocking way, again caught at Reynolds. Sarcasm apart, it meant Burley must know more about him than could have been learned from the first formal introductions when they'd been shown into the room. The thought now occurred that one way the major might recognise him was if son Roger had done the identifying—which was possible if son Roger'd been instrumental in his capture. It was a small but vital clue.

Perhaps Burley sensed he'd made a slip. He smiled persuasively. 'You won't find my sons are involved either,' he said. 'Unless wanting to have a free Cornwall is an offence. I've done my bit for Merry Old England, you see, and got a medal to prove it, but what's it done for me? Nothing but bleed me and my farm dry, that's what, and tossed us aside afterwards. Well, we're tired of it. When we're independent, we'll rise again.'

The mockery had gone, replaced by a cold bitterness, the words reminiscent of Em's but without her youthful enthusiasm. Reynolds sensed the interview spinning away into another long harangue on independence. He took a chance. 'We're also looking for a missing man,' he said. His voice had never sounded so harsh. 'A certain Paul Newland. Formerly Penderver. Ever heard of him?'

'No.' The major brought the word out sharply. Reynolds noted how his knuckles whitened as his hands closed on the wheels of his chair. A gold signet ring gleamed.

'What about the name Penderver?' Derrymore's turn to intervene. 'A good Cornish name. One to be proud of. Family used to live hereabouts, I believe. Part of

380

your own background.'

As the Major started to protest that he'd never heard of the Pendervers, they knew his name, what would he be wanting with another one, Burley was good enough for him and his sons, Reynolds leaned over the table and pointed. 'Then tell me this,' he said, softly now, menace just showing, 'why are you wearing a ring with the Penderver crest?'

At best it was a guess; he'd caught only a glimpse of the insignia but thought it looked familiar. Remembering Dr Howard's description of the coat of arms, backed by the picture Nick had coloured, he took a risk. He scored a hit.

The major reared back, his eyes hooded like a snake's. Before he could regain control of himself, Derrymore added, 'You mentioned sons. Let's have them in. We need to question them as well. I see you have a way to summon them, so if you'll permit ...' He picked up the bell and rang it so loudly that its peals could be heard echoing through the house.

Roger and another man burst through the door so quickly they must have been listening outside. They ranged themselves behind their father, protectively forming a bodyguard. The second man was shorter than his brother, but with the same square jaw and short-cropped hair. Presumably Nigel. 'What's going on?' he shouted. 'My dad's too old for this.'

Backed by his sons, Major Burley rallied to take the initiative. 'What is it you're really after, Inspector Reynolds?' he barked. There was no doubt of the sarcasm this time. 'Oh, don't be surprised that I know who you are. I read, you know. I've heard of you. I don't know who that fellow is,' pointing at Mabley, 'but I hear that he,' the ring flashed again at Derrymore, 'was at our meeting last night. Out of uniform. Spying, I suppose. Typical. But it won't work.'

This last came out in a roar. 'You can't pin anything on me or my sons; you've no proof. And you know as well as I do you've no right to be here. Take yourselves off before I set the dogs on you.'

At this the two sons advanced round the table. Seeing them close together, side by side, Reynolds had the strangest feeling. For a moment he was in the darkness of that metal box as the lid first opened. Except one figure was missing, the man with the woollen cap and the raucous voice. Then he was back in that airless room, measuring the distance to the door, calculating what their chances were if the two sons went for them. No matter that Major Burley was playing a dangerous game; for the moment he was winning. He'd called their bluff and left them with nothing.

They withdrew in respectable order, no chaotic rout, a slow and steady pace, Reynolds at the rear, while the Burleys, father and two sons, followed at a distance. When they reached the door, and were in the clear again, Derrymore turned to face them. 'We'll be back,' he told them soberly. 'That I can promise.'

The implied threat seemed to set the major off. He began to rant, frothing almost, the pent-up anger spilling out uncontrollably. Underlying his arguments was his refusal to be intimidated. When he was running the show there'd be no more harassment of him and his sons by jumped-up officers parading as the law. Cornwall would have its rightful place in the sun, that was what mattered, a Celtic inheritance of two thousand years due to be restored. He and his sons would achieve it, thanks to their friends and supporters. Reynolds had no idea of the numbers on their side. It was a tirade that threatened to topple into madness.

For the last time Reynolds and Derrymore exchanged glances. They were sure now they had their men, but still not the firm evidence to hold them. That must be left to another investigation beyond their control. Of all their time together, this was the lowest point.

Major Burley's shouts must have roused the dogs. Three padded round the side of the house, then, seeing strangers, came bounding forward. They hadn't been about before; someone, one of the sons, must have loosed them while the visitors were inside.

They stopped by the old man's chair, dangerous, hackles raised. A word would set them to the attack. And the car was still a distance off.

It was then that Mabley, who'd remained in the background all this while, started forward. 'My God,' he shouted. 'That's old Kern.' He dropped to one knee. 'Here boy, here boy,' he called as the dog came running towards him, tail wagging. A black and tan dog. A Dobermann.

And just as suddenly, they had their proof.

The two sons broke first, diving for cover in different directions. Letting them go for the moment, to be rounded up later, after Derrymore used his phone to call up reinforcements, the three headed for the outbuildings, the dog bounding beside them. They could hear the major bellowing as he followed in his wheelchair, trundling along faster than they'd have thought possible.

They knew what they were looking for, the last piece in the puzzle, the missing Paul Newland who they hoped would be here too. They ran along paths which they now saw had been covered with stamped-down cinders, making a smooth surface through the mud for the wheelchair. These paths extended in straight lines from one shed to the next. The door of the last shed was firmly closed, although the other buildings had no doors at all. Instinctively they headed in its direction.

As they reached it, they heard the sounds of bolts being pulled back, and a man appeared, a flood of obscenity and hatred pouring from him and poisoning the air.

He was powerfully built, square-jowled, tall. But it wasn't just the harsh, almost guttural voice, that froze them, or the knitted cap pulled down over his brow; it was the living likeness to the photograph still in Reynolds' pocket, the mysterious Paul Newland found at last.

In this moment of crisis, Derrymore kept his head. 'I arrest you, Paul Newland,' he said, 'for the following crimes.' He began to intone them, until Major Burley's laughter brought him up short.

The major was close behind them now, and his laughter had a harsh, crazed sound to it; it set the nerves on edge. 'You can't arrest him,' he was crowing. 'And I'll tell you why. This isn't Newland. This is my youngest son.'

And as they spun round to face him, 'Meet Tancred Burley,' he shouted, 'shot and left for dead in the service of his country too, a greater soldier than I was. And a perfect example of the disgraceful neglect the central government shows its heroes. Whoever your Paul Newland is, he isn't here.'

It was an even bigger shock. Before they could recover, Mabley cried out a warning. A gun had appeared in Tancred

386

Burley's hand. 'Shall I give it to 'em, Dad?' he called, his harsh voice suddenly childlike. 'He got away before, that one,' he waved the gun in Reynolds' direction, 'but I shan't miss again. I don't like to miss.'

He raised the gun to fire. They saw the impression of a smile on his face, they heard his father's laughter. Then simultaneously, as Reynolds and Derrymore tensed themselves, ready to dive at Tancred's feet and knock him to the ground, Mabley shouted in a hoarse voice to the dog.

A brown and black flash erupted; the Dobermann leapt towards Tancred Burley, its teeth bared. Then the shot passed harmlessly over their heads, and Tancred gave a throttled scream as the dog's fangs fastened, knocking him over backwards. The gun clattered to the ground. And suddenly there was silence.

For the moment the puzzle surrounding Tancred Burley's likeness to the photograph of Paul Newland must wait. Quickly they tied Tancred and his father up with loose pieces of rope, making a better job of it than the Burleys had done with Reynolds. Leaving the two men in

387

Mabley's charge, with the Dobermann to back him, Derry and Reynolds ventured inside the shed. They didn't have to go far. In an inner section once used for hay, they found the real Paul Newland, tied to a wall.

Thin, his eyes staring from a haggard face, he lay in a daze in his own filth, at first too weak to move when they unfastened him and too incoherent to speak. But even in this condition his similarity to his distant cousin was startling. And when he recovered he would hold the key to the mystery.

'So we were right. And wrong.'

Reynolds' summing-up was rueful. 'Newland was instrumental, but not in the way we thought.'

'It's a rum world.' Derrymore was as rueful. 'That dog,' he said. 'I kept wondering why you were on about it for so long. I know it was important, by gum it was, but,' he sounded embarrassed, 'I never thought for a moment it would remember a former master. I made that up. Yet it did. And what's more, it repaid all Em's love for it. And now Mabley's got it back as he said he always wanted, good luck to him. It makes you think.'

And of course there was much more to be explained than that.

Chapter 20

The main concern was how Newland came to be tied up in the Burleys' shed. And what part he'd played, if any, in the atrocities following his disappearance. When he recovered enough to speak, he gave them most of the answers.

His voice was so dissimilar to Tancred Burley's that the likeness between the two was immediately lessened. Their hair was also different; while Newland's hairline was indeed receding, Tancred's head was completely bald, a great red scar scored across the scalp.

Paul Newland's character was also different. His sister had called him charming but weak, easily led, naive. As he continued with his story they began to understand how originally he'd talked his way into Marge's good graces. But it was his naivety that had brought him to Tregarth Manor in the first instance.

In an old book he'd come across some reference to his original family name, and evidence of their previous status. The legend of their adventuring with Drake had fascinated him. Rather than confiding in his wife, he had, as she'd told them, used the excuse that he was on a buying trip for his antiques business—which, as Reynolds had guessed, was close to bankruptcy. He'd come to Cornwall to track down all he could about his family, spending the first few days in the records office. Em's unexpected help about St Theodosius' had been a bonus; it had directed him where to start his search.

All this they knew or had worked out for themselves. But, 'What exactly,' Derrymore interrupted, asking the leading question that had bedevilled them for so long, 'were you searching for?'

At this question Newland looked even more hangdog, his forehead beaded with sweat. When he explained, in faltering words, both Derrymore and Reynolds almost laughed.

'It's pitiful really,' Reynolds confided afterwards. 'I think he still believes it.

Once poor Em mentioned the church, he recognised it as the one where his ancestors were buried. He was sure he'd find it in the family tomb. The Penderver treasure.'

Derry shook his head. 'No wonder his sister said he was crazy,' he said, adding quickly, 'Oh, I know I was excited first off, when Dr Howard mentioned it, but no rational man would be conned into banking his whole future on such a cock-and-bull story. Why, he even made promises to his son on the strength of it.' An unforgivable offence, in Derry's opinion.

Newland admitted he'd merely met Em on the Tuesday to look at her copy of Hillard, but when he'd asked her to sell it, she'd refused—enhancing Mabley's story that she'd been angry when he'd suggested the same thing. Having identified the church, he took off next morning to find it. Relying only on Hillard, he didn't know then that there were two churches on the same site, and when he saw the new one busy with its fête, he wisely decided to bide his time before making enquiries. Unwisely he filled in the waiting period with a visit to one of his newly discovered relatives.

He'd planned to visit them all in turn, he said, possibly out of curiosity. The reason he himself gave was incredibly naive—he thought they might like to meet the proper head of the family! He chose Tregarth Manor Farm first, simply because it was closest to the church. He'd no idea of its proximity to his old family home, and he'd no intention of telling the Burleys what his real purpose was; unfortunately for him, they soon guessed.

Initially his cousins had been welcoming, kindly offering to put him up while he was in the neighbourhood. Right from the start the similarity between him and Tancred was made much of; he'd been flattered by the attention. Only gradually had it dawned on him that Major Burley was not all he seemed, his interest in Cornish independence, for example, spilling over into obsession. At the same time be began to realise that Tancred, his double, was more than odd; he had unexplained bursts of violence, becoming unmanageable even by his father, who was normally the only person who could control him in one of his moods. When the major began to press Newland for details of his intentions, and when Newland in turn discovered he was being followed, he became alarmed. He tried to leave, was prevented by having his car taken away on the pretext that it needed servicing—that big new BMW which he'd bought on hire purchase, his status symbol he now admitted, his advance, as it were, on his good luck, a mistake he now agreed, causing him more grief than pleasure.

By then, even he saw how dangerous the major and his sons were. When he resisted all their efforts to wring his secret out, they tied him up, starved him, tortured him even—here he pulled up the sleeve of his shirt to show the cigar burns on his arms. Clinging to the belief that as long as he remained silent he was safe, he held out, hoping that eventually his wife would report his absence or his tormentors might give up.

He'd no idea at all of what else they'd done, although they, or rather Tancred, had begun to ramble on disjointedly about punishments and revenge. In the beginning he thought that was all it was, a violent man's ramblings. Only when Reginald Burley had warned him his family were in danger if he didn't talk had he accepted that they would kill him too. Sick with terror, he made one last effort to win them over by offering to share the treasure with them.

Although he was convinced he was now as good as dead, strangely enough his captors let him live, probably because they thought he hadn't told them all he knew. After their unsuccessful break-in at the hall they decided to lie low. They kept up the pressure on him, though, even having someone stand watch over him all the time, finally telling him his wife and children were dead because of him. When he heard that, he now wept, he wished he were dead as well. Now that he was free again, he told Reynolds and Derrymore brokenly, all he wanted was to collect his wife and family and drive their battered car back to their own safe little home, never to return. And if there were a fortune buried in the family tomb, he wanted no part of it. For him, it was no longer a fortune, it was a curse.

Major Burley was left to fill in the gaps. When he was brought to the incident room, his two older sons were already in custody. Tancred had been institutionalised. Derry was in charge again, all irregularities overlooked; even headquarters couldn't take this moment of glory away. Upshaw had withdrawn all charges and taken himself off, grumbling that he wasn't needed, but showing more grace than might have been expected. Derry was left to conduct the final investigations with the same thoroughness he'd shown at the beginning. There was only one drawback. Keeping carefully to the letter of the law, he made sure the interrogation was strictly official, apologetically excluding Reynolds as was correct—but that didn't preclude his recounting all the details later.

The major's first concern was his sons, Derrymore explained. In an attempt to plea-bargain, he offered to take the blame if they, or at least Tancred, wouldn't be charged. 'You won't get much out of them if you don't get it out of me,' he told Derrymore, gesturing with his ring finger. 'They do what I say.'

Only when he'd established that Tancred at least would never be brought to trial, by reason of insanity, did he make his confession, although the phrase best fitting his recital was unrepentant self-gratification.

From the start he made it clear that he despised Newland. He wanted that on the record. A stupid, common fellow, in no way worthy of the Penderver name. As for being head of the family, that was the major's own role. And any of his sons was better suited to claim it; at least they'd been brought up as landed gentlemen. What if their own circumstances were reduced? He'd always been sure they'd rise again. By the by, had the sergeant noticed the names he'd given his boys, family ones, he crowed, fitting their rank and former fame. Even if their claim came through the female line, there was nothing to stop him changing his name back to Penderver—the fact that Newland had done the reverse had made him despise the upstart all the more. And Newland was a blabbermouth, thinking he was so clever yet with every word and gesture giving himself away. The only problem was, what exactly did he know?

Asked next about Newland's fortune-hunting, he too remained adamant that the treasure existed. He'd read about it himself; had heard about it all his life; his grandmother and great-grandmother had both believed in it. The opportunity to find it seemed God-given.

Burley knew the treasure must be 'big'; he repeated the word. For him it meant important in more than financial terms. It would make him and his sons famous, crowning his years of work for the Cornish people, one of their own back in power again. When finally Newland had the audacity to offer to share with him, he'd exploded.

'Share,' he now thundered, striking both fists on the table in the former Sunday school so fiercely that the windows rattled. 'What was there to share? Anything belonging to the family by rights belongs to us. We remained in Cornwall, we live here. His side forfeited their inheritance when they left. Newland deserved nothing.' He still seemed oblivious to the fact that in Cornwall alone there might be hundreds with the same rights.

Asked specifically about the murders, he claimed the first death was a mistake. He knew Em well, he said. Among his records they'd already found her name prominently listed as a contributor to his cause—Derry had been correct in his guess about where her cash had gone. Now he admitted he'd been milking her for a long while, and not just for money; he'd been feeding off her hopes and aspirations, promising to back her politically when she returned from college, pretending to use influence he didn't have. When, in the first days, Newland had innocently mentioned Em's help, Burley had been horrified.

Suppose Newland had as foolishly spoken to her about his intention to visit Tregarth Manor; Em knew who he was and where he lived, might become suspicious if Newland didn't return. He had to stop the leak.

On looking back, he said, he should have asked one of his other sons, rather than Tancred, to deal with Em, except he was afraid she might recognise them. Tancred usually stayed close to home because of his disfigurement; no one in the movement had ever seen him, or perhaps remembered he existed. He'd chosen Tancred especially to frighten her. That was all he wanted, he insisted, to frighten her into silence.

Here he went off into a diatribe about how close he and Tancred were, closer than his other sons—oh, they were all loyal, good boys at heart, he repeated, as if they were ten years old instead of almost fifty, but only he and this youngest son had gone through similar wartime experiences with similar terrible results, he in Italy in the Second World War, and Tancred in the Falklands. They shared the same beliefs; Tancred was more than close, he'd become his arms and legs.

As the first move, he returned to his story, he'd detailed Tancred and one of his brothers to watch Rainbow Park, easily done from the coastal path. They knew from Newland that he'd been staying there and that Em worked at the site. Tancred was to wait until she left that evening, and tackle her on the way home. They hadn't expected her to leave about midday, or for her to have so many other visitors that Friday afternoon. It was hanging about waiting for the visitors to depart that had got Tancred so worked up.

While Roger parked the car near the same lay-by that Derek had used, Tancred had set off through the fields, avoiding Derek on the way and arriving in time to see Reynolds show up, and after him, Marge. Yes, Roger had watched Derek return to his van, and yes, Tancred had seen him and Em making love in the back garden. That too had upset Tancred, giving him ideas. The major didn't enlarge on these but Derrymore knew what he meant.

The real trouble, however, was that Em didn't frighten easily. She'd argued with

Tancred, asking why he was so interested in Newland; Newland meant nothing to her except trouble. Then the dog had turned nasty, and after Tancred had given it a good kick, stunning it so he could tie it up, she'd really gone for him.

And the trouble with Tancred was he didn't know his own strength. He'd merely given her a good shake, intending to calm her down and make her listen. After he was sure she was dead he'd dragged her body inside the kitchen with the vague idea that it wouldn't be found there, then, tying his belt around the dog's neck, he'd run away with it back across the fields.

All a mistake, Major Burley again repeated. But, 'It wasn't Tancred's fault,' he argued. 'Most of the time Tancred is gentle, easily persuaded. It's only when he becomes overstimulated, that he goes haywire. It's like when he was in the war. They trained him to kill; he was wounded, and they decorated him because he killed so many of the enemy. Killing's what he's good at. And then, once he'd started, one death led to another. It was like a drug. After a while he couldn't stop.'

'So Mrs Pascoe and old Trev, were examples of "overstimulation"?' In his disgust Derrymore could hardly bear to continue with the interview. 'How do you justify trying to get hold of Nick Pascoe? What about the car bomb and the fire at Rainbow Park? Were they examples of how Tancred couldn't stop?'

The major's replies were factual, a soldier's battle plan. The grandma was perhaps unnecessary, he said, but she'd asked for trouble by getting in the way. He thought of her as a civilian casualty. Same with old Trev. As for their intention to kill off the boy—he shrugged. 'It was all over the village that Nick Pascoe had been boasting about what he'd seen. And he'd been spotted talking to that Reynolds fellow. Reynolds had paid him five pounds for information. God knows what he revealed.'

Asked now about the attack on Reynolds, he explained that the ex-inspector had also been observed at Rainbow Park that fateful Friday morning. His showing up at Em's place so soon afterwards, his equally early appearance at the dump after Newland's car was trashed—Tancred's speciality—made him a threat. Besides, he'd ensured the boy got away when Tancred had him almost cornered in the barn, a disappointment Tancred couldn't accept.

'We had to be certain Reynolds wouldn't interfere again,' the major explained, as if that were the sensible solution. 'A car bomb was our chance to kill him and the boy at one go.' He laughed, then frowned. 'We didn't expect it to go wrong,' he said.

He himself gloated that he'd made the bombs. 'I was a sapper in the war, a damn good one,' he told Derrymore. 'It didn't take me long to rig something up. No, Tancred didn't plant it; I relied on Nigel for that. We all had to be involved, you see. You know the old Cornish motto of course, one for all, and all for one; it's part of our lifestyle.'

He nodded his head gently in contemplation, rousing himself to add that he couldn't trust a delicate job like that to Tancred, although he'd thrown the fire bomb.

'At a caravan full of kids? With only their mother to protect them?' Derrymore's voice was full of rage. The gold ring flashed as Major Burley pointed a contemptuous finger. 'Newland stood out longer than I thought,' he snarled. 'It was the only way to break him. They were expendable.'

Once Newland finally revealed the object of his search, the major had immediately guessed where it was hidden. 'I knew about the two churches, of course,' he went on. 'I knew where the family vault might be. All three of my sons went off that night to find it, only to discover Reynolds there instead. Tancred did right to take him prisoner, even though his brothers had begun to protest there'd been too many killings. Mutiny in the ranks, which I crushed at once. Reynolds had thwarted us too often; I agreed with Tancred that he deserved to die. But I never dreamt that he'd escape us again; that really was unpardonable.'

This confession alone was enough to put him and his sons away for the rest of their lives.

A few lesser problems still remained, one of them the neighbour's conflicting testimony about the quarrel and the dog's barking. What she'd probably heard was Em's shouts when Tancred kicked Kern to silence him, and the row that'd followed. The only thing wrong was her timing.

Second and third were Derek's last lie and the unexplained telephone call to Marge. Strangely, they were connected,

403

although not quite in the way Reynolds had envisaged. When questioned again, Derek too confessed, for the last time.

What he'd intimated to Mabley was true, he said; he hadn't known the whole story when he'd made his final statement. In the days after Em's death he also had time for reflection. He'd reassessed his marriage, reassessed his life, reassessed exactly what Em had meant to him. When he'd seen Rachael in tears one day he'd had the courage to comfort her.

'Poor little thing,' he now explained to Derrymore, sitting on the edge of his chair in the Sunday school, his fingers knotted. 'She was terrified. She didn't know at first what her husband was up to but gradually she began to be afraid it must be something bad. When she told me what she'd done, I was appalled. Because I'd given her away.'

'Same old Derek.' This time Derrymore sounded more understanding. 'From the start I thought that guilt was his undoing. And isn't it strange that he got on so well with Rachael Newland when, for all his efforts, Mabley didn't.'

Even more strange, Reynolds thought, was that the two men became such good friends that Derek confided in Mabley without knowing who the Australian was. It was one of those odd twists, along with memories of Em herself, that Mabley would take back with him when he returned to Australia after the case was finished and brought to trial. And it was perhaps Mabley's way of making amends that when he left he gave Kern to Derek. 'Something to remember her by,' he said. So after all Em's dog remained in Cornwall, with the man who'd loved her best. It was perhaps fitting.

Rachael Newland, reunited with her husband, was less willing to explain her part. But it was ultimately her confession that caused the most surprise. It made sense at last of Marge Clithero's claims of intimidation. It was also the reason why Derek told Mabley that he'd lied again. What he meant was that, after she'd confided in him, he would have lied to shield her. Having her husband back hadn't changed her much, Derrymore said: she still kept her Quaker look, although her eyes sparked more. It took a lot of persuasion to make her give a statement. And she would only do so without her husband's knowing. 'He never told me everything,' she said, with her by now familiar snap, as if she had a point to make.

'When Paul didn't ring me on the Wednesday as he promised he would each day,' she told Derrymore, sitting in the makeshift incident room while her husband watched the children outside, 'I was worried. Something about the way he acted before he went made me uneasy. That's why I'd made him agree to keep in touch.'

She glanced at the sergeant, as if expecting him to feel sorry for her. 'So I rang his sister instead.'

She looked grave, suggesting it was an effort on her part. 'As usual. Izzie broke out in a rage,' Rachael said, 'saying Paul was hopeless and I was as bad, both of us babes in the wood, expecting to be looked after. When she added she supposed he'd frittered away the money she'd just given him, it came to me that he must have told her more than he'd told me.'

Her mouth turned down, and she looked so sour, Derrymore said he felt expected to comfort her. After a short interlude, when all he could think of was praising her for coming forward, 'I didn't let Izzie know I minded,' she went on in her smug fashion. 'I listened to her meekly. At the end, when she slammed the receiver down, saying why didn't I try to ring him instead, as if I was too stupid to think of that myself, I did what she suggested. Except I pretended to be her.

'I didn't even know he'd bought a new car until Mrs Clithero described it,' she added virtuously. 'I guessed he must have used some of Izzie's money to pay for it and I was furious. I covered my anger well by saying it was hers, which I now admit was stupid because she was bound to deny it. But it was my way of getting back at them both, you see. I said all the things Izzie would have said, even to blaming it all on me, and laid it on thick that Paul was emotionally unstable. I added all that other stuff about the police and threatening Mrs Clithero because I wanted to know more than ever where Paul was. That's why I showed up myself. But I wouldn't have done any of it if I'd known what a fuss it would cause.'

Like Major Burley, she seemed to think the excuse justified her actions. There was still no way of knowing if she was telling the whole truth, and she'd wasted enough official time and patience ... When Derrymore told her she'd be charged she couldn't believe him. 'Not little me,' she wept.

As for Izzie Worthington, it was only what she expected, she said; Rachael was a conniving bitch. And what Paul had told her wasn't so much after all. When he came to see her just before his Cornish trip, as in the past she let him talk but didn't ask specific questions. Only when he assured her that this time the deal was special, he stood to make a lot of money, she knew it was doomed to failure. Now she'd been told what it was, she agreed it was typical of him; pie in the sky, without substance or reason. Where he got hold of it, she didn't know or care; for all she knew some pub drinking-companion had spun him a yarn. But when he came to the point, the same old one, just a loan to see him through, he'd repay it with more than interest, she'd agreed. All right, he'd squandered her loan on a car that was burnt to a crisp, and he'd welshed on his promises. He always would. And she would always agree, she said bitterly. What else could she do?

After the church fête was safely over,

the vicar relented. The church hall needed reflooring anyway, he said, they might as well hunt one last time and settle the rumours once and for all. A team of experts from the university took on the task, and great was the excitement when under the flagstones, where the chute ended in the 1920s coal cellar, a stone slab was discovered beneath the dust, bearing the Penderver crest.

Identified as the family vault, the lid was reverently levered out of place. Underneath, the coffins of the Pendervers lay in ordered rows. But if there had ever been any treasure, it wasn't there now, and the secret of its whereabouts had gone with them to their graves. The stone lid was replaced and the flooring put back, although in deference, a plaque was attached to the wall above the ruins of the curving staircase, saying that this was the tomb of a great Cornish family of Tudor times.

In the end Nick had the last word on the subject. One of Dr Howard's books open in his hands, he came flying into the study where Reynolds was attempting to catch up on his proofs. 'Listen to this,' he said, perching on the arm of Reynolds' chair. He read aloud, by now needing only a little prompting for the difficult words.

' "When Queen Elizabeth, the last Tudor, died, her cousin James inherited. He wanted to make peace with Spain." '

Putting the book down, he said seriously, 'In case you've forgotten, Elizabeth hated the Spanish because they were Catholic. I know all about that from my gran. But King James was easier on the Catholics and wanted to be friends with Spain. It's important,' he added, 'that's why I'm telling you.'

He turned to the book with its splendid illustrations. ' "It wouldn't have been wise for the Pendatons to keep such a well-known object," he read, his voice rising to a squeak, "the spoils of an illegal war in Elizabeth's time. It might have been claimed back by its previous owners. Or Pendaton might have had to pay for it, in more senses than one. His repentance might have been caused by piety or, more likely, used to prove his support for the king's policy. He sent the Cadiz cross back to its former home." '

'There you are,' he said, as Reynolds took the book to read the passage for himself. 'It's almost the same story, only the name's different. Dr Howard said the Pendervers were sea dogs too and went to fight the Spanish; perhaps they brought back a cross as well. But do you know what I think? If Paul Newland was looking for a Cadiz cross,' he stumbled over the words, 'he should have known it wasn't his. So he and his cousins needn't have quarrelled about it it didn't belong to either of them. It belonged to Spain. And didn't I read that well, big words and all? I understood almost all of them.'

It was Mazie who had the last word about Nick. She and Derrymore had decided he couldn't go back to live with his gran. Mrs Pascoe had recovered as much as she was likely to, meaning she could walk and talk and look after herself, even watch her favourite programmes on television, but in no way was she capable of looking after a growing boy likely to revert to his old ways and heading for future trouble.

Nick himself was torn. The old life still had its appeal; he missed the freedom, he said. He also missed his gran. But most of all, he admitted, he didn't want to leave Reynolds.

For his part, after weighing up the

difficulties, and calculating the risks, Reynolds also admitted he wanted Nick to stay. He would miss him too, the house would be empty without him, but what could he do? Farmhouse existence wasn't his style; he couldn't live there with Nick and his grandmother.

'Then,' said Mazie, rising to the occasion and taking the law into her own hands, 'let them come and live with you. Your house is big enough, his gran won't be in your way. She can act nominally as your housekeeper and we'll get a daily to do the work. Nick will have a chance of proper schooling, and a proper home with a father figure to keep him in line.' She didn't have to say, 'And you'll put some meaning back into your life.'

The publishers hope that this book has given you enjoyable reading. Large Print Books are especially designed to be as easy to see and hold as possible. If you wish a complete list of our books, please ask at your local library or write directly to: Magna Large Print Books, Long Preston, North Yorkshire, BD23 4ND, England.

This Large Print Book for the Partially sighted, who cannot read normal print, is published under the auspices of

THE ULVERSCROFT FOUNDATION